Weave of Absence

A WEAVING MYSTERY

CAROL ANN MARTIN

AN OBSIDIAN MYSTERY

OBSIDIAN
Published by the Penguin Group
Penguin Group (USA) LLC, 375 Hudson Street,
New York, New York 10014

USA | Canada | UK | Ireland | Australia | New Zealand | India | South Africa | China
penguin.com
A Penguin Random House Company

First published by Obsidian, an imprint of New American Library,
a division of Penguin Group (USA) LLC

First Printing, October 2014

ISBN 978-0-451-41362-8

Printed in the United States of America
10 9 8 7 6 5 4 3 2 1

To my beloved sister Rachel.
You are so, so missed.

Chapter 1

Marnie was getting married.

After the initial shock passed, I decided I was happy for her. More than that—I was thrilled . . . and maybe just a tiny bit envious too. Marnie had met Bruce only a month ago, and she was getting married in June—two months from now. Meanwhile, I'd known Matthew my entire life. Our mothers being best friends since college, our families had spent holidays together since we were kids. For much of that time he'd been just a friendly acquaintance to me, same as I'd always been to him. And then a year ago I'd had to admit that I'd fallen in love with him. Unfortunately, while my feelings had changed, his hadn't. Recently, though, we'd started getting together for dinner once, sometimes even twice a week. But I couldn't call it dating. It was just an occasional dinner with a friend. And in case I got the wrong idea, he still called me "kiddo," driving home the point that he had no romantic feelings for me. Unfortunately, the only wedding bells in my near future were going to be my friend Marnie's.

What I had to do was think positive, I told myself. *If it happened to Marnie, it could happen to me.*

I stepped off the ladder, folded it, and carried it to the cupboard in the back. When I returned, I scanned the room with satisfaction. All evidence that this place was my recently opened weaving shop, Dream Weaver, was gone. I'd spent the entire day turning it into a party room.

I mentally ran down the items on my list. Balloons? Check. The ceiling was covered in white and silver helium-filled balloons. Drinks? Check. The sales counter was now a self-serve bar. On it was a bucket of ice, filled with half a dozen bottles of sparkling wine. Alongside were three neat rows of champagne flutes. Shower gifts? Check. Farther back, in the area I'd designated as my weaving studio, was a pyramid of gifts all wrapped in silver and white. (As you might have guessed, those were the colors I'd chosen as the theme of the party.) Nibbles? Check. I'd put away my collection of lovely handwoven afghans and set out trays of fresh fruit around a chocolate fountain on the sideboard, and on the nearby table was a prominently displayed white-frosted cake. On the top tier was an embroidery ring to which was glued a diamond-shaped paperweight—my idea. It looked like a giant version of the engagement ring Marnie had so proudly shown off one week earlier.

As a finishing touch, I'd hung a large banner above the counter. Originally, I'd planned for it to read CONGRATULATIONS, but my friend Jenny had quickly informed me that one should congratulate the groom, not the bride. To the bride, one offered one's best wishes. Anything else was sure to bring bad luck. So now the banner read MUCH HAPPINESS IN YOUR NEW LIFE, in big pink letters. Jenny, it seemed, was not only a clairvoyant but a superstitious clairvoyant.

"Done," I said, more to myself than to Liz Carter, who was standing by the counter. She had shown up half an hour ago to "help," but had headed straight for the bar. I glanced at the bottle she'd cracked open. It was already three-quarters empty.

"The place looks beautiful," she said, adding, "if I do say so myself," as if she had done any of the work. "All that's missing now are the guests." I detected a slight slur to her voice.

"And the bride to be," I said, glancing at my watch. "Everybody should be here soon." I made my way to the bar and poured myself a glass of soda water, then added a splash of white wine, an ice cube, and a slice of lemon. I leaned back against the counter. Maybe I could relax for a few minutes before everyone showed up. But relaxing wasn't easy, worried as I was about my friend. She'd been so secretive about Bruce, not even telling me he existed until she was already engaged, and then refusing to introduce him. I couldn't help but wonder about that. Did he have some terrible flaw she didn't want me to know about? Was she ashamed of him?

"I haven't met Marnie's fiancé yet. She said you introduced them. What's he like?"

She peered at me above the rim of her glass. "He's nice, and very successful—a financial advisor from Seattle. He just sold his business and came out East looking for the perfect place to retire."

"In that case, I'm surprised he's here and not in Miami."

"He says he loves the temperate climate here. It rained all the time in Washington, even in winter." She shrugged.

"To each his own," I said.

She took another sip. "I'm happy for Marnie. I'm just surprised."

"So was I," I said. "It all happened so fast."

"It did happen fast, but that's not what I'm talking about. I mean, Bruce Doherty is such a . . . an attractive man. And Marnie is—well . . ." Bruce was good-looking? That meant she had not kept him a secret out of embarrassment. I jumped to my friend's defense.

I cut her off. "Marnie Potter has wonderful qualities. She's just about the nicest person I've ever met. Any man she marries should consider himself very lucky."

"Maybe he has a mother fixation. Or perhaps it's her cooking," Liz continued as if she hadn't heard a word I'd just said. Considering the amount of alcohol she'd already imbibed, she probably hadn't. "She is such an incredible baker. You know, if it wasn't for her baking, I doubt Jenny's coffee shop would have done as well." Jenny was the owner of Coffee, Tea and Destiny.

"She's not just a great baker. She's also a gifted weaver. I owe much of my success to her too." When I'd first opened my shop, Marnie had agreed to sell her weaving through me on consignment. To this day, her pieces regularly outsold those from all my other suppliers. Then, after Jenny rented part of my floor space and opened her shop next to mine, Marnie began baking for her. It wasn't long until she started hanging around after dropping off her baked goods. Soon she was spending entire days here, and even doing most of her weaving in my shop rather than in her home. "I need the company," she'd insisted, but I knew better. It was just like Marnie to do me a favor, all the while pretending I was doing her one. Before I knew it, she was in my shop practically all the time, helping me with customers and accepting only a fraction of the pay she should really be getting—thank goodness, because God knows I couldn't afford to pay her more.

"Anyone who knows Marnie will tell you she'll spoil that man to death," I added.

I wasn't sure whether the sound Liz made was a chuckle or a hiccup. "Maybe somebody should warn him to stay away from her baking, otherwise he'll end up fat like her."

The woman was beginning to seriously irritate me. "You don't like her very much, do you? So why did you set them up?"

She bristled. "It's not that I don't like her. I was chatting with her at the church picnic last month, when Bruce wandered over. All I did was introduce them. I didn't exactly expect them to start dating."

Liz's reaction assured me of one thing. Bruce was not the bad catch I'd imagined. So, the mystery remained. Why had Marnie kept him a secret? I studied the woman, wondering if there was maybe a bit of jealousy in those malicious words. After all, she was not only single but also a few years younger than Marnie—in her mid- to late forties. I didn't know her well, but from what I had learned, her life seemed empty. She traveled extensively, but lived alone. When she was in town, she volunteered a few hours a week at the local library. Except for Marnie, she didn't have many friends. And from the sound of it, the two of them were not as close as I'd imagined. She might have hoped to get the man for herself.

I was going to say something snippy, but at that moment the door flew open and Jenny walked in, struggling under the weight of a large gift-wrapped box.

"There you are," I said, thanking my lucky stars that she had chosen that moment to arrive. Another minute and I might have blurted something I'd later regret. "I was beginning to worry about you."

"Sorry I'm late. I ran all over town for silver wrapping paper, and finally had to drive to Belmont." She noticed Liz. "Oh, good. I see you had some help. Hi, Liz."

"If you call drinking help," I muttered under my breath. Jenny gave me an understanding smile. Did Liz have a reputation for drinking? Hmm. After a year of living here, I still wasn't up-to-date on all the local lore and gossip. But I was catching up fast. I grabbed one end of the box and we carried it across the room to where the rest of the gifts were piled, dropping it alongside the others with a thud.

"I hope there was nothing fragile in it."

She chuckled, shaking her head, sending her sandy hair bouncing. "No wonder I couldn't find silver wrapping paper anywhere in town. Will you look at that pile? There must be two dozen presents here. Lucky Marnie." She stretched her back, glancing around. "Nice. You did a great job with the decor."

"What did you get her? That box weighs a ton."

"Marnie's been complaining that her bakeware is starting to fall apart. I got her a complete professional set."

"That's generous of you."

She shrugged. "Not really. She hardly charges me for all the baking she does for the shop. I'd be surprised if she makes a decent profit. And I know she's still paying off the loan she took out for her kitchen." Last year, Marnie had hired an architect and had an extension built in the back of her house. Now she was the proud owner of a professional industrial kitchen.

"That would be just like her. She hardly charges me for all the time she works in the shop. She insists that she'd rather be here than by herself at home all day." A thought came to me. "Now that she's getting married, do you think she'll still want to work for us?"

Jenny blanched. "Oh, my God. If she quits, I might as well kiss my business good-bye."

That possibility troubled me too. It might not be as disastrous to my shop as it would be to Jenny's, but still, I couldn't imagine going to work every day and not having Marnie to keep me company. Funny thing—she'd started coming in because she was lonely, and now if she stopped coming, I'd be the one who would be lonely.

Marnie had never admitted her age to any of us, but she was constantly complaining of hot flashes, so I guessed her to be in her early fifties. She was overweight, had Lucille Ball hair, wore bright blue eye shadow, and loved animal prints and anything spandex. She was the last person in the world I would have expected to like so much. But to my surprise, she'd become like family to me. My mother, who was my only real family, lived an hour or so away from Briar Hollow, the small town at the foot of the Blue Ridge Mountains where I now lived. Poor Mom—she'd been so worried for me when I left Charlotte. To this day, she couldn't understand why a woman my age—mid-thirties—would leave a perfectly good job as a business analyst to become a weaver. Her only consolation was that Matthew lived here too. Her greatest hope was that he and I would fall in love, get married, and give her lots of grandchildren. And since I'd inadvertently blurted out that I had feelings for Matthew, her hopes had become a near obsession. *Me and my big mouth.*

The sound of the bell above the door startled me back to the present.

"Hey, Della," called Melinda Wilson from the doorway. The beautiful blonde was in her early forties, a baker from nearby Belmont—the only baker I knew whom Marnie would not mind catering her party. A few years ago, when Melinda's husband was killed in Afghanistan, she'd moved to Belmont and opened a bakery. If not for Marnie taking a job there, it might have gone bankrupt. In the year she'd worked for Melinda, Marnie had taught her many of her best recipes. Now the two women's baked goods were so similar, Melinda's could almost be mistaken for Marnie's. Almost, but not quite.

"Need any help?" she asked, looking around. She'd dropped off the food a few hours earlier, mentioning that she would do her best to come to the party.

"Melinda, I'm so glad you could come."

"I had to do a lot of rescheduling, but I really wanted to be here for Marnie's party." She looked around. "Wow, you've been busy. The place looks great." And then noticing the food trays, she set off to check that everything was just right.

"How long has this food been sitting out here?" she asked.

"Not long," I said. "I took it out of the fridge no more than fifteen minutes ago. Which reminds me, I have to bring down more bottles of wine."

Suddenly, half a dozen other women traipsed in. The few who had not dropped off their gifts earlier carried them over to the pile. The door had barely closed when it swung open again as more guests arrived.

"Everybody, the bar is over there," I yelled over the cacophony of chatter, and then pointed for good measure. A group of women wandered over.

Another group walked in, and soon the room was full. Wine was flowing and conversation bubbling—or vice versa—when suddenly my telephone rang twice and then stopped. This was the agreed-upon signal that I'd prearranged with Mercedes Hanson, a pretty teenager who lived a few houses down from Marnie.

"Marnie's on her way," I called out. "Everybody to the back of the room, and be quiet." There was a rush to the area where I'd relocated the looms. Jenny hurried to the front to lock the door and turn off the lights. Then she scurried to join the group. We waited in hushed silence until, a few minutes later, the door swung open and the lights switched on.

"Surprise!"

For a second I thought Marnie was going to have a heart attack. She wasn't a young woman, and since she was overweight, something like that could happen. Her hand flew to her chest and her face turned white. And then she burst out laughing. I exhaled. She'd live, I decided, laughing myself. Behind her, I noticed a good-looking man blinking in shock. Bruce Doherty, no doubt. I hadn't expected that he would show up too. I was about to meet the mystery man. At that moment, Mercedes burst through the door and grabbed Marnie's arm, hopping with excitement.

"I wish I could have seen the look on your face. Were you surprised?"

"You bet I was. Any more surprised and I might have dropped dead from the shock," she said, her hand still on her chest. "So this whole Della-hurt-her-ankle-and-needs-me-to-rearrange-the-display was a ruse?" she said.

Mercedes grinned. "It was my idea. Della couldn't think of any other way to get you here without making you suspect what was really going on."

Marnie glanced at my shoes. "Considering the skyscrapers you wear, it sounded plausible." I ignored the comment. Since I'd moved here, I'd held on to my city shoes. And from the way most of the townsfolk reacted to them, you would have thought I was the only woman who wore four-inch heels. "Although," she continued, "I did think it was strange that you wanted that done on a Sunday night."

"I worried you'd come in early and ruin the surprise." I turned toward the man, smiling. "You must be Bruce."

"I am. And you must be Della—so happy to meet you at last." He looked around at the group of women. "I think I just crashed a hen party. Seeing as I'm the only rooster here, I think I'd better go."

"Don't be silly. Why don't you stay and meet everyone? I'm sure all of Marnie's friends are dying to get to know you." I threw Marnie a look. "She certainly kept you hidden long enough."

He smiled and the corners of his eyes crinkled attractively. I could see why Marnie had fallen for the man. He was tall, a bit over six feet. And at one time in his life he must have been well built. Now he carried a few extra pounds around his waist. His hair was dark with a little gray at the temples. He had blue eyes, an easy smile, and perfect teeth—the kind that must have cost a fortune in orthodontia. He looked like he was in his early to mid-forties, which, if my guess was right, would make him about a decade younger than Marnie. All at once, Liz Carter's words came back to me: "He's so good-looking and she's so . . ." I flushed with shame, realizing the same thought had just flitted through my mind. *So what if he was younger? He wouldn't be the first man to marry an older woman.*

"Oh, please don't go, sweetheart. I'd love you to stay," Marnie insisted.

"If you're sure you don't mind," he said, following us to the center of the room. Women flocked over and introductions were made. When the crowd dispersed, I noticed Melinda Wilson across the room. She was staring intently at Marnie's fiancé, as if trying to catch his eye. *I must be imagining things,* I thought. But at that moment he happened to glance her way, and his gaze froze.

I watched her tilt her head imperceptibly, as if signaling him to come over. And then her eyes darted around the room nervously.

"I think I'll go grab myself a glass of wine," Bruce said to Marnie. "Be right back." But instead of heading for the bar, he went straight to the table where Melinda was standing. He picked up a napkin and took his time choosing a few nibbles. I watched as Melinda nodded curtly and looked away. Her mouth wasn't moving, but I had the strangest impression that she was speaking through her teeth. Bruce's back was to me, so I couldn't swear to it, but I had the impression he was too. It struck me that I was watching a covert conversation. All at once I became aware that Marnie, who was standing next to me, had grown quiet.

"Marnie, how about I get you something to drink?" I said quickly. "Does a tall glass of champagne sound like a good idea?"

"Like a mighty fine idea, if I do say so myself." I led her toward the bar, praying she hadn't noticed the shenanigans going on just a few feet away.

I poured her champagne, and we clicked glasses. "Isn't my fiancé a handsome man?" she said, gesturing toward Bruce. She was so in love, she could barely take her eyes off him.

"He certainly is."

A group of women gathered around us, kissing Marnie and offering their best wishes. When everyone had a turn, Mercedes grabbed Marnie by the hand and dragged her toward the pile of gifts.

"You have to open your presents."

"Are those all for me?"

"They sure are," said the teenager. "Mom couldn't be here, but she bought you a present. It's from both of us. I hope you like it." Mercedes's mother was a dot-com millionaire. I suspected that anything she would have bought would be outrageously expensive. I followed, keeping a discreet eye on Bruce and Melinda. They were still carrying on their secret conversation, unaware that a few pairs of eyes were beginning to stare at them with suspicion. One pair of those eyes belonged to Helen Dubois. Helen was a middle-aged local woman—in her late forties or early fifties—who had recently joined one of my weaving classes. She stood rigidly across the room, her eyes focused on Bruce with a peculiar intensity. The blood had drained from her face, leaving her so pale she might have seen a ghost. I made my way over to her.

"Helen? Are you all right?"

She nodded, still staring at Marnie's fiancé. "Yes, yes, I'm fine," she said, sounding far from it.

She looked ill, wavering on her feet as if she might faint.

"Can I get you a glass of water, or maybe something to eat?"

She turned to me, as if suddenly noticing me for the first time. "What did you say his name is?"

"You mean Marnie's fiancé? His name is Bruce. Bruce Doherty. Why? Do you know him?"

She shook her head and then, snapping out of her trance, she said, "What I could really use right now is a drink." She put up a hand, stopping me. "Don't bother. I can get it myself." And she headed toward the bar.

I followed her until I noticed Liz Carter across the room. She was staring at Helen through narrowed eyes, not unlike the way Helen had been staring at Bruce. She put down her glass and, cutting through the crowd, made a beeline for Helen. She tapped her on the shoulder and pulled her aside. "Oh, Liz, I need to speak to you. Maybe I'm going crazy, but I think Bruce—" She suddenly noticed me standing a few feet away and froze.

"Sorry, ladies. Didn't mean to eavesdrop," I said and crossed the room.

There was no reason to worry about Helen. As long as Liz was there to participate in the gossip, she would be fine.

Thank goodness. Helen shouldn't be left alone. She looked unwell. Maybe Liz would turn out to be of some help after all. I turned my attention back to the party.

"Hey, Della," Nancy Cutler said, coming over. Nancy was a bookkeeper who commuted to Charlotte daily for her work. "I think we're getting a bit low on the bubbly." She brandished a half-empty bottle. "This is the last one."

I'd left a number of bottles upstairs in my apartment refrigerator to chill, and had completely forgotten to bring them down. "I've got more at home," I said. "I'll be right back."

"Need any help?"

"No, thanks. I can manage."

My apartment was above the store, so a few seconds later I was already halfway up the stairs. The main reason I'd bought this building last summer was that not only did it have great commercial space, but it also had two rental units on the second floor. I'd kept the larger one, a two-bedroom, for myself and was renting the second one, a smaller, one-bedroom apartment. Convenience and added income. What more could a penny-pinching entrepreneur ask for?

I unlocked the door and dashed down the hall to my old-fashioned kitchen—complete with a farmhouse sink, black Formica counters trimmed in nickel, and antique glass-door cabinets that reached to the ceiling. This kitchen was the second reason I'd bought the place. I'd fallen in love with it the moment I'd laid eyes on it.

I pulled half a dozen bottles of wine from the fridge and rushed back downstairs, almost colliding with Nancy Cutler as she dashed out the door.

"Sorry," she blurted. I held on to the bottles.

"Nancy? What's wrong? Why are you leaving?" But she was already halfway down the sidewalk, moving at speed-walking pace. "Nancy?"

She either ignored me or didn't hear me as she hopped into her car and drove off with a squeal of tires—as if she couldn't get away fast enough. *What the heck was that all about?* I stepped back into the party and looked around. Melinda had wandered away from Bruce—*thank goodness*—but now Helen Dubois had taken her place. However, there was definitely no secret flirtation going on between her and Bruce. She was stabbing him in the chest with her finger, her face tight with anger. He was backing away from her, making placating gestures, all the while glancing around nervously.

What was that all about? I set the bottles on the counter and called, "Jenny, can you take care of the wine for me?" I rushed over to Helen and rested a hand on her arm.

"Helen, what happened to your glass of wine? Let me get you a fresh one." Without waiting for her to agree, I wrapped an arm around her shoulder and guided her gently toward the bar. When I glanced back, Bruce was adjusting his tie, relief painted all over his face. A moment later he was standing next to Marnie, a protective arm around her. Strangely, I had the impression the arm he had thrown around her shoulder was more for his protection than hers. Still, it was about time the man paid some attention to his fiancée.

"What in the world were you two arguing about?" I whispered.

"I'm sorry. I didn't mean to create a scene. It's just that—"

Suddenly, Liz Carter appeared next to her. "There you are," she said, interrupting Helen. "One minute you're telling me about the exhibit you're organizing, and the next thing I know you're gone. Tell me more about your plans. Maybe I can help. I'm good at that sort of thing."

The two women walked away, Helen having completely forgotten my question. Or had she? It might have been my imagination, but when Liz cut short our conversation, Helen had seemed to welcome the interruption.

"Good party," said a voice next to me. I turned to see Margaret Fowler, my upstairs neighbor and tenant. She was a pretty brunette in her early twenties. An avid weaver, she had hit it off with Marnie and me from the moment we all met. "I wanted to get here at seven thirty, but I had to drive to Charlotte and back. I only got here a few minutes ago." She looked apologetic.

"Don't worry—you didn't miss a thing."

"Was Marnie totally shocked?"

"I'll say. I was worried she might suspect something, but obviously not. She looked as if she was about to have a heart attack."

"Too much of a surprise, by the sound of it." She chuckled and looked around. "Everybody seems to be having a good time, especially Marnie. Look at her. I don't think I've ever seen her look so happy."

"She does look happy, doesn't she?" Marnie was holding up cookie sheets—probably part of Jenny's gift—and she was glowing with happiness.

"Oh, that's my present," Margaret said, as Marnie picked up another silver-wrapped gift. She excused herself and as she darted over, Jenny appeared at my elbow.

"Can you feel it?" she asked, two deep lines between her brows.

"Feel what?" I asked, confused.

For as long as I'd known her, Jenny had claimed to have an ability to read auras and sense danger. I'd always dismissed her "feelings" as nothing more than a vivid imagination mixed with a better than average ability to read people.

She scanned the room, glowering. "Something bad is about to happen. I can feel it in my bones."

Chapter 2

The next morning I woke up with a massive headache. I couldn't blame it on the wine, since I'd had only two glasses all night, and both of them were diluted with soda water. On the other hand, I'd gone to bed late and spent most of the night worrying about Marnie. I threw back the covers and stumbled to the kitchen to make myself a strong cup of java. As I rummaged through the cupboard, I happened to glance at the clock. *Five o'clock?* I pulled up the shade. Sure enough, it was still dark outside. Well, there was no point in climbing back into bed. If I hadn't slept all night, I sure as hell wouldn't fall asleep now. Once I was up, I was up.

I made a pot of strong coffee, and while it brewed, I changed into a pair of black pants and high heels. It was April, still a bit early for linen, but I figured *what the heck?* and threw on the cream-colored shirt I'd made from some of my own hand-woven yard goods. Every time I wore it, I got loads of compliments. And when I told people that the fabric had been made right here in my shop, the explanation invariably created more interest in my weaving classes and in my merchandise.

I carried a cup of coffee down to the shop and looked around. The nickel-plated antique cash register was back in its place on the long wood counter facing the entrance. On the tea table a few feet away, a collection of place mats was prominently displayed. On a rocking chair were half a dozen throws, beautifully arranged in a rainbow of colors. Next to it, in a large basket on the floor, were a number of rolled-up woven rugs. Everything was in its place. The party room had disappeared and my beloved weaving shop had returned. I'd been so tired when I locked up last night that I hadn't fully appreciated how much help Jenny and Margaret had been. They had stayed after the party, and with the three of us, the cleanup had barely taken an hour. On my own, it would have taken me half the night. Thank goodness for friends.

When my real estate agent had first showed me this building, the square footage of the store had seemed huge. It was, in fact, twice the size I needed for my tiny business. When I mentioned to Jenny that I could never fill that space, she had come up with a great idea. She'd offered to rent a portion of the space and open her own shop alongside mine. I'd loved her suggestion so much that I'd gone right out and made an offer on the building. Two months later I'd moved in.

After studying the room, we'd decided to divide the two businesses with two walls of shelves, separated by an opening that would provide a doorway into the back portion, Jenny's shop. These bookcases would give us both extra storage. I could use mine for yarns and weaving paraphernalia, and she would stock all of her special blends of teas and coffees in hers.

The beaded curtain in the doorway had been a gift from Marnie, as was the antique penny arcade gypsy woman in the corner of the coffee shop. It was old, from the twenties or thirties, and added a touch of mysticism to the atmosphere, which was perfect since, along with her coffee and teas, Jenny also offered tea-leaf and tarot readings, hence the name of her shop, Coffee, Tea and Destiny. I'd since grown accustomed to the sound of the beads chiming as they brushed against one another.

I took a last gulp of coffee and marched over to my dobby loom. My latest project was an entire collection of white household linens with a fine navy chevron border, which I had persuaded a few of my weaving friends and students to help make as a surprise for Marnie. With half a dozen of us collaborating on the project, it was only a matter of weeks before the entire trousseau would be finished. I was still on the first piece, a dishcloth. I bent over the loom and studied the weave. It was tight and uniform. Perfect.

I picked up my shuttle and loaded it with a new

bobbin of navy yarn. Soon I was lost in the pleasure of weaving. There was something soothing about weaving—the rhythmic movement of my hands as I tossed the shuttle through the shed from one to the other, the walking of my feet on the pedals. To me, it was a form of meditation. Whenever something bothered me I sat at my loom and wove, and somehow all my stress seemed to evaporate. This morning, it almost made me forget my worries about Marnie's fiancé—almost, but not quite. Now that I had met him, I was certain Marnie had avoided introducing him because she worried I wouldn't like him. And judging from my first impression of him, she'd been right.

The next time I looked up was when the front door opened, throwing the bell above the door into a frenzy of excitement.

"What are you doing here so early?" I said as Jenny came in. She was wearing a long lacy tunic over a pair of leggings, and silver earrings in the shape of spiderwebs. When I'd first met her, I'd been envious of her great figure and sexy bohemian style. Much as I was trying to adopt a more casual style myself, it was still a struggle to stop wearing business suits. All that proved was that you could take the girl out of the city, but you couldn't take the city out of the girl. "You look amazing," I added.

She waved away my compliment. "The question should be, why are *you* already here? Another sleepless night?"

I put the shuttle down and got up to stretch my back. "You got it."

She glanced at her watch. "Oh, rats. It's already ten past eight. I'd better go put the coffee on. Be right back," she said and hurried to her area.

"I'll just run out for a second," I called after her. "Keep an eye on my shop, will you?" I pulled on a sweater and walked briskly down the street for a copy of the *Belmont Daily*. Picking up a copy of the paper to read over a cup of Jenny's coffee was part of my morning routine. There was something reassuring about this mundane habit, as if this regular morning activity helped assure me of a good day. I folded the paper under my arm and went back to the shop.

"It's only me," I called out, closing the door behind me.

"Coffee will be ready in a couple of minutes," Jenny yelled back, followed by a burst of noise from the grinder.

I walked over to the beaded curtain that separated our stores and brushed it aside. "Any chance the good doctor might come around? He could just feed me the caffeine intravenously."

Her face glowed, the way it always did at the mention of her boyfriend. "Sorry. He's at the hospital. You'll have to take it the old-fashioned way."

Shortly after her ex-husband's death last summer, Jenny had met Ed Green, a doctor from nearby Belmont. They had been inseparable ever since.

Why couldn't Marnie have met a nice man like him? "It's not like I'm fussy," she'd once told me. "I'll be happy as long as the man has a pulse." No wonder she had fallen so hard for this character. He had not only a pulse but good looks to boot.

The aroma of freshly brewing coffee drifted out from the back. A moment later, Jenny popped her head through the curtain.

"Here you go," she said, carrying a small basket of pastries and two mugs. She set everything on the counter. "I'm beginning to worry about Margaret," she said, looking at her watch. "She should've been here by now. By the way, the muffins are from Saturday, so they're not the freshest."

"I'm sure they're fine." I looked at the selection. "What kind have you got here?"

"Cranberry-orange and carrot-raisin."

I picked one. "What do you think of Bruce Doherty?" I asked.

But before she could answer, the door swung open and Marnie came in, carrying half a dozen boxes of freshly baked goods and effectively putting an end to that conversation. She set them on the counter.

"You look happy this morning," Jenny said, catching my eye with a meaningful gaze. She wanted me to keep my mouth shut. "How did you like the party?"

"I don't know how to thank you girls. Bruce was so touched by the way my friends all made him feel so welcome."

Especially Melinda, I thought.

"Don't thank me," Jenny said. "It was all Della's doing."

"It was my pleasure," I said.

Jenny lifted the flaps of the top box. "Fresh scones!" she said. "I could kiss you."

Marnie grinned. "I had such a good time last night, I couldn't get to sleep. So I spent the night baking."

"What about Bruce? He doesn't mind you getting up in the middle of the night and leaving him alone in bed?" Jenny asked.

Marnie did a double take. "What in the world are you talking about? Bruce doesn't spend nights at my place—not until we're married." She smiled secretly. "He respects me too much for that."

This struck me as more than just a little bit odd. Two mature people who were already engaged did not—at least did not usually—hold off on spending nights together. And I especially did not buy Bruce's being okay with that, unless . . . I wondered what he was doing with his nights, and with whom he might be doing it.

I glanced at Jenny and found her looking at me, her brows raised quizzically. She gave me a slight nod, which told me that she was asking herself the same questions.

Marnie picked up a couple of the boxes. "I'll drop these off in the back and be right back. I have something to show you. Wait till you see!" Jenny picked up the other boxes and followed. A moment later Marnie was back, carrying one of the boxes.

"I should have told Jenny to leave this one here. This is what I want to show you."

The front door opened and a couple of women walked in, nodding their hellos on their way to the coffee shop.

"Morning, Della. Morning, Marnie."

"Good morning, ladies."

Marnie waited until they disappeared behind the beaded curtain and then she opened the box. "Take a look at this." She lifted out a parcel wrapped in dark blue onionskin paper. She pulled the paper back, and I was looking at a neatly folded piece of striped fabric. She spread it out, revealing a blue square stitched to one corner. Inside the square was a patchwork of stars in a circle.

"What do you think?" she asked.

It looked like an early version of the American flag. I ran my hands over it, smoothing the wrinkles along the way. The fabric was rough and full of slubs—linen, most certainly homespun, and old, very old. The white had yellowed with age, the red had faded to pink. But the most important detail, I noticed, was the number of stars that had been hand-appliquéd on the blue square. There were only thirteen.

"How old is this?" I asked.

"I did a Google search, and found out that this particular flag is what's called the Betsy Ross design. It was adopted in 1777, and remained the official flag until 1894. But because communication was slow in those days, some parts of the country continued to make them for some time after, so it could be from as late as the early 1900s."

I snatched my hands away, realizing that this piece of history could be worth a fortune. "Have you had it evaluated?"

"I have no idea how much it could be worth. I remember my grandmother telling me about it when I was a child. She got it from her mother, who got it from her mother. I got it from her when she died. I put it in a drawer and forgot about it. I came across it just a few days ago, when I was going through my stuff to figure out what I would sell and what I would keep when Bruce and I get married."

I leaned in to examine one corner where the fabric seemed to be unraveling. "This could be worth tens of thousands of dollars," I said, awed. "You'd better get an expert to look at it as soon as possible."

"That's what Bruce said when I showed it to him. He wanted to take it into Charlotte right away and get the curator at the Charlotte Museum of Art to take a look at it. But I wanted to show it to you first."

"Put it back in the box and keep it somewhere safe. You shouldn't even let anybody touch it until it's evaluated."

The bell above the door tinkled. I turned around to see Matthew strolling in with Winston, his

French bulldog. My heart leapt and I just knew I was grinning like a fool. I turned my smile down a few degrees.

"Hi, Matthew," Marnie said.

Matthew was tall, nearly six feet, which meant that when I stood next to him in my high heels, I *almost* reached his shoulder. His hair was dark, and his eyes could change color—from a light golden brown when he was in a good mood, to almost black when he was furious. I'd seen them both ways, but lately they were more often the former. I dared to hope that meant the friendship he felt for me might be growing into something more. He walked over to the counter.

"I have to go into Charlotte today," he said. "So, if you don't mind, could you keep Winston until dinnertime?"

"As if you need to ask," I said.

Winnie padded over and dropped his butt to the floor, staring at me. He had a flat, wrinkled face on a squat, muscular body. His large soulful eyes softened his otherwise ferocious mug into that of an adorable teddy bear.

From the day I'd opened my store, Matthew had been dropping him off each morning. It was an arrangement that made everyone happy. Matthew needed peace and quiet while he wrote, whereas poor Winnie was miserable without attention all day. And truth be told, I liked having him around. What I liked best about it was that once Matthew had finished his daily word count, he'd come by and pick him up. So I got to see him twice a day. And once in a while, I'd get an invitation to dinner out of it. What this girl wouldn't do for a date.

"How's your book coming along?" Marnie asked. "This is your second one, right?"

"It's going well. I just hope I finish it on time." A year ago, a publishing house had accepted Matthew's proposal for a book on criminology. He'd quit his teaching job at UNCC, moved back to Briar Hollow, and settled down to write. He'd finished his first book and was now hard at work on a second one. "I never realized how stressful these deadlines can be."

"Tell you what," I said. "You can just leave Winnie with me until you're finished." I ruffled the fur on Winston's head. "You love spending time with me, don't you, big boy?"

Winston rolled over on his back, no doubt hoping for a belly rub. I fished through my drawer for a doggy biscuit and he scrambled back onto his feet and lunged for it. And then he trotted over to his cushion, chewing contentedly.

"What have you got there?" Matthew asked, noticing the flag. He leaned forward to get a good look.

"It's Marnie's," I said. "Isn't it gorgeous?"

Marnie explained, "It's a sort of family heirloom. I'm not sure exactly how old it is, but I know it goes back a few generations."

He studied it in silence for a few seconds, then said, "You should have this looked at by an expert."

"That's what we were just talking about," I said.

He paused, looking thoughtful. "I have a friend at the Charlotte Museum of History. Actually, he's the curator. If he can't tell us, I'm sure he knows some expert who would know."

Marnie's eyes widened. "Really?" She seemed about to agree and then she frowned. "I don't know. Bruce really wanted to take it to Charlotte himself."

"Didn't you say Bruce would take it to the Charlotte Museum of Art?" I said. "Surely the museum of history would be a better place to bring an antique flag. Besides, Matthew knows the curator. I'm sure Bruce won't mind."

"I'm on my way to Charlotte to see my agent now," he interjected. "I'll be driving right by there. I could drop it off on my way. But I don't want to cause an argument. If Bruce wants—"

"No, you're right," Marnie said, cutting in decisively. "Bruce won't mind. In fact, he'll probably be happy he won't have to make the drive." She repackaged the flag and handed it to Matthew. "Please be careful with it."

"I promise." He gave me a peck on the cheek, patted Winnie on the head, and walked out. A minute later he was gone, the roaring of his car engine fading in the distance.

Marnie looked at her watch. "Is it already eight forty-five? I'd better get going."

"Where are you off to?"

"I'm having breakfast with Bruce at the Long-view," she said, naming a local bed-and-breakfast that had recently expanded into a boutique hotel, complete with an adjoining fine-dining restaurant. "Don't worry," she continued, heading for the entrance, "I'll be back before ten o'clock." The door swung shut behind her.

She walked away with new energy, her flaming red hair bouncing with every step. Damn that fiancé of hers. If he broke my friend's heart, he would have to answer to me.

"Do you know what I think, Winnie?" He looked up at me. "I have a feeling something bad is about to happen." Good grief. Had I really just said that? That proved it. I was spending way too much time with Jenny. I was beginning to have woo-woo feelings. Next, I'd be seeing auras.

Chapter 3

My paper was spread open and I was sipping my coffee and reading an article about yet another museum robbery. There seemed to have been a string of them all across the state over the last couple of years. Every month or so, another priceless painting or historical artifact went missing. This latest one had occurred two nights ago at the Charlotte Museum of Art. So far, all the police would say was that a thief, or thieves, had broken into the museum during the night and escaped with a collection of contemporary paintings by local artist Herb Jackson.

Before I could read any more, the same group of Jenny's customers who had come in a short time ago walked through my shop on their way out.

"I love that shirt you're wearing," one of them called to me.

"I'm glad you like it," I said. "I made the fabric myself, right here on my Irish wide-width loom." I pointed across the store to the huge loom, which I hadn't used in a few months.

"Really?" the woman said. She and one of her friends came over for a closer look. "It's gorgeous." She looked around. "Do you sell these shirts?"

I hadn't even considered stocking them, but quickly I said, "I haven't got any ready-made. They're special-order items. If you place an order, I'll be happy to whip one up for you."

"How much would that be?"

We discussed price, and I explained the labor involved. Before she left, I had her measurements, plus a deposit. Luckily, I had recently completed a large order of yard goods for Bunny Boyd, a famous interior designer. The commission was the largest I'd ever had and one of the most interesting. She was restoring a historical mansion and wanted all the period fabrics replicated. I had yards left over, and it wouldn't take me more than a few hours to sew a shirt. Since I'd been getting so many compliments on mine, I would use the rest of the fabric to make extra shirts. The women left, and just as I noticed my cup was empty, Jenny appeared in the doorway with a fresh pot.

"Ready for a refill?"

"I'm beginning to think maybe you do read minds after all."

"I never claimed to read minds. I read auras."

I grinned. "And palms, and tarot, and tea leaves."

"You'll see. One of these days you'll be a convert," she said, pouring. "It's so quiet today. I suppose it's a good thing, considering Margaret hasn't come in. I've only had a handful of customers. I wonder why."

"Maybe it has something to do with the party we had last night. Most of your customers are friends of Marnie's, and everyone was here."

"You have a point. People went home late."

"By midafternoon you'll be crazy busy as usual. Don't worry." We turned as Margaret walked in.

"Speak of the devil."

"Hi, Della. I'm so sorry I'm late, Jenny. I don't know what was wrong with me. I slept right through my alarm. I promise it will never happen again."

"We were just wondering how come you hadn't showed up."

Margaret blushed. "Sorry," she repeated. "I shouldn't have had so much to drink last night."

I'd met Margaret last summer when she was closing her weaving studio and had listed her extra-wide loom on craigslist. I'd bought it, and when she learned that I had an apartment to rent, she'd become my tenant.

"Don't feel too bad," Jenny said. "The place is deserted today. I hope it gets busier soon."

She glanced at her watch. "I'd better get to work. Good thing I live upstairs. I only got up ten minutes ago and I'm already here."

I chuckled. "That's one advantage of living above your place of work. You just have to roll out of bed and keep rolling all the way down the stairs."

Margaret headed for the back. "That was a good

party last night—too good," she said, over her shoulder.

"I'm glad you enjoyed yourself. Marnie looked like she was having the time of her life," I said.

She stopped abruptly and returned to the counter. "Speaking of Marnie, what did you guys think of that fiancé of hers?" By the tone of her voice, I suspected she didn't like him any more than I did. "Isn't he a bit young for her?"

Jenny hesitated, then spoke. "I wasn't going to say anything, but, yes. He is sort of young—not that we can hold that against him," she said with a smile. "What really worries me, though, is his aura. It was filled with danger." I refrained from smiling, but too late. Jenny had already noticed the twitch at the corner of my mouth.

"I know you don't believe in auras, but his was gray, almost opaque. And you know what that means—trouble. I'm telling you, there's something not right with that man." In my opinion, anybody who noticed the way he was behaving, having a surreptitious conversation with Melinda Wilson at his fiancée's engagement party, would've come to the same conclusion. And it had nothing to do with auras.

Margaret nodded. "I totally agree. He's trouble."

"What makes you say that?" I said.

Margaret shrugged. "I got the impression he was just waiting for all the women in the place to flock to him."

"One of them sure did," Jenny said.

"What I can't figure out is why Melinda would behave that way. Isn't she a good friend of Marnie's?"

Jenny looked at me. "I was talking about Nancy Cutler. Why? What did Melinda do?"

"I can't believe you didn't notice. She and Bruce were carrying on this covert flirtation. Well," I added, "I can't swear that they were flirting, but something was definitely going on." I described what I'd seen.

"But—" She looked stunned. "I know Melinda has been widowed for almost a decade, but according to everyone, she's still carrying a torch for her dead husband. It doesn't make sense that she'd flirt with her friend's fiancé."

"Like I said, maybe it wasn't flirting, but something was going on, and it was something neither of them wanted to be caught at."

"Well, it was Nancy's behavior that really surprised me," Jenny said. "She asked me for a pen and paper. I was standing right next to her, so I know she scribbled down her name and telephone number, and then she scampered over and whispered something in his ear and handed him the note."

I widened my eyes. "Did he take it?"

"He sure did, but not before sneaking a look around the room to make sure nobody was watching. And then he slipped it in his pocket."

"Seriously? That really surprises me. Nancy Cutler is just about the last person I would suspect of making advances to a man—especially one who's involved with one of her friends."

Nancy was a bit spinsterish—not that I would say this out loud, but she was not attractive. She had moved back to Briar Hollow a few months ago after years of living in Chicago and then more recently in Charlotte. She was probably in her early forties and might have been more attractive if she tried. Other than that, I didn't know much about her. It seemed to me that every time I saw her, she was wearing tweed skirts and twinsets. She wore her hair tied back in a smooth chignon, and her makeup was nonexistent. "She looks more like a stern schoolmistress, not exactly the flirtatious type. I don't think I've ever even seen her smile. Maybe there's some other explanation. We don't know what she said to him. It might have been something completely innocent."

"Oh, I don't think she was flirting," Margaret said. "One minute she was talking to him, and the next she turned around and walked away as fast as she could."

"I wonder what that was all about," I said.

"What do you think we should do?" Margaret said. She looked from Jenny to me. "If you two are right about him and Melinda, shouldn't somebody warn Marnie?"

"Are you serious?" Jenny looked stunned. "I don't think that would be very wise. What if we're wrong?"

"A minute ago you were so sure," I said.

She grimaced. "I know. Poor Marnie. I just hate to hurt her."

I crossed my arms. "I, for one, think Margaret is right. Somebody has to tell her. She'll be hurt. There's no question about it. She might even hate us for it, but she'll come around. If we don't tell her now, it will be much worse later." My comment was met with a long silence.

"I still don't like it one bit," Jenny said, throwing up her hands. "But you are closer to her than I am."

"How about we sleep on it for a few days?" Margaret said.

Jenny nodded. "Good idea. It's not as if she's getting married in the morning. And who knows? Maybe she'll figure it out on her own. And when that happens, we can be there to support her." She saw the look on my face and added, "I'm being a chicken. I know." Before I could try to change her mind, she turned to Margaret. "We'd better get back and start preparing for the lunch crowd— supposing we have one." They disappeared behind the beaded curtain and I returned to my weaving.

As I got into the rhythm of working the loom, my mind wandered back to the events of the party and then to the argument I'd witnessed between Helen Dubois and Marnie's fiancé. Whatever it was about must have been important; otherwise I couldn't imagine Helen getting into a public confrontation in the middle of a celebration. What could have made her so angry, I wondered?

There was only one way to find out. I would

have to ask her myself. I calculated quickly. The next time I was scheduled to see Helen was five days from now—on Saturday, when she was to come in for a private weaving lesson. I was not about to wait that long. I beat in the weft on my loom and put away my shuttle.

"Margaret," I called, hastening to the beaded curtain. She looked up from behind her counter. "Can you keep an eye on the shop for a while? I'll be right back."

"No problem," Margaret said, looking puzzled. "Where are you going?"

But I hurried away without answering.

I parked my red Jeep in front of Helen's house and as I approached the front door, I quickly worked out how to explain why I was popping by so unexpectedly. Helen had mentioned wanting to show me some yarns she was thinking of using. I'd simply tell her I happened to be in the neighborhood and decided to stop by and take a look at them. I knocked and waited a few minutes—no answer. I knocked again.

When I pressed my ear to the door, I could hear music from somewhere inside. Surely she was home. Why wasn't she coming to the door? I thought back to what I knew of Helen's private life. Marnie had told me the woman had been single her entire life and that she lived alone. So if anybody was here, it was likely her. I knocked one more time, harder now, and waited. Still nothing. A bad feeling came over me.

"Hello?" I called out. "Helen? Are you home? It's me, Della." I knocked a few more times and as the minutes ticked by, my feeling of dread grew.

What if something had happened to her? She could have slipped in the shower, taken a tumble down the stairs. Accidents happen in the home all the time. I wasn't about to break into her house, but I couldn't just walk away either. I stepped off the stoop, and tiptoeing behind the shrubs, I made my way to the living room window and peered in. As my eyes grew accustomed to the dimness, I made out the furnishings—a large open armoire with a television inside, a coffee table with a pile of books, a sofa— *There she is*.

Helen was sleeping on the sofa, still dressed in the same blue party dress she'd worn last night. Maybe she'd had too much to drink. I was about to walk away when it occurred to me that no matter how drunk she had been, she should have slept it off by now. The party had been hours ago. And nobody could sleep through all that knocking. I peered in again. Was it my imagination or was there something odd about the angle of her head? All at once my dread turned to panic.

I grabbed my cell phone from my bag and punched in 911.

Chapter 4

"**D**ead," the older officer said. He was a rugged man with black hair and eyes. He stood and raised his eyes from the body to me. "I'd say strangled, by the looks of it."

From the quick glimpse I'd had of Helen's bloated purple face, I'd already surmised as much, but hearing it from the mouth of an official suddenly made it real. A wave of nausea washed over me and the floor shifted. I grabbed the wall for support, taking long, deep breaths.

"Whoa. Careful there. Maybe you should have a seat before you keel over," the second officer said. She was a pleasant-looking blonde with intelligent eyes. She guided me to the kitchen, where I wouldn't have to look at poor Helen. *Thank goodness*. She pulled out a chair at the table for me and then sat down opposite me.

"That's how the killer got in," she said, as if to herself. I glanced at where she was looking. The sliding door to the backyard was not quite closed. A sliver of an opening remained. She bent over and checked the handle and lock. "Shit. Anybody could have come in. It's broken." She stood. "Hey, Harrison," she called, "come look at this." Her partner rushed in, and she pointed it out. As he continued to inspect it, she sat down again and retrieved her notebook from her shirt pocket.

"I'm Officer Lombard, by the way," she said.

"Della Wright," I said, struggling to keep control of my emotions.

She nodded. "I got your name from dispatch." She poised her pencil to take notes. "Can you tell me what time you got here?"

"I must have gotten here at . . ." I glanced at my watch. "It must have been close to nine thirty. I knocked and knocked, but she didn't answer. I could hear music inside, so I knew she had to be here. I started getting worried. That's when I peeked through the living room window, and . . . and—" My voice broke and I wiped away a tear. "I just saw her last night. I can't believe . . ."

"You say you saw her last night. Where was that?"

"I was giving a party, a bridal shower for a friend of mine who's getting married. Helen was one of the guests." She jotted a few words into her notebook.

"Dispatch said you called at nine twenty-two, so you contacted them almost as soon as you got here?"

"I—I guess so. I couldn't have been knocking more than a few minutes."

"You say you were worried. Any special reason?"

"I could hear music, and I'd been knocking—hard—for a few minutes. I couldn't imagine that she didn't hear me."

"Was the victim expecting you?" Hearing her referred to as a victim hit me again, and I had to swallow a few times before answering.

"I was giving Helen weaving lessons," I said. "She wanted me to look at some yarn she'd bought. She wasn't sure it would work for the project she was planning and needed my advice." I sighed. "Poor Helen," I said under my breath for the umpteenth time.

"So the deceased was expecting you."

I avoided answering by asking a question of my own. "Do you have any idea how long she's been dead?"

"The coroner will be able to tell." If that was the case, they might never solve this murder. They were likely to be on the wrong track from the start. I must have made a face because the officer peered at me questioningly.

"Something wrong?"

I scratched at a dried fleck on the table. "I know Dr. Cook. He's a good doctor, but not a great coroner." She watched my nervous fingers and I pulled my hands into my lap.

"What makes you say that?" she asked.

"Maybe I shouldn't mention this, but he's just too nice. He refuses to believe that not all people are good. I've only lived here for a little over a year, and I already know of two cases where he pronounced the deaths as natural, only to find out later that they were murders."

She twiddled her pencil between her fingers. "I wouldn't worry too much. I doubt in this case he'd make any mistake. The victim was clearly strangled."

"Poor Helen," I said again.

"You own the weaving store on Main Street, don't you? Is that where I can reach you if I have any other questions?"

"Dream Weaver, yes." I gave her both my business number and my cell number.

The interview came to an end, and I left the house just as Dr. Cook arrived. He nodded as he walked by, carrying his old-fashioned medical bag. The poor man looked harried. I imagined he'd feel even worse in about two seconds.

I climbed into my Jeep, feeling despondent. Helen might not have been a close friend, but her death was still upsetting. All the more so since I had been the one to discover her body. I had moved to Briar Hollow to escape the big city, in search of peace and quiet. If a person could be murdered in Briar Hollow, was there anywhere in the world that was safe?

I rammed the stick shift into drive and headed back to the store, nearly going through a red light at the only intersection in town. *Whoa. There's no point in my ending up dead too.* A few minutes later

I swung the Jeep into the alley behind my building and pulled to a stop. I climbed out, pausing for a steadying breath before going into the shop.

It was only a few minutes past ten o'clock, my regular opening time. Marnie would probably already be in, and she could read me the way Jenny read tea leaves. And Helen had been one of her friends. I couldn't just blurt out the tragic news. As soon as I opened the door, Winston came bouncing up, wagging his tailless butt in joyful exuberance. He threw himself at me.

"Hey, Winnie." I rummaged through my pocket and found a lint-covered doggy treat. He snapped it up in midair and trotted back to his cushion, munching with satisfaction.

"There you are," Marnie said with a smile. "Where did you disappear to?" I hadn't noticed until now, but since Marnie had met Bruce, her mood had greatly improved. When I'd first moved here, she's been known as the local grouch—her way of camouflaging her too generous spirit, as far as I was concerned. But I had a feeling that her recent pleasant disposition was about to take a dive.

"How was your breakfast date?" I asked, in search of a way to tell her about Helen.

"Oh, it wasn't a date. It was just breakfast." Even though she smiled as she said this, I had the impression that something was bothering her.

"Hey, is something wrong?"

"Of course not. What could be wrong?" She

gave me a smile that was too bright, which only made me more suspicious.

"Come on, Marnie. You can't fool me. I know you better than that. Something is clearly upsetting you. Is it something to do with Bruce?"

She glowered. "Oh, it's nothing. At least I hope it's nothing. For some reason, Bruce got it in his mind that Briar Hollow is not the right place for him to retire after all. He was trying to talk me into moving farther south."

"That's rather sudden. I thought he loved it here. Did something happen to make him change his mind?"

"Not that I know of. Yesterday, Briar Hollow was the most wonderful place in the world. Now, this morning, he can't wait to get out of here. Anyhow, what can I do? I hope he changes his mind again and decides we can stay here." She crossed her arms and seemed to suddenly notice my discomfort. "Are you all right? You're looking awfully pale."

"I'm fine," I said, not very convincingly, and her frown turned to concern.

"You're so white. Maybe your blood sugar is low. Let me get you something to eat."

"Don't go." I struggled to find the right words and ended up just blurting it out. "I'm sorry to have to tell you this, but Helen is dead."

She just stood there, frozen. Maybe she hadn't heard me right.

"What? That can't be. She was fine last night."

Her face fell slowly, as if she was still waiting for me to jump up and announce that I was just joking. "She's dead? But how?"

"She was killed. I'm so sorry, Marnie."

"Killed. You don't mean . . . murdered?"

"I'm afraid so."

She felt for the seat of the chair behind her and collapsed into it, probably paler than I'd been. "Helen—dead." Tears rose to her eyes. "But what happened? How?"

I couldn't bring myself to tell her she had been strangled to death. "I'm sorry, Marnie. I know she was a good friend. Do you want me to get you something? A cup of coffee? A muffin, maybe?"

"Do the police know who did it?"

"I don't think so."

"How did you find out?"

"I happened to go by her place this morning, and when she didn't answer—"

She cut me off, horrified. "Are you telling me you found her? Don't tell me any more. I don't want to know." She pulled herself out of the chair. "No wonder you look sick. Here, you sit. I'll get you a coffee."

I must have been having a delayed reaction, because I began to shake. It started with my knees, but pretty soon I was trembling all over. "Thanks. But any more caffeine and I'll be vibrating like a jackhammer."

She hurried toward the back of the shop on wobbly legs. Winston stared after her, looking confused.

"It's okay, boy." I threw him a treat and he snatched it in midair. "Go back to sleep. Marnie will be fine." I hoped I was right about that.

I could have gone to pick up a muffin myself, but I knew my friend well. Keeping busy was her way of coping. Two minutes later she was back, Jenny and Margaret on her heels. From the expressions in their eyes I knew she had already given them the bad news.

"You're still as white as a sheet," Marnie said. "Here, I brought you something to eat." She handed me a coffee and set a plate of muffins on the counter. "Cranberry-orange, your favorite. It'll make you feel better."

"I'm all right, Marnie. Don't worry about me. Here, why don't you sit down?" I hardly thought eating would help in this case, but I picked a pastry if only to satisfy her, and broke it into small pieces. Meanwhile, she was struggling to keep from crying.

"I still can't believe it."

Jenny gave me an I-told-you-so look. "And you said I was crazy when I predicted something bad was going to happen," she said in a low voice.

"You knew Helen was going to be murdered?" Marnie asked, her eyes round with shock. She had always been a strong believer in Jenny's ability to divine the future. "And you didn't warn her?"

"No, of course I had no idea Helen would be killed. If I'd known, I would never have let her go home by herself. All I had was a premonition that something bad was going to happen."

Margaret looked about to add something, and froze. For one terrible moment I was certain she was about to tell Marnie about how we mistrusted Bruce. I gave her a fierce look and shook my head imperceptibly. There couldn't be a worse time than now to tell her something like that. She had just lost a friend. To my relief, Jenny broke the tension.

"You know me," she said. "I get feelings, but they're generally vague."

Marnie stared at her. "I get feelings too, you know. And I get the feeling right now that you three are hiding something from me. Will one of you please tell me what's going on?"

We were saved from having to answer when the bell tinkled and two of Jenny's regulars walked in. They marched over to the counter like women on a mission.

"We just heard about Helen Dubois," said the first, a dark-haired woman with a shade of orange lipstick my mother wore decades ago. "Is it true? That you found her?" It never ceased to amaze me just how fast news—especially tragic news—got around in this small town.

"It was very upsetting. I can't bring myself to talk about it. I'm sure you understand." I wasn't about to let myself be maneuvered into a gossip session.

"Oh, how perfectly awful for you," said the second woman, this one a silver-haired lady wearing three strands of pearls. She wasn't going to give up so easily.

Luckily, Jenny took charge. "Hello, Agatha, Norma. Marnie brought in some homemade scones this morning, and I remember how much you like them. How would you like a cup of fresh coffee to go along with that?"

"Oh, er, that would be lovely," the dark-haired woman said, sounding disappointed. They followed Jenny to the coffee shop, throwing backward glances over their shoulders.

"I guess we'd better be prepared," Marnie said, watching them walk away. "It's going to be a busy day. Nothing gets business hopping like a local murder."

"Are you sure you want to stay? If you prefer to go home, I'll understand."

"No. The last thing I want is to be alone. I'd have nothing to do but think. I'd rather keep busy."

"Are you sure? People will be in all day, wanting to hear the details. They'll want to talk about her, share memories. That might be too much for you."

She raised her chin. "It'll be better than being alone." She picked up the phone. "I'll give Bruce a call. He always knows how to make me feel better."

I busied myself tidying up the displays, all the while lending a discreet ear to her conversation. After telling him about Helen's death, all she said was "yes," "no," and then her tone took on a happier note. "Really? You mean it? See? I knew you'd feel differently if you gave it a bit more thought."

She hung up. "Bruce changed his mind about moving away."

"He did? I'm really happy for you." She joined me at the armoire and pulled out a stack of hand towels and began refolding them. I kept an eye on her as we worked. I caught her tearing up a few times, but she just blinked away the wetness.

In my short time in this sleepy little community I'd learned that any death—especially a murder—always hit the townsfolk hard. Most of them had lived here all their lives. They felt protective of their own, and when one of them became the victim of a crime, everyone shuddered, wondering who among them could be the culprit. Marnie was holding on to her emotions for now, but I knew she'd fall apart the second she was alone.

A group of customers walked in and I busied myself helping them. Another couple of women walked in, and before I knew it the store was full and we were running ourselves ragged. Around twelve thirty, there was a sudden lull. When the last customer had finished paying, I handed her the bill and opened my drawer to get a new sales pad, riffling through the papers in the drawer. Instantly, Winston's ears perked up. Whenever I opened that drawer, he figured he was getting a treat. I threw him a liver cookie. He gulped it down and then looked at me expectantly.

"Sorry, buddy. No more."

"What are you looking for?" Marnie asked.

"We're out of sales pads. I must have forgotten to order new ones."

"Why don't I run out and pick up a couple of

generic receipt pads from Mercantile's?" she said. "They won't be as nice as the ones you usually buy, but we can stamp the name of the shop at the top until your new order comes in." She looked so eager to go that I realized she needed the break. A walk would do her good.

"Go. In the meantime I'll call the printer and place the order. Get enough to carry us through the next couple of weeks."

"Will do."

I opened the cash register, pulled out a few bills, and handed them to her. She grabbed her bag and a second later the door closed behind her. I made my way to the back and peeked through the beaded curtain. A group of ladies were huddled around a table, no doubt talking about Helen's murder. I caught Margaret's eye and waved her over. She whispered something to Jenny and made her way through the tables to me.

"Did I read you right? Were you seriously about to tell Marnie that we don't trust her fiancé?"

"Somebody has to tell her," she said defensively.

"I agree, but for God's sake, not now. She's already got enough on her plate. I don't think she could handle more bad news."

"I suppose. But what if Helen's death pushes her even deeper into the arms of that man? Do you think we should take that chance?"

"What are you talking about, deeper? She can't get much deeper than engaged. Besides. How do you propose we tell her? 'Hey, Marnie, you know that man you're head over heels in love with and planning to marry? Well, I'd hold off on that if I were you because I saw him flirting with another woman'?" I gave her the eyebrow. "I know exactly what she'll say. She'll tell us to butt out, that we're nuts and to stop meddling in her life. And not necessarily in that order."

Her gaze rose to the ceiling. "Unless . . ."

"Unless what?"

"Maybe Jenny can give her a reading. She usually goes to her before making big decisions."

"Did she ask her before getting engaged?"

"No." She scowled. "He sprang the big question over a romantic dinner. He even went down on one knee and popped open a little blue box. Of course, she said yes right away. Can't blame her for that. Any woman would have done the same."

I had to agree with her there. I might be compelled to let out an enthusiastic yes if Matthew so much as knelt to tie his shoelace. "A reading is a great idea. Let the cards tell her. That way she can't blame us." There was a hint of sarcasm in my voice, but if Margaret picked up on it, she didn't show it. "I'll suggest it to Jenny later."

I returned to my counter and called in my order of sales pads. Then I went to my loom and threw the shuttle halfheartedly for fifteen minutes or so. When I looked down at the rows I'd just completed, I saw that the thread tension was all over the place. Some rows were so tight I could barely tell where a stitch started or ended. Others were practically loose enough to be mistaken for fishnet. The result was a wavy texture worse than anything I saw in my beginner classes. I yanked out the yarn row by row, until I had a pool of thread at my feet. As I was rolling it back onto the bobbin, the bell sounded. I turned to see Marnie walking in, followed by Officer Lombard. I rose from my chair and joined them at the counter.

"Sorry to drop in this way," said the officer. "I have a few questions I forgot to ask. You said the vict—" She stopped and corrected herself. "The deceased was at your party last night?"

"That's right." I wasn't sure where she was going with this. "She arrived around seven thirty and left early—oh, I'd say it must have been nine or so."

"Did you happen to notice who she was talking to during the party? Or if she argued with anyone?"

All at once I had a flash of Helen and Bruce arguing. She was poking him in the chest with a finger, her face twisted in anger. Could Bruce have something to do with Helen's death? No. That was crazy thinking. But there was no way I could tell the police about that argument, at least not in front of Marnie.

"Della?" I startled. Officer Lombard was studying me. "Did you just remember something?"

"Oh, uh, no. I was just trying to. I was so busy making sure everybody's glass was filled and that the food kept coming, that if anything did happen, I didn't notice." A lie by omission was still a lie, I reminded myself. I hoped I didn't look as guilty as I felt.

"Could you give me a list of all the people at the party?"

"I can do that right away," I said, pulling out the guest list from the drawer. "It'll only take me a second to copy it down for you."

"Don't bother. I can photocopy it at the station and bring back the original." I handed it over. "Thanks." She perused it and then folded the page and slipped it into her notepad. "I'll have it back to you tomorrow." She turned to Marnie, who had been listening quietly during this time. "Did you happen to notice the deceased talking to anyone last night?"

She shook her head. "No. Not at all." She began putting away the sales pads in the drawer. I tried to read her expression, but she was shuffling things around, lining them up neatly, seemingly intent on organizing everything in the catchall drawer. I couldn't swear to it, but I had the impression she was avoiding the officer's eyes. I knew my friend well, and I'd say she looked at least as guilty as I felt.

Chapter 5

As soon as the police officer left, Marnie seemed to relax.

"Marnie," I said tentatively, "are you certain you didn't notice Helen talking with anyone at the party?"

"What are you suggesting?" she snapped. "Are you saying I just lied to the police? Why would I do that?"

"I'm not suggesting anything of the kind. I just thought you looked nervous when Officer Lombard asked you if you saw anyone talking with Helen at the party. That's all."

"Well, if I looked nervous, that must mean I'm hiding something, right?" She grabbed the empty cup from the top of the counter and stormed away, but not before adding, "For your information, everybody feels nervous when the cops are around, and doubly so when they're being questioned. That doesn't mean they just killed someone." A second later she marched off to the coffee shop.

Just killed someone? What the hell? Why would

Marnie even imagine that I would suspect her of something so vile? It was ridiculous. As for her excuse for being nervous, that was not so far-fetched. Everyone *was* nervous around cops, including me. The instant I spotted a squad car while I was driving, my heart went into overdrive. I pulled out the rubber stamp and one of the sales pads just as Marnie returned with a fresh cup of coffee and looking contrite.

"I'm sorry," I said. "Please don't be upset. Of course I don't suspect you. I'm just worried about you. That's all."

"Give that to me. I can do it," she said. She set her cup on the counter, splashing half of it all over the pad. "Now look at what you just made me do." And just like that, a stream of tears ran down her cheeks.

"Don't worry. It's no big deal." I grabbed a stack of paper napkins and blotted the spill, glancing at her as I did. She'd been holding on since hearing the news of Helen's death, but, now, all that pent-up emotion was boiling over. "See? All fixed." I threw the napkins into the wastebasket, and patting her arm, I said, "Listen, Marnie, you should be home right now. You should take a nap, do some weaving or baking—whatever makes you feel better." She snatched a balled-up tissue from her sleeve and dabbed at her eyes. "Let it out," I said. "Keeping your feelings bottled up isn't going to do you any good. Go ahead and have a good cry. That's what I'd do if I'd just lost a friend."

"No, really, I'm fine." She blew her nose and tossed the tissue into the wastebasket. "See?"

"This is what you call fine? I'd hate to see what you look like when you're feeling bad."

She cracked a weak smile. "Maybe you're right," she said. "I need a few minutes to compose myself. But I really don't want to go home. I'll just go to the back and have a sit-down for a few minutes." I didn't think a sit-down, as she called it, would be much help, but there was no point in insisting. When Marnie made up her mind, there was no changing it. She picked up her bag and headed for the coffee shop. A moment later she had disappeared behind the beaded curtain. I wondered if Jenny would offer her a reading now, and prayed she'd wait until Marnie was more in control of her emotions. A bad reading now could send her over the edge. I hurried to the beaded curtain, and when I peeked in, Jenny had an arm around Marnie and was pulling up a chair for her. I had nothing to worry about. Her movements were full of sympathy. She would never do anything to make Marnie feel worse. I returned to the counter.

All morning I'd been dying to call Matthew. I picked up the phone and punched in his cell number. I had so much to tell him. There was Helen's murder and the argument I'd witnessed between her and Marnie's fiancé last night. His phone rang half a dozen times before he answered.

"Hi, Della. What's up?"

"Where are you?"

"I'm just getting out of the city. As long as I don't hit traffic, I should be back in Briar Hollow in about an hour. My meeting went way faster than I thought."

"Oh, sorry. I don't want you talking on your phone while you're driving."

"Don't worry about it. I'm on hands-free. What's on your mind?"

"I don't know if you've heard. Helen Dubois was murdered."

There was a sharp intake of breath. "When did this happen?"

"She was at my party last night, so it had to have happened some time during the night or early this morning."

"Let me guess. You found her body?"

"Er . . . yes. I just happened to drop by her place. And when she didn't come to the door, I looked in the window."

"That can't have been very pleasant. How's Marnie taking it?"

"She's holding up as best she can. I've been trying to get her to go home, but she won't hear of it. Listen, why don't you come over for dinner tonight and I'll tell you everything?"

"Does that mean you're cooking?" he asked, sounding less grim.

"Not unless you want frozen pizza. That's about all I have at the moment. I could always run over to the store and pick up something."

"I have a better idea. I can pick up dinner and bring it over."

"Sounds like a plan."

"By the way, I dropped off Marnie's flag at the history museum. My friend took one look at it and almost passed out. He brought it to the back and showed it to his assistant. I have a feeling that thing is worth a small fortune. You should have seen the staff when they gathered around. They looked like they were witnessing the unveiling of the *Mona Lisa*. He asked to keep it for a day or two, and promised to send it back to Marnie the minute he's finished examining it. I hope Marnie won't mind."

"You really think it's worth a lot of money?"

"Let me put it this way. My friend suggested Marnie might want to have it carbon-dated."

"Hold on a second. Carbon dating—don't they have to cut pieces out of it to do that? That would ruin its value."

"Maybe in some cases, but he noticed that one of the corners is a bit frayed. He said he could take a few threads without causing any damage."

"Is that all he'd need?"

"I wouldn't worry. If the Vatican allowed the Shroud of Turin to be carbon-dated, I'd say that Marnie can allow the flag to be tested without worry. Anyhow, it'll be up to Marnie. He can venture a guess as to its value, but if she wants a more exact figure, she'll probably want to do further testing."

"I suppose so." I chuckled. "Would you mind if I tell Marnie the good news? It might lift her spirits a bit."

There was the blast of a car horn and Matthew swore under his breath. "Some idiot nearly rammed into me. Listen, I'd better stop talking and concentrate on driving. Since I'm coming over for dinner, I won't bother picking up Winston before that. See you around six." He clicked off.

I put the receiver down just as Marnie returned. I wondered if Jenny had given her a reading. Probably not. Margaret would have waited for me to make the suggestion to Jenny.

"I have some good news for you," I said. "Matthew dropped off your flag at the museum, and they think it's worth a lot of money."

"Really?"

"They offered to have it carbon-dated. They wouldn't mention something like that unless they were quite certain."

She wiped a hand over her brow. "It's all so crazy. I had it sitting in a dresser drawer for years. I had almost forgotten about it. And now I'm worried about sending it out to experts."

"They said they'd have it back to you in a couple of days. But you should have it insured as soon as possible."

"Again, insurance," she said, sounding surprised. "I went through my whole life without ever worrying about it, and now, that's all I seem to be hearing about—mortgage insurance, life insurance, and now property insurance."

"What do you mean?"

"Bruce is concerned about my financial security. Isn't that sweet of him? He offered to go over my investments with me the other day, and when he saw how little I have in my retirement account, he suggested we get joint life insurance. That way, if he dies first, I'll be financially secure for the rest of my life. I can't believe how protective of me he is. We're not even married yet and he's already looking out for my safety."

"That is nice," I said. "What's joint life insurance?"

"Hmm. I don't know much about life insurance in general, but this one sounded like a smart choice. He said it was also called a first-to-die policy. We only pay one premium, but whichever one of us dies first, the other collects the face amount. The agent said it was a no-brainer for couples concerned about each other's financial security."

"I think I have heard of those," I said. "How much is the face amount?"

"A million dollars."

My eyebrows jumped. "Wow. You'll be rich if he dies first." *Or he will be if Marnie predeceases him.* I had no idea why that idea popped into my mind, but now that it had, I couldn't shake it.

"I know it's an awful thought, but that's what he said too. At first he only mentioned getting a policy on his life, and then he remembered about joint life." The bell tinkled and a couple of women walked in, cutting our conversation short.

"Welcome to Dream Weaver," Marnie said, walking over. Meanwhile, all kinds of crazy notions were whirling through my mind. I pushed them away and plastered on a smile. She guided them to the armoire where a stack of handwoven Turkish towels were displayed.

The rest of the afternoon went by in a continuous stream of clients. As grateful as I was for the business—by day's end I had sold more in a few hours than I usually did in a week—I was even more grateful for the reprieve it seemed to offer Marnie. As long as she was running around helping clients, she didn't have time to grieve. But as soon as the shop became quiet, around five thirty, the mournful look returned to her eyes. She looked around for something to do, and noticing the dish towel I had been working on at my loom, she examined it.

"This is beautiful," she said. "I love the navy on white. But you know what would look really pretty is purple on white."

"Purple? Are you sure? I've never been asked for purple before."

"I don't know about anybody else," she said, "but I'd love it." She grabbed her purse and blew me a kiss. "See you tomorrow, sugar pie." She was trying to sound breezy, but didn't quite make it.

"What are your plans for the evening?" I asked.

She paused at the door and sighed. "I sure hope

Bruce will be okay with a quiet evening at home. I don't have the energy to do anything but veg in front of the TV. I'll try to find out about the funeral arrangements for Helen. I'll let you know." The door closed behind her, and I was left wondering about her comment. Had she somehow guessed that the towels I was making were for her? Was this a hint that she'd prefer purple? Regardless, I would just finish this towel and put it in stock, then start a new set for Marnie. But it wouldn't be nearly as much fun if the surprise was spoiled.

Winston stirred. He looked up at me with big questioning eyes.

"Ready to go for a walk, big boy?" He jumped to his feet, suddenly alert. "Going for a walk is your favorite thing, isn't it? Along with treats, belly rubs, and head scratches." I pulled out his leash and he almost convulsed with joy. "Hold on for a second." I clipped it on and called out to Jenny in the back. "I'm off. Do you want me to lock the door as I leave?"

"Don't bother. We're just leaving too." She and Margaret appeared in the doorway. "Good God. We had such a busy day. By four o'clock we were out of muffins and apple turnovers and cakes and pies. All we had left was plain bread, tomatoes, lettuce, and bacon. I never made so many BLTs in my life."

"We were crazy busy too," I said, picking up my bank deposit.

I followed them out and locked up. Margaret

waved good-bye to us and ran up the stairs. I turned to Jenny.

"I have an idea. Instead of warning Marnie about Bruce, why don't you give her a reading? That way, you can couch the advice in the form of a prediction."

"Margaret told me about the idea. I think it's brilliant. I'll do that."

"By the way, Marnie noticed the dish towel I was working on and commented that it would look lovely with purple on white. I think we should make everything that way for her."

"Purple?"

"I know. But if that's what she wants . . ."

She shrugged. "Purple it is, then. I'll call all the ladies and let them know."

"What are you up to tonight?" I asked. She smiled secretively and I guessed the answer. "Don't tell me." I closed my eyes and brought my fingertips to my temple. "I see you having dinner with an attractive doctor. Yes, I see him kissing you—"

She chuckled. "Ha, ha. Very funny. Laugh all you want, but you'll see. Someday you'll believe in my abilities. I have an idea. Why don't you join us? I'm only making pasta—nothing fancy. "

"Thanks, but Matthew is coming over for dinner."

"Ooh. Are you planning to seduce him over some of your fine takeout?" she said, alluding to my lack of culinary skills.

"Not fair. I've been learning to cook, and I can

make a mean beef bourguignon, I'll have you know. But I'm afraid seduction is not on the menu tonight. I'm planning to tell him my concerns about Marnie's fiancé."

"Great. Maybe he'll have some words of wisdom to share."

"So how was your day? Did you make a lot of money?"

"It was so busy, we hardly had time to breathe. We had a few short lulls, none of them for more than a few minutes. All in all a good day, maybe double the usual amount of business."

"I forgot to tell you," I said. "Officer Lombard stopped by earlier. She asked for a list of everyone who attended the party."

"Does she think somebody from the party might have killed Helen?"

"Your guess is as good as mine. She seemed interested in who was talking with Helen at the party, and if anyone had argued with her."

"And?"

"And, I did see her arguing—with none other than Bruce." A new idea occurred to me. "You don't think he has anything to do with her death, do you?"

Jenny gave me an incredulous look. "Now, you're being completely paranoid. The man might be a flirt, but that doesn't make him a murderer."

"You're probably right," I said. "I'm so worried about him hurting Marnie that I'm painting him as a worse villain than he is." At that moment a car came to a stop a few feet away and I recognized Ed Green, Jenny's boyfriend, at the wheel.

"Oh, there's Ed," she said, beaming. "See you tomorrow," she called, sliding into the passenger seat. I watched them drive away, wondering if Jenny was right. Was I becoming paranoid? Every time anyone so much as mentioned Bruce's name, I grew more suspicious of him. I glanced at my watch. If I wanted to freshen up before Matthew got here, I had better get a move on.

"Let's go, big boy. We have to go do that bank deposit and get back in time to get pretty for Matthew." He looked at me as if I had rocks in my head. "Come on. The sooner we get home, the sooner you get a treat." He broke into a gallop, dragging me along at the end of his leash.

Chapter 6

I was ready. I had changed into my blue dress, one I knew Matthew liked. My makeup was fresh—smoky eyes and a new color of lipstick called Kissable Pink. And I looked hot. Hopefully, he would think so too. A bottle of Chardonnay was cooling in the refrigerator, and in case he preferred red, I also had a bottle of Brunello. I had just finished setting the table when the phone rang. I glanced at the call display—my mother.

"Honestly, Della, I don't know how you do it," she blurted. "Why is it that if there's a death anywhere within a hundred miles, you're going to find the body?"

"Nice talking to you too, Mom."

"I'm sorry, sweetheart. It's just that I worry for you. Promise me you're not going to start poking around, trying to find out who killed that poor woman. That can only get you into trouble, or worse—dead."

"I suppose you read about that online?" A few years ago, I'd taught my mother to use the

Internet—a momentary lapse of judgment on my part. Now, my sixty-nine-year-old mother could check on the latest news or gossip from Briar Hollow with no more than the stroke of a key. She'd even arranged for local news to stream directly into her in-box. Any little thing that happened near me sent her into a panic. Okay, so a murder wasn't exactly any little thing, I admit. Still, she often made me feel like a teenager with overprotective parents.

"Did you know the woman?" she said, ignoring my question.

"I'd only met her a few times. She was the local librarian and had just registered for one of my weaving classes."

"A librarian. Honestly, what is this world coming to? Why in the world would anybody want to kill a librarian? The article didn't say how she died, just that her death looked suspicious. But I'm right, aren't I? She was murdered, wasn't she?"

"Until the coroner confirms it, I don't really know." There was no point in getting my mother more riled up than she already was.

"What does Matthew think?"

"I haven't had a chance to talk to him about it yet. He was in Charlotte all day. But he's coming over for dinner. I'm sure we'll discuss it then."

Her tone went up an octave. "He's coming over for dinner? Are you cooking for him? Does that mean what I think it does? Are you two starting to date?"

"Yes. No, no, and no," I said. "It'll be takeout. It only means that we're friends and, no, we are not starting to date."

She clucked her tongue, and I had a vision of her wagging her finger at me. "If only you'd take my advice and flirt with him. He's such a nice boy."

"Matthew is hardly a boy, Mom."

"And he'd make a great husband," she added, ignoring my comment.

"Stop it, Mom. I don't want to hear this."

"Fine. I won't say another word. But let me at least say this. When Matthew tries to talk some sense into you, will you please take his advice? One of these days, Della, you're going to find yourself in real trouble."

"Don't worry, Mom. I have no intention of getting involved in a murder case."

The long sigh at the other end of the line told me she didn't believe a word I'd just said. Truth be told, she had a right to her skepticism—not that I was actually planning anything, at least not until I had a suspect. All at once, it occurred to me that I did have a suspect. Bruce Doherty and Helen had argued at the party. Of course, I was stretching a bit here, but seeing as he was engaged to Marnie, wasn't it my duty as a friend to look into the background of this man? All for Marnie's sake, of course. The best part was that I could keep my hands clean, if I could convince Matthew to investigate the man. Hmm. That idea might be worth exploring. With his police connections, it would be easy as pie for him. Before teaching criminology, Matthew used to work with the FBI. When he moved here, it didn't take long for the local police department to hear about his experience and start asking for his help on some of the more complex cases.

"Della? You still there?" My mother's voice brought me back.

"Sorry, my mind was wandering. Oh, will you look at the time?" I said. "Matthew will be here any minute and I'm far from ready." Another fib. Why did I always find myself lying to my mother? I was a bad, bad daughter.

"I hope you're wearing a dress. Men like to see women in dresses."

"Yes, I am."

"And I hope you're wearing makeup. Sometimes you don't wear enough eye makeup."

"I do my makeup very nicely; thank you."

"And make sure to do some listening for a change. Don't hog the conversation all night. Let him put in a word now and then."

"I'm hanging up now, Mom. Love you. Bye." I dropped my phone into my bag, just as the buzzer rang. Winston galloped past me, coming to a screeching halt at the door.

"It's me." Matthew's voice came through the receiver. A moment later, he appeared, carrying two bags of takeout sporting the mountain-range logo of the Longview. He looked drop-dead gorgeous in a plaid shirt and a pair of faded blue jeans.

"Dinner for two," he said, handing me the bags. "Southern fried chicken, mashed potatoes, and gravy as a main course, and pecan pie for dessert." He gazed down at me.

"Sounds yummy," I said, tearing my eyes away from his before I lost myself in them. "After all those calories, I'll just have to starve myself for the rest of the week."

"You're in perfect shape. I wouldn't worry about it if I were you."

He thought I was perfect? I felt a blush rising and turned away. "Would you like red or white?" I asked, leading the way to the kitchen and handing him the bottle opener.

"White," he said.

I opened the fridge, pointing to the bottle inside. "Help yourself." I plated the food and carried the dishes to the dining room. And then I lit the single candle I'd set in the center of the table and dimmed the lights.

"Wow. Aren't we being fancy?"

All at once I felt foolish. A second later, when the candle went out. I turned the light back on.

"That's much better. Now we can see what we're eating," I said. For a moment I thought he looked disappointed—projection, no doubt.

He cleared his throat. "Helen Dubois, the dead woman—she was a good friend of Marnie's, wasn't she?"

"She was. Marnie put up a good front. She insisted on staying at work all day. But I could tell she was upset. Even the news about your friend agreeing that her flag is worth a fortune barely cheered her up."

"That's understandable," he said, as he poured the wine. "Losing a friend is a painful experience." He offered me a glass and raised his. "To happier days." We sipped. "By the way, you didn't tell me how Helen was killed."

"She was strangled, by the looks of it. I only had a quick glance, but her face was bloated and almost purple."

"Well, if that's how she died, chances are the killer was a man, and a strong one at that."

I shuddered as a picture of Marnie's fiancé with his hands wrapped around Helen's throat flashed through my mind. "Strangled. I can't imagine a worse way to die. I'd rather be shot."

"Nice thought." He gave me a crooked smile. "I'd rather die in my sleep."

"Let's not talk about murder and death while we're eating, please—if you don't mind."

"Don't tell me you're getting squeamish. I always thought murder was one of your favorite subjects."

I ignored that comment and dove into my meal with enthusiasm. "Good chicken," I said between bites. "By the way, I told you that Marnie is getting married, remember?"

"Yes, of course. I realized after I got back in my

car this morning that I'd forgotten to congratulate her."

"Don't you know? You never congratulate the bride—only the groom."

"I'll keep that in mind," he said, chuckling. "Didn't this all happen really fast? Didn't you tell me she just met the guy?"

"It's way too fast if you ask me. But that's only one of the reasons I'm worried. I don't like that man one bit."

He paused, fork in midair. "You usually like everyone. What did he do to make you dislike him?"

"If you'd seen the way he was behaving at last night's party, you wouldn't like him either."

"Tell me."

"I had some friends over—a sort of surprise wedding shower in Marnie's honor. I wasn't expecting him to show up, but he was with her when she came—"

"You can't seriously be holding that against him."

"That has nothing to do with it. It was the way he behaved. It was the first time most of Marnie's friends met him. I know it was mine. Instead of standing by Marnie's side, he went off and started flirting with one of the guests."

"Flirting? In front of everyone? That's rather rude."

I hesitated. "Well . . . in all honesty, I can't swear that they were flirting, but it sure looked like it to me. And then, as if that wasn't enough, he got into a nasty argument with another of the guests." I told him about the secretive way he and Melinda Wilson carried on their conversation, but before I got to the confrontation with Helen, he put up a hand.

"Melinda Wilson . . . I've heard that name before."

"She's a baker from Belmont—a friend of Marnie's."

"Nice friend. Although, in all fairness, even if you're right and they were trying to cover up the fact that they were talking, that doesn't automatically mean they were doing something illicit. They weren't necessarily arranging to meet."

"If it was all so innocent, why were they being so covert?"

"Don't get upset. I'm just saying. Any possibility you misread their body language?" He must have been reading *my* body language right, because he abruptly changed the subject. "Okay, let's move on. Tell me more about the argument he had."

"I couldn't hear what he and Helen Dubois were arguing about—"

"Whoa. Are you talking about the same Helen Dubois who was murdered?"

"That's right," I said. "Now do you get it?"

He leaned back in his chair. "Tell me more."

"I was across the room, so I didn't hear what they were saying. But I can tell you she looked mad as hell, jabbing him in the chest with her finger. Meanwhile, he was glancing around nervously."

"Sounds like more than just a mild disagreement."

"That's what I think too," I said, knowing that my next words were bound to get a rise out of him. "Which brings me to my problem." His eyes narrowed. "Officer Lombard came to the shop to ask me who Helen was talking with last night and if I'd seen her arguing with anyone. And . . . well . . . I sort of lied. I said I was too busy all evening to notice."

His eyes suddenly turned dark, a clear sign I was about to get a good talking-to. "Why the hell did you do a stupid thing like that?"

"You would have done the same thing," I said. "Marnie was standing right next to me when the policewoman was questioning me. What was I supposed to do? I couldn't very well blurt out that I thought her fiancé was a murderer." I tried to read his eyes as they lasered into mine.

His brows rose. "Murderer? Are you suggesting he killed Helen? What gave you that idea? Just the fact that he and Helen had an argument at your party?"

"Well, if he didn't, don't you think it's quite a coincidence? He's seen arguing with a woman, and then a few hours later she turns up dead. Isn't that one of the first things the police do? Look for people with whom victims recently argued?"

He picked up his fork again and resumed eating. "You're adding one plus one and coming up with ten. If the only evidence you have against him is that he was arguing with the victim the night before she died, that's no evidence at all. Certainly nothing worth concluding he's a killer." His next words were exactly what Jenny had said. "He might be a flirt, but that doesn't make him a murderer."

"I just remembered something," I said, snapping my fingers. "Bruce announced to Marnie over breakfast this morning that he wasn't so crazy about living in Briar Hollow after all. And this is after weeks of telling her how much he loved it here." Okay, so this was a bit of an exaggeration, but he had talked about loving the weather here. "He said he wanted to move. Don't you think that's strange?" He quirked an eyebrow. "Well, I think it is," I continued. "He has a huge argument with Helen Dubois. The next morning he announces that he doesn't like it all that much here after all. Then, as soon as Marnie announces to him that Helen Dubois is dead, he suddenly changes his mind about wanting to move. What do you make of that?"

"Interesting," he said. "But that hardly proves anything. For one thing, if he murdered her, as you want to believe, he would have already known she was dead. So his decision to stay in Briar Hollow probably had nothing to do with Helen Dubois's death."

I deflated. "I hate when you get so logical."

"I thought my logic was one of the things you like best about me," he said. I glanced up from my plate. His smile was all mischief, and my heart skipped a beat.

"Hardly," I said, assessing whether this was an attempt on his part to flirt or if he was just being the bratty kid that used to drop ice cubes down the back of my T-shirt. Definitely the brat, I decided. "Still," I said, "don't you think we should investigate?"

"We? You know how I feel about you playing detective."

"Okay, so not we. You."

"I am not going to investigate someone for the reasons you just outlined."

"Well, here's what really has me worried. Bruce talked Marnie into taking out a life insurance policy for one million bucks."

That got his attention. "Are you telling me she named him as beneficiary?"

I nodded. "Now do you get it?"

He took another bite of chicken and chewed in silence for a moment. "If it was anybody else, I'd flat out tell them there was nothing to investigate. But I have to admit, you do have an instinct for these things. I'm probably going to regret this, but . . ."

"Thank you. I'm telling you, there's something wrong with the man."

Suddenly Winston hurtled straight into the table, trying to look over the top. The next few seconds seemed to play in slow motion. Glasses fell over, splashing wine everywhere. Then the table dipped, and plates, glasses, and cutlery went crashing to the floor.

"Winston!" Matthew said. The dog froze. He studied the mess in silence and then slunk away with his head low. "You should feel guilty," Matthew called after him. He squatted, picking up broken pieces of porcelain.

I hurried to the kitchen to get a mop. "Don't be upset with Winnie," I said. "The table is old. I should really get a new one."

"I'll take a look at it. Maybe I can fix it." As soon we finished clearing up the mess, Matthew assessed the damage. "I'll swing by with some tools tomorrow and it'll be as good as new."

"I guess that brings us to coffee and dessert," I said. As I ground coffee, Matthew brought the conversation back to Bruce.

"Where does this Bruce guy live?"

"He's been staying at the Longview for the last month, maybe longer. I don't know much about him." I shrugged. "Marnie says he was a successful financial advisor, sold his firm, and came out here looking for a place to retire."

"Retire? How old is the guy?"

"I don't know for sure, but I'd say he must be around forty-five or so—maybe even younger."

"Really?" He leaned against the doorway, folding his arms. "I thought you were going to say he was in his sixties or older. But if he's only in his forties, he's awfully young to be retiring." He said this as if retiring young suddenly made Doherty more suspicious. He continued. "In my experience, a successful financial advisor will postpone retiring for as long as he can. He'll take on assistants or even partners. That way he can enjoy as much free time as he likes and still keep the money rolling in. Maybe the guy wasn't doing as well as he wants everyone to believe."

"There's something else too." I felt like a real jerk for saying this. "Not only is he younger than Marnie by about a decade, but he's handsome. And you know Marnie. She's the salt of the earth, and anybody who gets to know her loves her, but she wouldn't exactly win any beauty pageants."

"That doesn't mean a thing. Some men like a woman with some meat on her and with some experience."

"How do you like your women?" I asked. As soon as the question was out, I wanted to bite back the words. Then I reminded myself that everybody kept telling me I should flirt with him. His eyes met mine with a mischievous glint.

"Oh, I don't know. I like them pretty. Pretty is better than ugly. And I like them smart. Smart sounds better than stupid."

"Very funny. Well, there are plenty of pretty and smart girls around. How come you're still not dating anybody?" Now I knew I was pushing it.

"Maybe because the girl I like isn't available."

He was still looking at me, but I couldn't read his expression.

"You're in love with a married woman?" I was shocked. When I'd first moved to Briar Hollow, I'd imagined that something might have been going on between Jenny and him. To my relief, I'd soon found out that all they shared was a friendship. If Matthew was in love with a married woman, that would explain why he was still single. And more importantly, why he was taking so little notice of me.

"I didn't mean unavailable in that way. She just doesn't like me the way I like her." He tilted his head and stared at me. "Why aren't you attached?"

I blushed. "Oh, I guess I'm just too involved with starting my business to have time for love and romance." I cleared my throat and changed the subject before he could see how his question had rattled me. "About men liking older women, I might agree with you except that I saw the way he made a beeline for Melinda Wilson at that party. And you know how beautiful Melinda is."

"I still think you could be wrong. Any idea where he's from?" he asked.

"Seattle, according to Liz Carter. She's the one who introduced Bruce to Marnie."

"He shouldn't be too hard to trace."

"I'm so glad you'll look into him."

"Hold on. Don't get all excited. I'm just going to run his name through the system, see if he has a criminal record. And, to be honest, I know this is a complete waste of time. I fully expect him to come out clean. If it was for anybody else, I would never agree to do this."

"Thanks. I'll owe you one. And what should I do about the police? You know, about not mentioning that I saw him arguing with Helen at the party."

"Tell me again what you saw."

I described the scene, right down to the way Helen Dubois was stabbing Doherty in the chest with her finger while he looked around nervously.

"Maybe he was embarrassed. Being caught in an argument in the middle of a party would be uncomfortable. He would have wanted to put an end to it as fast as he could."

"Maybe," I said, unconvinced.

"Don't worry. I promised I'd look into him, and that's exactly what I'll do. What's his surname?"

"Doherty." I spelled it out for him and he scribbled it on a piece of paper.

"So where's that dessert? I picked pie because I know that's your favorite," he said, and the atmosphere lightened.

"Wish I could say I cooked it," I said, chuckling.

He poured the coffee while I served the pie. A few minutes later we settled in the living room and ate in companionable silence. At one point I happened to glance at him and was surprised to find him staring at me with a contented smile. It occurred to me that if he had been sitting next to me rather than across from me, he might have leaned over and kissed me right about now. I debated moving over to the sofa, and just as I was gathering my courage, he stood.

"Well, that was a pleasant evening, but I think I'd better get going. I have a lot of writing to do tomorrow." Winston trotted over to him and he bent down to scratch his head. "Want to go home, big boy?"

Winston went into a break dance. *Traitor*. Why did he have to look so happy?

Chapter 7

I was at the store at eight o'clock the next morning, opening my copy of the *Belmont Daily* and in desperate need of a cup of java. If I didn't get one soon, I would go into serious caffeine withdrawal. Hopefully Jenny would be here soon. I glanced at the headlines, expecting to find the usual small-town article—something about a local spelling bee, or maybe a high school football game, but to my surprise, today's big, bold letters screamed BREAK-IN AT THE LONGVIEW. And underneath in slightly smaller print, THIEVES GET AWAY WITH VALUABLE PAINTING.

Oh, no. I knew just the painting they were talking about. *Poor Bunny.* Bunny was a local success story. She was born and raised in Briar Hollow, and then, a couple of decades ago, she moved to New York and became an interior designer. Now she was a nationally known television personality and star of her own decorating show. A few years ago she had come back to Briar Hollow, bought the local bed-and-breakfast, the Longview, and with her impeccable taste in decor had soon turned it into a profitable business. Then, last fall, she had poured a ton of money into the place, giving it a new identity as an elegant boutique hotel with an adjoining dining room and hiring a top-notch chef. Just a few weeks ago, she'd proudly told me about her latest purchase, an original Grandma Moses that she planned to display in the hotel lobby.

"I think what this town needs is a touch of glamour," she'd said casually when I'd questioned the wisdom of such an extravagance. "Don't worry. You know Grandma Moses's style. Nothing of hers is sophisticated. Her work is charming in a quaint country way—perfect for Briar Hollow."

She had misunderstood my concern. I was worried about the expense, not the style. Still, she was right. Briar Hollow was not Manhattan. And Main Street was not Fifth Avenue. Before the Longview's renovations, our best local restaurant had been the Bottoms Up, a combination eatery and bar complete with pool table.

Bunny's acquiring the painting for the Longview had created a lot of local buzz. So much so that half the people in town made a special outing just to dine at the restaurant and look at the painting. And the Longview's new restaurant became an instant success.

All I could say was that I hoped she had insurance. At that moment I noticed some movement at the front door. It flew open and Jenny strode in.

"Did you hear the news?" she said. "Bunny's been robbed. They took her Grandma Moses."

"I was just reading about that this very minute. Poor Bunny. She must be so upset."

"I swear, Briar Hollow is becoming as dangerous as any big city—murders, robberies . . ."

"I'd hardly compare our crime rate to that of Charlotte," I said. "That's one of the reasons I moved here."

She paused, resting her elbows on the counter. "I know. It's just unnerving is all. I feel so awful for her. I know she loved that painting."

"Have you spoken to her?"

"No, not yet. I tried calling her, but her phone is busy."

I snatched my cell from my bag and punched in her number. "Still busy," I said.

"She's probably getting calls from everybody in town."

"How much was that painting worth? Do you have any idea?" I asked.

"At least a few hundred thousand dollars, I'd say. I Googled Grandma Moses when she first bought it, and let me tell you, her paintings are not cheap." She straightened. "I have to make the coffee. This robbery means another marathon day of gossiping. I'd better get ready for the crowds."

"Some people's bad luck," I said. "As if she didn't already have enough with what happened last year." The previous fall, Bunny had been engaged to the local multimillionaire. But instead of becoming her husband, the man was now serving a life sentence.

"I know. Crazy, isn't it?" She headed toward the back, shaking her head.

Soon the aroma of brewing coffee filled the air. The bell above the door tinkled again and Marnie came in, carrying her daily delivery of fresh pastries.

"Morning, sunshine," she said, sounding surprisingly upbeat. And then, winking, she added, "I have something I know you love in here. Apple turnovers. I had a bag of apples that were getting a bit wrinkled. Not good enough to eat raw but perfect for baking."

"Thanks. That's really sweet of you, but I'd better not. I had dinner with Matthew last night—fried chicken and pecan pie from the Longview." I patted my stomach. "I'm going to have to let out a few seams."

She harrumphed as she walked by on her way to the back. "Right. You are so very fat. I wish I was so fat."

"You're the one with the fiancé, so don't come crying to me," I said. I was tempted to ask if she'd learned anything about Helen's funeral arrangements, but decided to hold off. The question would only kill her good mood.

"You could have a boyfriend too if only you learned to flirt a bit. Speaking of"—she turned and marched back, dropping her boxes on the counter—"how did your dinner with Prince Charming go?"

Oh, dear. I knew exactly where this was heading. She'd be giving me another of her speeches. Why was everybody so convinced I needed lessons in flirting? "For your information, it went very well," I said, looking for a way to change the subject. "Did you hear about the robbery? Bunny's Grandma Moses painting was stolen."

"Really? How awful." She knitted her eyebrows. "You know, there's been quite a string of robberies lately."

"That's news to me."

She nodded. "Oh, yes. They're happening all around Charlotte, in museums, in private homes, everywhere."

"Right," I said, remembering. "I was reading about that just yesterday."

"Bruce left his paper at my place last night," she said. "I went to bed early and slept for a while, but after doing all my baking I couldn't get back to sleep. Damn menopause. When it's not hot flashes, it's insomnia. So I sat up and read for a while." I suspected her sleeplessness might have had more to do with the news of Helen's death than hormones. "Seems the cops suspect all those robberies are the work of the same person," She continued, picking up her boxes. "Well, you and I have nothing to worry about. We don't have anything worth stealing."

"You're right about me, but from the sounds of it, that flag of yours is worth a pretty penny."

She looked startled. "It completely slipped my

mind. I was supposed to find out about insuring it. I'd better do that as soon as possible." She frowned. "But I don't even have an exact value on it yet."

"The curator said he'd be able to give you at least a rough idea of its value. Call your insurance broker. He'll be able to advise you."

"Yeah. Right. I know what he'll do. He'll slip me some hugely expensive policy, hand me a pen, and say, 'Sign here.'" She headed toward the back, looking irate.

"Wait. I want to hear all about your evening with Bruce." But she had already disappeared behind the curtain.

I returned to the article about the robbery. The painting, it seemed, had been wired, making it almost impossible to steal without triggering the alarm. When asked if the police had any suspects, they had answered with their customary "We're working on it." I picked up my cell and tried Bunny's number again—still busy. I dropped the phone back in my bag and returned to my project.

With the number of customers who'd come in yesterday, I'd hardly made any progress. I still had about fifty rows to do before I could take this one off the loom. I studied it. The dishcloth would be gorgeous. I'd pulled out the uneven threads until all that remained was perfect. But my misgivings about Marnie's fiancé had erased much of the pleasure of working on her wedding present. In spite of that, I picked up the shuttle and went back to work.

"Here's your cup of coffee," Marnie said, returning with a tray a few minutes later. I left my loom and joined her. "I know you said you didn't want one, but if you don't eat it, you'll hurt my feelings." With that she set a plate with an apple turnover on the counter.

"You know I can never turn down your baking," I said, groaning. "Did you see Bruce last night?" I asked.

"He came over for a quiet dinner at home." She smiled, and I was amazed to see her twirling a lock of hair, much the way a teenage girl might do. The woman was *so* evidently in love, and she was *so* going to get her heart broken. Her face clouded over. "I was pretty tired. I guess the news of Helen's death hit me harder than I thought, so he went back to his place early. Anyhow, you enjoy your coffee. I'll be right back. Jenny promised to give me a reading today and she's not too busy right now."

This I did not want to miss. I took another bite from my turnover, grabbed my coffee, and headed to the beaded curtain, hoping to listen in. Jenny shuffled the deck and then instructed Marnie to cut it and pick a card. For the next minute all I could hear was the sound of cards slapping against the table. Then, more shuffling and card slapping.

"Here we go," Jenny said. Before I could hear more, the front door opened and Margaret strolled in.

"Morning, Della," she called out. "What's going on?"

I signaled her to be quiet. "Jenny is giving Marnie a reading," I whispered.

Her eyes lit with sudden understanding. She lowered her voice, "Ooooh. I'm so glad Jenny took our suggestion. It's a great idea." She tiptoed over and we both strained to hear. I made out some whispering, none of it loud enough to understand.

"I can't hear a thing," Margaret said after a few minutes. "I'll go grab a cup of coffee and be right back." She stepped into the coffee shop. A minute later she returned. "I heard her tell Marnie to be careful, that she has a habit of trusting too easily." She gave me a thumbs-up.

"That's good. I hope she told her to be careful of tall dark-haired men who come bearing engagement rings."

"That might be a bit too obvious," she said.

"Perhaps, but she'd better make it really clear. Otherwise, you know Marnie—she'll give it some different interpretation. How did she seem?"

"Hard to say. She was just listening and nodding."

I strained to hear once again, but couldn't make out a word. "Damn it. Why do they have to speak so low? I want to know what Jenny is saying."

"Don't worry. Marnie will tell us, probably in excruciating detail."

I walked over to the counter and took a sip of my now-cold coffee. Margaret followed me. "You saw his behavior at the party, didn't you?" I said.

"Nancy Cuttler was flirting with him," she said.

"And he seemed to be flirting back. Then she just turned around and fled. It was weird."

Jenny said she had slipped him a piece of paper, I remembered. And what was Nancy's sudden panic all about? "So that's what happened. I ran into her when I was bringing in more wine."

"And then Helen Dubois went over to him. At first they seemed to be having a normal conversation, then suddenly she got really angry. I couldn't hear what she was saying, but he looked scared to death. He kept backing away from her and glancing over at Marnie." Her eyes grew wide. "Oh, my God. You don't think—" She shook her head. "No, that's just crazy."

"I don't think what?"

"You don't think he could have killed Helen, do you?"

The thought had crossed my mind. But chances were he had nothing to do with it. "For all we know, Helen could have been giving him a piece of her mind for carrying on that covert conversation with Melinda while his fiancée was just a few feet away."

"I hope you're right," Margaret said, looking doubtful. "But what if he did? Shouldn't we do something? Say something to Marnie?"

"Tell her what? We have no idea what he and Helen were arguing about. As for him being her murderer, that's pure conjecture."

And then she repeated the same words I'd been saying over and over. "Poor Marnie. He's going to break her heart. I just know it."

"That's my biggest fear too," I said. "If only I could find out what he and Melinda were talking about—to find out if they were really flirting."

"That's easy. Ask her," she said, as if it was the most natural suggestion in the world. And then, sensing my incredulity, she added, "Even if she lies, you should be able to read the body language."

"You're right. Go straight to the source." I snatched my purse and rummaged through it for my car keys while talking to myself. "I'll remind her that she owes Marnie. Without her, her bakery would have gone under. Maybe she'll fess up."

Margaret looked surprised. "You mean you're going there right this minute?"

"No better time than the present," I said. "Bakeries open early. I'll be back before you know it."

Chapter 8

I drove slowly. I'd left without a plan, without any idea how I was going to broach the subject.

Hey, there, Melinda, inquiring minds want to know. Were you flirting with Bruce Doherty? You do realize, don't you, that he's the man who's engaged to your good friend Marnie, the same good friend who taught you everything you know about baking?

The closer I got to Belmont, the crazier my spontaneous decision to just drop by felt. *I've come this far,* I thought, crossing the city lines. *I might as well go through with it.* I drove by the first few stores and craned my neck, trying to spot a bakery. In my rush to get here, I had left without the address or even the name of the store. All I knew was that it was situated somewhere along Main Street. I was halfway into my second drive-through when I spotted it. I parked across the street and made my way over.

It was a tiny shop, squeezed between a butcher and a green grocer. The sign read MELINDA'S and underneath, in smaller letters, FRESH FROM THE

OVEN. In the window was a display of breads, cookies, and pies. I walked in and was instantly enveloped in a blend of mouthwatering aromas— vanilla, apples and cinnamon, lemon. For a moment I almost forgot why I was here. Behind the counter a freckled-faced teenage boy with a head of red hair and a gap-toothed smile was transferring a tray of muffins to the display counter.

"Good morning. How can I help you?" he asked, straightening his lanky frame.

"I'm here to see Melinda. Is she in?"

He bobbed his head toward a doorway behind the cash register. "She's in the middle of icing a batch of coffee cakes right now. I can tell her you're here if you like."

"That would be great." I gave him my name and he disappeared into the back room, returning a moment later.

"She'll be right out."

A few minutes went by. I studied the display cases. My stomach rumbled, and I was about to give in and order a piece of scrumptious-looking walnut torte when Melinda appeared. Her blond hair was pulled back into a tight ponytail under a hairnet. She came forward, untying her apron.

"Della. What a pleasant surprise." She grinned. "Tommy gave your name as Mrs. Wright. I had no idea it was you. What brings you to my neck of the woods?"

"I wanted to stop by and thank you personally for the lovely spread you prepared for Marnie's party. Your food was a huge hit. Everybody was talking about it. I must have gotten a dozen phone calls about it yesterday." Okay, so that was a lie, but it wouldn't hurt to butter her up. "You are a wonderful baker," I continued. "I've always been partial to Marnie's, but yours is every bit as good." I silently begged Marnie's forgiveness.

"What a nice thing to say. I'm glad you're happy. You paid for it. I have to say, if I'm any good, it's all thanks to Marnie. She taught me well, but I think I still have a ways to go before I can say I'm as good as she is." She paused. "You didn't come all the way out here just for that, did you?"

"I had an errand in town and thought I'd stop by," I said, trying vainly to think of some way to bring the conversation around to Bruce. "Also, I do have an ulterior motive. There was one kind of cookie you brought over, with butterscotch chips and nuts. They were so delicious. I've been dying to ask Marnie to make them, but I don't know what they're called."

"You must be talking about my pecan rolls."

"Whatever they were, I loved them."

"The only other cookies I brought were chocolate chip. If you give me a sec, I'll write down the recipe for you in case Marnie doesn't have it." She went behind the counter, got a pad and pencil and returned. As she jotted down the ingredients, I cleared my throat.

"I suppose you heard about Helen Dubois. Such a tragedy."

She gave me a blank look. "What are you talking about?"

"You don't know? Helen is dead." I decided not to mention I was the person who had found her body.

She covered her mouth in horror. "You can't be serious."

"I'm afraid so."

"How did she die?"

"It's not official yet, but the word is that she was strangled. The police have declared her death suspicious."

"You mean she was murdered? How awful. Do the police have any suspects?"

I shook my head. "They asked me if I noticed anything at the party. But I was so busy playing hostess, I didn't. Were you and Helen close?"

"I hardly knew her," she said.

"I've heard that she and Bruce Doherty argued that night. Did you witness that?"

"No."

"Did he say anything to you that night about Helen?"

She stopped and stared at me. "What are you talking about?"

"I saw you two having a long conversation near the food table. I was wondering what you were talking about."

"He and I shared a few words—hello, nice to meet you, that sort of thing. But I wouldn't say we chatted for any length of time." She gave me a wary look as if she were trying to assess whether I believed her. I did not.

"Really? How strange. I could have sworn you were carrying on quite a long conversation."

Her mouth tightened. "I don't even know the man. I can't imagine what I would want to talk to him about." She picked up her pencil and resumed writing. "Let's see. One cup of golden raisins. One cup of pecans."

"I'd never met her fiancé before that party. What was your impression of him?"

"Can't say that I got any impression one way or another," she said curtly. "Why all the questions? Are you working for the police now?"

I felt the blood rise to my face.

"Of course not. It's just that Marnie is my friend, and I have a bad feeling about this man. I want to know whether she's making a huge mistake marrying him. Melinda, if there's anything you know about him, please tell me. Marnie was good to you. Don't you think you owe her the truth?"

She seemed to debate with herself. Then suddenly she said. "I didn't want to say anything, but . . . he and I did talk. At first it was just polite conversation, at least on my part. But he became very rude, making comments about my figure and suggesting that we get together. That's when I walked away. If it had been anybody but Marnie's fiancé, I would have slapped him in the face, but I didn't want to make a scene at her engagement party."

My mouth dropped. Now that I had the information, I felt sick. I'd never felt so sorry to be right.

She tore the recipe from the pad and handed it to me.

"Thank you," I said. "I appreciate your honesty."

"No worries. If there's anything else I can do for you, drop by anytime. Hope you enjoy the pecan rolls."

I nodded to her employee and left. It wasn't until I was in the car that it occurred to me that if what she'd told me was the truth, the misbehavior was on his part, not hers. So why had she tried to convince me that they weren't talking? Unless Melinda wasn't as innocent as she wanted me to believe. I sat in my Jeep for a full minute. When I glanced at the shop, I spotted her staring at me. I turned the key in the ignition. I felt her eyes boring into me until I drove away. I returned to Briar Hollow, feeling like a cat that had been outsmarted by a mouse.

Winston came bounding over as I walked in. "Yes, I love you too, big boy." He jumped up, hoping for a treat, no doubt. "No, Winnie. Down." I disengaged myself and he slunk off, his eyes full of hurt. "Don't look at me like that. You know you're not supposed to jump on people." Feeling guilty, I fished a dog treat from my pocket and held it up for him. He galloped back, snatched it, and we were friends again.

"You just missed Matthew," Marnie said from behind her loom. She rose and came to the counter. "He said he'd pick up Winston around five. He had his tool kit with him, said he promised to repair your dining room table?" She gave me a crooked smile. "What exactly have you been doing on that dining room table?"

"Don't be ridiculous," I snapped.

"I gave him your apartment key. I hope you don't mind. He brought it back a few minutes later. He said the table was good as new."

"Great. Did Jenny give you a good reading?" I asked, taking off my jacket.

"She always gives good readings. Not that I always like what she has to say."

"Why? What did she say?"

"I bought myself a gorgeous dress in Charlotte last week—my wedding dress." She smiled shyly as she said this, and then she became serious. "Jenny said that I wouldn't get to wear my wedding dress."

"What is that supposed to mean? You won't get married?"

She looked horrified. "Don't even say such a thing. I bought my wedding dress one size smaller, and I'm on a diet. I think it means I won't lose the weight before the wedding." She shrugged. "Oh, well. I'd better find another dress in the right size."

"What else did Jenny say?"

She shrugged. "Not much. She said a man close

to me is surrounded by danger. I don't know who she could be talking about. The only man close to me is Bruce, unless she was talking about my next-door neighbor. That's it—she must have meant Barney. He has a bad heart." Just as I'd feared. Jenny had been too vague. Now Marnie was giving the prediction her own spin.

"Anything else?"

"I should watch out for somebody who wishes me harm."

"Uh-oh. I hope his initials aren't B.D."

She looked puzzled for a second, and then guffawed. "You mean Bruce? That's the most ridiculous thing I've ever heard."

"How sure are you that you can trust him?" I asked. "It's not as if you've known him for very long."

"I wouldn't be marrying the man if I didn't trust him. Besides, she didn't tell me the person I shouldn't trust is a man. The only man she mentioned was the one who is in danger." Her face clouded over. "Uh-oh. You don't think it's Bruce, not Barney, who's in danger, do you?"

"Are you sure you didn't misinterpret what she told you? Maybe she said the man close to you is dangerous."

She stared at me. "What are you talking about? You're trying to hint at something, aren't you?"

"No. I'm just wondering. Sometimes when we're in love, we don't want to see what's right in front of us. Remember? You were married once. You trusted your husband. And then years into your marriage, you found out that he had been having affairs all along."

"I was young when we got married. I was nineteen years old, going on sixteen. I'm a little older and wiser now." Older, yes, but I had my doubts about her being wiser. She continued. "When a man wants to hide something, he can hide it pretty good." That was my point exactly. I said nothing. She narrowed her eyes. "What are you getting at? You think Bruce is seeing other women?"

"I didn't say that. I just wondered how much you trust him. You only met the man a month ago. How can you trust someone enough to want to marry them in such a short time?" Color rose to her face, and I realized I'd been too insistent. "I've never been married," I added quickly, hoping she would think all I was voicing was my own insecurity. "I've never even lived with anyone. Just the thought of trusting someone completely would scare me to death."

"Ah, so that's what this is all about. Honey pie, when the right man comes along, you just know."

That was such hogwash. I had to turn around so she wouldn't see the expression in my eyes. I changed the subject. "By the way, did you hear anything about the funeral service for Helen?"

"I called the police this morning. I wanted to find out who's in charge of making the arrangements. They still haven't been able to locate any relatives."

"You mean she had nobody in the world? That's so sad."

"She never married. The only family she had was a sister—Sybille. She was about ten years younger. Their parents died when Helen was nineteen, and she became a sort of surrogate mother to Sybille, until she just—poof—vanished one day."

I looked at her skeptically. "Vanished?"

She nodded. "Nobody knows what happened. It's a mystery. Sybille was living in Chicago at the time. She was very successful, only in her early twenties and already head of human resources at the Art Institute of Chicago. And then one day she just didn't come home from work. Helen spent years looking for her. She hired private investigators. She put up a reward. She spent every dime she ever made on the case. Then about six or seven years ago she just gave up. I guess she came to accept what everybody else already knew. Sybille was dead. Helen went to court and had her declared legally dead."

"Was the case ever solved?"

"There are plenty of theories, but as far as I know, the police never found out. Helen and I didn't discuss it. This all happened back when I was married and living in Charlotte, so I never heard all the details. When I moved back here and Helen and I renewed our friendship, I tried to bring up the subject a couple of times, but she became so distraught—cried and cried. I thought it best to leave it alone. If she wanted to talk about it, fine. But I wasn't about to risk upsetting her again."

The story left me feeling sad for Helen.

Marnie's voice brought me back. "I was thinking," she said. "If nobody steps up, I might make the funeral arrangements myself."

"That would be really nice of you. If you need any help, I'm here."

She squared her shoulders. "I'll call the police again. Maybe they've located a relative by now." She picked up the landline and punched in the number.

Chapter 9

The door swung open and Liz Carter walked in, wringing her hands. "Oh, Della. I just heard about poor Helen. It's so, so terrible."

"I know. It's an awful tragedy."

"I don't know what to do about the library. I was volunteering a few hours a week, giving Helen a hand. There was way too much work for one employee. But that's all the town budget would allow, one employee. Somebody's got to be there, but I have no idea if I should call a locksmith and take over until a new librarian is hired." She looked at me as if she expected me to offer her a solution.

Marnie ended her phone call and hung up. "Hi, Liz," she said, coming around the counter. "How are you?"

Liz repeated what she had just told me. "I know how much Helen cared about that library. She was even organizing a special event to raise funds." The doorbell jingled as a messenger strode in, carrying a flat parcel.

He looked from me to Liz to Marnie. "I have a package for Marnie Potter."

"That's me," Marnie said. The young man handed her a pen and she signed the receipt. "I wonder what this is," she said, trying to read the label.

"It's from the Charlotte Museum of History," he said, stashing the pen behind his ear. He headed for the door, leaving Marnie staring at the box.

"It must be my flag." She snatched a pair of scissors and slid the blades along the tape.

Something Liz said just hit me. I turned to her and asked, "How could you have just heard about Helen? She was killed two days ago. That's all anybody around here has been talking about."

"I left town right after the party. I've been in Charlotte ever since. I just got back. I must have chosen the worst time to leave. Not that anybody could have foreseen this, but still, if I'd been here, I would already have figured out what to do about the library. Now it's been closed for two days, and as far as the exhibit she was working on, it's as good as dead." And then, realizing what she'd just said, she covered her mouth. "I can't believe I just said that."

"Why don't you call the mayor? He'll tell you what to do. I bet he'll be relieved when you tell him you're willing to take over until they hire someone. He might even offer you the job, since you're already familiar with the place."

She shook her head, taken aback. "Oh, I could never take Helen's job. It would feel so wrong. Besides I don't want to work full-time. Nine to five, five days a week? That's not for me." I remembered how much of her time Liz spent traveling. A full-time job would curtail her freedom. She continued. "But I don't mind helping out until they find somebody else." She glanced around. "Wow. This place sure looks different once you get all the party stuff out." She wandered over to the armoire and looked at the display of towels. There were small linen hand towels, regular-sized linen bath towels, and great big Turkish towels with fringed ends. "Everything you sell is so beautiful. One of these days I'll have to come by and pick something nice for myself." Her eyes fell onto the Betsy Ross flag Marnie was taking out of the box. She walked over to the counter. "What's that?"

Marnie beamed. "My grandmother gave it to me when I was just a girl, and I've had it stored away in a drawer ever since. I suppose you could call it a family heirloom. I'd completely forgotten about it, until I found it the other day when I was going through some old stuff. I sent it out to the Museum of History in Charlotte, hoping they could give me an idea of its value." As she said this, she tore open an envelope. "Oh. Look at this, a note from the curator." She perused the note in silence, her eyes growing wider as they moved down the page.

She grasped for the chair behind her. "I'd better sit down," she said, fanning herself with the sheet of paper. She dropped onto the seat and glanced at it again. "He says the flag looks authentic and that, in his estimation, it could easily be worth something in the high six figures." She stared at Liz and me, openmouthed.

I gasped. "High six figures? Wow! That's a lot of money."

Liz reached a tentative finger toward the flag. "Are you serious? Why . . . that piece should be in a museum." Her face lit up. "That gives me an idea. I told you that Helen was working on a special project, didn't I? She was hoping to raise money for the library. She was organizing this special one-week exhibition—a collection of old books, some first editions that are worth quite a lot of money, but nothing close to the value of your flag. She had a bunch of old pens too, and some old typewriters, a printing press. Just a whole lot of writing tools." She glanced at the flag again, her eyes full of wonder. "Would you consider lending your flag to the library for the exhibition? It would only be for one week. And I promise it would be quite safe. It would be inside a glass display case. Nobody would be able to touch it. The exhibit is scheduled to start next week . . . although I have no idea what's going to happen now."

"Of course I'll lend it," Marnie said without hesitation. "It's the least I can do for Helen. It would have made her happy."

"Thank you. I know just how I'll display it." Her eyes became dreamy. "I'll use it as a background for the most important piece, a first-edition biography of George Washington in six volumes by John Marshall. Won't it look absolutely stunning?"

"It sounds wonderful," Marnie said. "When do you need it? Would you rather take it right away?"

"Shouldn't you call your insurance broker first?" I suggested.

"Oh, by all means. Get it insured first," Liz said.

"Oh, you're right. He'll probably want to see it before issuing a policy," Marnie said. "I'll give him a call. The minute you can pick it up, I'll let you know."

"Great," Liz said, heading for the door. She paused with her hand on the handle. "By the way," she said, looking at me, "are you sure you want me to make a place mat for Marnie's trousseau?"

"I've got three other beginners like you making one each. And I'll help you."

She looked relieved for a moment. Then her forehead furrowed. "I hope you won't be angry at me, but I goofed. I let it slip about the trousseau we're making for her. Me and my big mouth. But Marnie says she doesn't mind it not being a surprise. Tell her, Marnie. That's what you told me, right? You're not angry at me, are you?" A second later the door closed behind her.

I swung around to Marnie and wagged a finger at her. "You sneak. You knew about my surprise. No wonder you dropped that hint about liking purple on white."

She gave a weak laugh. "Don't worry. I promise to love your gift no matter what the color."

"I already decided to keep the navy on white for myself and start a new collection for you. So you'll get your purple chevron."

"No, really. You don't have to do that," she insisted, but I could tell she was pleased. When at last she put the subject of the towels to rest, she said, "Didn't you think that was strange?"

"What are you talking about?"

"Liz asking us for advice on what she should do about the library. It doesn't make sense. She could have asked any number of people. Nancy Cutler is on the town council and the two of them are friendly. She could have called the mayor. Why would she come to us instead of going to them?"

"Sometimes people don't think clearly when they're distraught."

"Or maybe," she said. "Because she heard that you found her body and was hoping to hear some details."

"In that case, why didn't she bring it up? She didn't ask a single question about it."

"You're right," Marnie said, tapping her chin with an index finger. "She came here for a reason. I just know it. Hmm, I wonder . . ."

"Maybe she wanted to find out what Helen and Bruce were arguing about at the party."

"What are you talking about?" Marnie demanded. "Helen and Bruce didn't argue."

Shit, shit, shit. I would have paid to take my words back. But there was no point in denying it now. "Actually, they did, Marnie. I saw them arguing myself."

"It was not an argument," she said, confirming that she knew more than she'd previously admitted. This told me not only that she knew about it but might even have witnessed it herself. Marnie had lied, at least by omission, to Officer Lombard when she stopped by. "Helen was telling him about an incident she'd had at the library with a high school student."

"Come on, Marnie. It didn't look like a casual conversation to me. She was jabbing her finger in his chest."

"That's right. She was jabbing him the same way that teenager had jabbed his finger at her. She was demonstrating, for God's sake."

"How do you know what they were talking about? You were all the way across the room, unwrapping your presents."

"I happened to notice them talking and asked Bruce about it later."

I was speechless. The story was thin. It didn't explain the anger on Helen's face, nor the way she had stomped off in a fury. Even though all my instincts told me I was right and Marnie was wrong, I felt just the briefest of doubts. What if it had happened that way? What if all this suspicion I felt toward Bruce was based on nothing but my own fertile imagination?

Marnie was shaking her head at me. "You really are something else. I'm surprised you haven't already convicted Bruce of murder. You've got to stop going around mistrusting everyone all the time."

I was saved from having to answer when the door swung open and Bunny walked in. Her hair was limp, her makeup smudged, and instead of one of her usual expensive designer outfits, she wore a pair of jeans and a plain knit sweater. I moved forward.

"Oh, Bunny, I just read the news. How are you holding up?"

She brushed back a long lock of blond hair and gave a weary shrug. "I'm not exactly thrilled. But I'm thankful that at least nobody was in the room when it happened. Otherwise, who knows, Briar Hollow might have seen its second murder in two days."

"That's an awful thought. I hope the painting was insured," Marnie said.

"Of course it was. Not that it will be easy to get the insurance company to pay up."

Marnie's eyes widened. "What do you mean? If you had a policy, they'll have to honor it. You can sue them if they don't."

"Not if they can prove fraud." At our shocked silence, she said, "The painting was wired directly into the security alarm. Nobody could have taken it down without disarming it, and I am the only person who knew the code. So the police think . . ." She opened her hands in a helpless gesture.

"You can't be serious."

"As long as the case is unsolved and there remains a question about my innocence, the insurance company has the right to hold the face amount. My insurance guy was the second person I called, after calling the police. His company had an investigator there within hours. The man was there before the reporter from the *Belmont Daily*. And the questions he asked? He was stickier than the cops. Ugh." She shuddered. "I hope I never have to go through that again."

"Poor you."

She grimaced. "There must be half a dozen cops searching my lobby as we speak. I should really be there, but I had to get away before I had a public meltdown."

Marnie pulled the chair from behind the counter. "Here, have a seat. You look as if you're about to collapse." It was nice to see Marnie fawning over Bunny. When the two had first met, my friend had taken an instant dislike to the beautiful blonde. According to her, the woman dressed too flashy, wore her makeup too loud and her nails too long. But to everyone's surprise, the antipathy had slowly given way to a grudging respect and then to a warm friendship.

Marnie continued. "I tried to call you, but your phone was busy."

"Figures. It hasn't stopped ringing all morning. One of the cops finally took it off the hook."

"Why don't I get you a cup of coffee?" Marnie offered.

"Thanks, but I think caffeine is just about the last thing in the world I need right now." She put out a shaky hand as evidence. "But I'll have a cup of tea if you don't mind—jasmine, maybe, or chamomile."

"Right away." Marnie disappeared into the back.

She groaned. "God. I had no idea how tired I was until I sat. I've been up all night."

"All night? What time was it when you discovered the painting was gone?"

"I heard the robbers take it. At least I think I did. The last restaurant clients must have left around eleven, and we locked up about a half hour later. I went to bed soon after that. Around one o'clock in the morning I heard this loud metallic grating sound from right below my room. I couldn't make out what it was. Then there was a loud pop. I thought it sounded like a gun, or what I imagine a gun would sound like. My bedroom is right over the reception area, and the noises seemed to come from there," she said. "You know how quiet this town becomes at night. Normally the lobby is dead silent until morning. I considered calling the police, but thought I should take a look around first. I grabbed my bathrobe and went downstairs. That's when I saw the painting was gone." She let herself fall against the back of the chair, as if the retelling had exhausted her. I thought I saw tears quivering on her lashes, but she brushed them away so fast that I wondered if I'd imagined them. I had never seen Bunny looking less than perfectly composed.

"Come on, Bunny. Everybody around here knows you. You're the last person in the world the police would suspect of being involved."

She wiped a hand over her face, further smudging her makeup. "I hope you're right," she said, sounding doubtful.

"You know I am. And as far as the insurance companies, they're just trying to find an excuse to keep the money. I suppose it was worth a lot?"

"Almost half a million."

Ouch. "No wonder you're upset."

"It's not the painting, or even the money, that I'm upset about." She tightened her lips for a moment, struggling to keep her emotions in check. "I always thought of Briar Hollow as home. This is where I come to feel safe. If somebody can break into my home here, then I might as well stay in New York between filming seasons." It occurred to me that I'd had the same bleary thoughts after discovering Helen's body.

"Anybody would feel that way after a bad shock. But, you'll see, everything will fall into place. The police will catch the culprit, and they'll find your painting." She looked as if she didn't believe a word of it.

Marnie appeared carrying a tray with a cup and a plate of pastries. "Here you go. I brought you something to eat. It'll make you feel better." She set everything on the counter and handed the mug to Bunny.

"Thank you." And then she surprised me by accepting a chocolate cupcake. This, more than anything, drove home just how upset she was. As if she'd read my thoughts, Bunny said, "I normally never eat pastries, but I haven't had a bite since dinner last night—so, just this once." She broke a piece off her cupcake and popped it into her mouth.

"I wonder if it's the work of the same person," Marnie said.

"What are you talking about?" Bunny asked.

"Haven't you heard?" Marnie asked. She told her about the article in the *Belmont Daily*. "I'm surprised you didn't see it."

"I only read the *New York Times*. Tell me more about this article."

"They've been breaking into museums and private homes all over the state and making off with valuable artworks. The article didn't give any more details than that."

Puzzled, Bunny said, "But how would anybody know about my painting?"

"Are you kidding? A painting worth half a million dollars in Briar Hollow? That kind of news gets around," Marnie said.

"I know the local paper made a fuss about it. But it was hardly national news," Bunny said.

"Oh, word travels fast," Marnie said. "How many

people do you think heard about it? It made the front page of the *Belmont Daily*. And half the people in town had dinner at the Longview just to see it. Those same people could have told friends, who told other friends."

I didn't want to point out the obvious. Killers and robbers didn't all come from big cities. They sometimes came from small towns, too.

Bunny looked pensively into her cup. "The police have probably thought of the same possibility. They asked me for a list of all the restaurant and hotel guests we've had since the painting's been on display. It isn't enough that they questioned me and the hotel employees. Now they're going to harass my guests."

All at once it occurred to me that one of the guests staying at the hotel was none other than Bruce Doherty. I pictured the layout of the Longview in my mind. When Bunny had converted it from a bed-and-breakfast into a hotel, she'd transformed a part of the second floor into her private quarters. She'd simultaneously expanded the back of the building to almost double its previous size, creating an extra eight suites for a total of fourteen. The main corridor accessing all the suites ran from the lobby to a back emergency exit. I couldn't help wondering which room Bruce was staying in. Was he on the second floor? Or was he on the main floor, close to the reception area where the painting was displayed? I glanced at Marnie. She was twisting her hands, wearing a worried expression.

"Thank you for the tea, ladies," Bunny said, rising to her feet. "I think I'd better get back. Otherwise the police will imagine that I've skipped town." She attempted a smile, resulting in a lopsided grimace. She had no sooner left than Marnie snatched the phone.

"I'd better call Bruce and warn him," she said.

"Warn him?" I said.

Her forehead furrowed, and she put the receiver down. "Why are you looking at me like that?"

"I was just thinking," I said, "that's a strange choice of words."

Her eyes became suddenly ablaze. "What are you suggesting? That I'm warning him because I think he's involved somehow? Or maybe you think he and I conspired to steal the painting together."

"Don't be silly. You're my friend. I would never—"

"But you think Bruce is involved. Admit it. Not only do you think he's involved in an art heist, but you suspect him of being involved in Helen's murder. Don't bother denying it. You've been hinting at it ever since you found her body." She glared at me. "I don't know what you're trying to do, but you are not going to turn me against the man I love. Bruce is a good man, and I am damn well going to marry him—no matter what you say." She picked up the box in which she'd placed her refolded flag, grabbed her purse, and marched over to the door.

"Marnie, don't go. I'm only worried for you because I care."

"I suggest you stop worrying about me and start worrying about yourself. At least I have a man who loves me, which is more than you can say for yourself," she snapped from the entrance, and the door slammed shut behind her.

I knew she'd only spoken in anger, but her words stung all the same.

"What in the world is going on?" Jenny asked as she parted the beaded curtain. "I could hear the shouting all the way from the back." She looked around. "Where's Marnie?"

"Gone." I told her what had just happened. "I wouldn't be surprised if she never spoke to me again. I really messed up."

"That doesn't sound like her. It makes me wonder if she already had doubts of her own about him. That could be why she was so angry."

"You don't think I said too much?"

"Maybe a little. Still, if she suspects that you're right, it will be difficult for her to accept that she made a mistake. It would mean having to break things off with Bruce." She sighed. "It's much easier to get angry at you. Hopefully, you made her rethink her relationship. Give her time. She'll come around."

"I hope you're right." I thought about this for a second. "Do you think I should give her a call?"

"Not now. She needs distance to think things through."

"By the way, how did the reading go?" I asked. "From what she told me, I think you didn't make it clear that Bruce was not to be trusted."

"That's the funny thing," she said, frowning. "I saw a lot of emotional turmoil around her, but the only danger I could see was for a dark-haired man. But I did advise her not to trust too easily."

"But the whole point of that reading was to warn her off Bruce."

She tilted her head, peering at me. "Hold on. I promised to give her a reading, and that's what I did. I honestly thought I'd see danger surrounding her, but I didn't. What did you want me to do? Lie? I can't predict things I don't see. That would be dishonest."

I tried to stifle a monumental eye roll. But too late.

"Marnie said you had finally come around to believing in my gift," she continued, looking hurt.

"I'm not saying I *don't* believe," I said weakly. I'd already offended one friend today. The last thing I wanted was to upset Jenny too.

"Oh, gee, thanks. You just made my day." She glared at me, and then she spun on her heel and returned to the coffee shop. She didn't so much as pop her head out for the rest of the day. At five thirty, she marched by, announcing that she was "taking off" and slamming the door shut behind her. I groaned. *Great going, Della.* I'd offended two friends in as few hours.

The door opened again and Matthew strode in. "What's with Jenny? She practically froze me out when I said hello." Winston went barreling over to him, wagging his tailless behind. "Whoa, there, big fellow. I know. I know. I love you too." He raised his gaze to me. "Got a paper towel or something? He's slobbering all over my shoes."

I handed him the box of tissues, relieved that I wouldn't have to explain Jenny's behavior. I felt about as dumb as a doorbell and didn't really want to point out my own stupidity. He came closer and I got a whiff of his aftershave. It was faint, but sexy as the devil.

"I just stopped by the butcher," he said, wiping his shoes. "And I picked up two nice porterhouse steaks on the off chance you might want to have dinner with me. If you say no, I'll have to feed the second one to Winston." Winston looked at me and whimpered. I knew what he was hoping I'd say. But I wasn't about to turn down an invitation from Matthew.

"Sorry, big boy," I said scratching his head. "But I promise not to eat the whole thing. I'll leave you a few bites. How's that?" He gave an appreciative growl.

I grabbed the cash from the register, stuffed it into my purse. I would make my bank deposit in the morning. "Ready," I said.

When I first decided to leave the city a little over a year ago, Matthew and I struck a deal. He'd move into my modern Charlotte condo, which was conveniently located just a short drive from the university where he taught. Meanwhile, I'd move into his house. The arrangement was perfect, but it lasted only until Matthew's book submission was accepted. He'd then decided he would be better able to write here, in peaceful and quiet Briar Hollow.

I'd known from the moment we made this arrangement that it was temporary. But I had lulled myself into believing things could go on this way indefinitely.

Now, coming back to Matthew's house almost felt like coming home. This was the same kitchen where I had repainted the cabinets and refinished the floors. The same place where I'd first come to realize I was in love with him. As soon as he came back to Briar Hollow, though, I'd learned how impossible it was to share a house with a man who didn't feel about me the way I did about him. So I hired a real estate agent, and in no time, I found the building where I now lived and worked.

"You know where everything is," Matthew said, waving toward the pantry. "Make yourself at home while I turn on the grill. Maybe you can season the steaks in the meantime."

I got the meat from the fridge, rummaged through the cupboard until I found the spices, and set to work. He came back in search of a lighter, and then returned again a moment later looking for matches, muttering something about "damn lighters never working."

I popped the potatoes into the hot oven and washed the lettuce. I had just finished making the salad dressing when he stepped back into the kitchen wearing a satisfied grin.

"I finally got it going. How long till the potatoes are ready?"

I glanced at my watch. "Maybe another half hour."

"Sounds good. I'll put the steaks on in about twenty minutes. In the meantime, how about a glass of wine?" Without waiting for my reply, he poured two glasses and handed one to me. "To you," he said. We clicked glasses, and I struggled to keep myself from blushing as he looked deeply into my eyes.

"Good wine," I said, flustered under his intent gaze. "Which reminds me. Do you have any wine vinegar?"

"Sure." He pointed me toward the cabinet next to the fridge, where I very well knew he kept his oil and vinegar. "Anything else you need?"

"I'm good. I just needed a drop of it." I unscrewed the cap and poured in a tablespoon. "There. All done." I busied myself getting the plates and cutlery. He dipped a finger into the salad dressing and popped it in his mouth.

"This is good," he said, sounding surprised. "Look at you. You're a regular pro in the kitchen these days," he said, coming closer and wrapping an arm around my shoulders.

"Just so you know," I said, "I have a new recipe from my mother and if you're going to make fun of my cooking, I won't invite you over to test it.

And it just so happens to be one of your favorite dishes—chicken Parmesan."

"I wasn't making fun of you. I'm impressed. You're so domestic these days—a regular Julia Child."

"That proves it. You *are* laughing at me."

He gave my shoulders a squeeze and I almost melted. The heat of his arm around me, the scent of his aftershave—it was too much. When I turned to face him I was suddenly breathtakingly close. My eyes met his. I leaned in, hoping—no, willing him to kiss me. I closed my eyes, held my breath, and the next thing I became aware of was his lips brushing against my forehead. And just as quickly, he let go of me, leaving me reeling.

"Medium or rare?"

"Wh-what?" I stuttered, flustered.

"How do you want your steak? Medium or rare?"

"Oh, er, medium."

He picked up the platter of seasoned meat and headed for the door. "Medium it is." And the door banged shut behind him.

I took a few bracing breaths and regained my composure.

Over dinner, I turned the conversation to Bruce Doherty.

"I wondered how long it would take for you to get around to him," he said, chuckling. "I kept my promise and made a few calls. I didn't find out much, but what I did learn you'll find very interesting." I was already on the edge of my seat. He took his time, sipping his wine and chewing another bite of steak.

"Are you going to tell me or are we playing twenty questions here?"

"It turns out that Bruce Doherty was indeed an investment advisor. He owned his own firm for thirty years until he sold it two years ago."

"But that doesn't make any sense. He doesn't look a day over forty-five. That would mean he was running his own investment company by the time he was fifteen years old."

"There are a couple of possibilities. Bruce Doherty might look considerably younger than he really is. Or he could have had a face-lift. It isn't entirely unusual for men these days, especially if they are looking to prolong a profitable career." As logical as that sounded, I didn't believe it for a minute. "Another possibility, and this is the one that's far more likely . . ." He paused and wagged a finger at me. "I don't want you to panic now."

"Great. Just the thing to say when you want to scare someone."

"What I think is that Bruce Doherty might not be his real name."

I was struck dumb. Of all the ideas that had crowded my mind, this one had never occurred to me. It conjured up a number of entirely new possibilities, each one more frightening than the other.

"Oh, my God. He's using an alias," I blurted.

"I've got to call Marnie right now. She has to stay away from him."

"Hold on a second. All we have right now is questions. You can't do or say anything until we know more. What if it's the first possibility?"

"You mean the face-lift? Come on, Matthew. You don't believe that any more than I do."

"Still, you can't go and accuse someone unless you're one hundred percent sure."

I folded my arms and glared at him. "So what do you want me to do? Sit back, while that man—"

He put up a hand. "I already called the Washington State Investment Board earlier. They have pictures of every person licensed to trade stocks and bonds or sell mutual funds in the state. They confirmed that a Bruce Doherty does exist, and they're e-mailing me his picture. I should get it at the latest by the end of the day tomorrow. That should tell us if we're on the right track." He looked down at my plate and noticed my untouched steak. "If you don't start eating your food, I won't tell you anything else."

"There's more?"

"Eat," he said. I took a bite. "That's better," he said. "Those are nice steaks. It would be a shame to let them go to waste."

He was right. The steak was delicious, but I had to force myself to swallow. I couldn't shake the picture of Bruce with his hands around Helen's throat. As soon I dispelled that image, it was replaced by one of him strangling Marnie.

"Stop worrying. There's nothing either one of us can do right now."

"How can you expect me not to worry? I won't be able to sleep a wink tonight. Poor Marnie. By the way," I said, changing the subject, "Bunny stopped by the store earlier. Did you know her Grandma Moses painting was stolen?" He nodded and I continued. "The police think she did it, because the painting was wired directly into the security system, and she was the only one with the code."

"That hardly proves anything. Getting around a security system is a piece of cake for a professional thief."

"Really? Knowing her, she probably spent a fortune for some fancy security system, and now you're telling me it's a waste of money?"

"All I'm saying is that when a burglar sets his mind to something, he can usually figure out a way to do it."

"I just hate that she's under suspicion. Don't the police know who she is? She works in some of the most expensive homes in the country. If she was convicted of theft, even if it was for theft of her own painting, she never get another decorating contract again."

"She has nothing to worry about. You know cops. They suspect everyone in the beginning."

"Listen to this. Bunny happened to mention that the police want to question all the hotel guests. Marnie grabbed the phone to warn Bruce—her words, not mine—as soon as she left. And then she stormed out when I commented that 'warn' was a strange choice of words. What do you make of that?"

"Don't be too hard on her. You've been known to overreact at times too."

"Hey! I resent that. I am not in the habit of over-reacting." Before he could come up with specific examples, I changed the subject. "I wouldn't have said anything to Marnie, except that she got this concerned look in her eyes, as if she was worried about him being questioned."

"Hmm. Do you think she's beginning to suspect him?"

"Funny, that's what Jenny suggested. But even if she is, she's more likely to make excuses for him or, worse, protect him. I wouldn't put it past her to provide him with an alibi if he needs one."

"You're jumping to conclusions. From what I know of Marnie, she'd more likely shoot the man than protect him."

"You can't imagine how much in love she is."

"I wish somebody would feel that way about me," he said with a twinkle in his eyes. I wanted to blurt out, *"Just open your eyes. Can't you see that I'm in love with you?"* But, as usual, I kept that information to myself.

"This is no time for joking," I said. "Don't forget that Helen Dubois had an argument with that man, and just a few hours later, I found her dead. I'm beginning to think I should just come right out and tell Marnie everything we know."

"Normally, I'd agree with you. But in this case, I'd say there's no point."

"What do you mean there's no point?"

"If you tell her without having something to back up your claim, the first thing she'll do, after slamming the door in your face, will be to pick up the phone and tell him. Then she'll be in even graver danger."

"Oh, my God. I never thought of that. If he wants to get his hands on her life insurance, he'll kill her right away."

"That's why I keep telling you to wait."

"Okay," I said, subdued. "But you've got to bring me that picture the minute you get it."

"I will. I promise."

Now that we had a firm plan, I felt a bit better. Matthew would get the picture tomorrow—twenty-four hours from now. Surely nothing could go wrong in just one day.

Chapter 10

I spent a sleepless night, tossing and turning. My mind raced, conjuring one frightening scene after another—Marnie lying on her sofa, her face purple and bloated. As this image faded, it was replaced by one of Marnie at the altar in a white wedding dress, splashed with blood, staring into the eyes of a stone-cold killer. By five o'clock, I gave up trying to sleep. I tossed back the covers and crawled out of bed. After making myself a pot of coffee, I wandered down to the shop.

I was appraising the results of my latest marketing effort. I'd brought in the handwoven shirt my client had admired the other day and used it as the central piece in a display. I'd moved the hand towels out of the armoire and set the shirt in their place. Around it I'd hung a few of Margaret's magnificent shawls, and on the other side, a half dozen of Marnie's afghans. This was the first time I'd created a fashion grouping, and much to my relief it looked lovely. With any luck my customers would think so too, and the orders would come rolling in. I returned to the counter, where I'd left the pot of coffee I'd made, and poured myself another cup. When I got to my third, I came to the conclusion that no amount of caffeine would sweep the cobwebs from my brain this morning.

I made my way over to my loom. It wasn't yet six. Jenny wouldn't be here for another two hours, Marnie not for three or four. That's if she showed up at all. Hopefully she would, and by then I should have made some serious progress on her white and purple dishcloths. When she saw how hard I'd worked on them, she would get over her anger.

I had originally planned for four dishcloths. One was finished, which meant my loom was dressed for three more. I measured the amount of purple yarn I would need, wound it on a bobbin and popped it into the shed. Soon I was swept away in the rhythm of working the loom.

Before I knew it, the bell tinkled and I glanced at my watch—ten to eight. *Already?*

It was Jenny. "You're here early," she said, coming over to see what I was working on. "Is this one of the dish towels you're making for Marnie?"

"It is."

"I'd better get going on the hand towels, then. Otherwise, everyone will be finished with their pieces except me." The bell rang again, and this time Margaret walked in and wandered over to join us.

"Nice," she said, admiring the dish towel. "I've

finished dressing my loom for a set of place mats. I'm glad I didn't start the weaving. I understand she wants purple?"

"That's what she wants."

Margaret shrugged. "Oh, well, to each his own. Did you start the coffee?" she asked. Jenny shook her head, and Margaret said, "I'll go put it on."

Jenny turned her attention back to me, and frowned. "Are you okay? You don't look so good."

"Gee, thanks." I stood and stretched my back. "I couldn't sleep," I said, searching her face. To my relief I saw none of the miffed attitude of yesterday—just concern.

"I hope it wasn't over the . . ." She pointed to me and then to herself. "I don't know why I got so upset. It's not as if I should have been surprised. You're a pragmatist. You don't believe in tarot and tea leaves."

"I'm sorry. I wish—"

"Nothing to be sorry about. You are who you are. And there's nothing wrong with that. I'm the one who should be sorry."

"It's okay. As you said, you are who you are too. And I shouldn't have expected you to lie to Marnie." She beamed me a smile.

"Well, I'm glad that's over." She made a hand-wiping gesture. "There, all forgotten. Now, how about a cup of coffee?" When she returned with the coffee, I repeated what I'd learned from Matthew.

"He thinks Bruce Doherty is an alias?" she said,

aghast. "Oh, my God. Maybe you were right about that life insurance policy he made her take."

"That's the part that really scares me."

"Maybe Margaret is right. We have to warn her right now."

"We can't do that," I said, explaining Matthew's theory that telling her would only place her in even graver danger. "Like Matthew says, she won't believe a word unless we have proof. And he should be receiving a photo of the real Bruce Doherty from the Investment Board today."

"I can't believe I just gave her a reading and saw none of that in there." Luckily, I was able to keep a straight face. "Although," she continued, "that would have more likely shown up in Bruce's—or whatever his name is—cards than hers. Are you sure we can't tell her?"

"Not until Matthew brings me the photo. I promised. Besides, unless we have indisputable proof, Marnie would never believe us."

At that moment the telephone rang and Jenny picked it up.

"It's Marnie," she said, covering the mouthpiece. Into the phone, she said "Yes" a few times and then, "What?" All at once the blood seemed to drain from her face, leaving her looking gray.

"What's wrong?" I asked, but she only waved me away, gripping the receiver tighter.

"How bad is it? Are you sure you're all right?"

"Did something happen to Marnie?" I mouthed

again. She turned her back to me, covering her other ear with her hand.

"But how could that have happened?" She listened a bit longer, and then whispered a few words of encouragement. "You'll be all right. Don't worry about that." At last she replaced the receiver in its cradle. "Marnie had an accident," she said. "She fell down some stairs. She's got one arm in a sling and she's having trouble walking—something to do with one of her knees and her hips. She won't be able to come in today."

"But how?" I asked, as a vision of Bruce pushing her down a flight of stairs popped into my mind.

Jenny nodded knowingly. "Whatever you're imagining, I think you're probably right. She said Bruce took her out to dinner at some fancy restaurant in Belmont last night. It's on the second floor of some old house. As they were leaving, she stumbled and fell down the stairs."

"You know what's going on, don't you? He's trying to kill her," I said. "He's got that insurance policy on her and he's trying to get rid of her. We can't wait. We have to go and tell her about him right this minute."

Her eyes filled with horror. "I think you're right. But there's one problem. You said it yourself. We can't tell her until we have that picture. But what we can do is make sure she's not alone with that creep for one second."

"Good idea."

"I just thought of something," Jenny said. "I don't have anything to serve my customers."

"Why don't you zip up to Belmont and buy whatever you need from Melinda? Her baking is similar to Marnie's. Most customers won't even notice the difference."

"I don't have a car."

I turned to Margaret.

"Don't look at me," she said. "My car is at the garage. And it's going to stay there until I can afford to pay for the repairs."

I sighed. "I suppose I could go." As uncomfortable as seeing Melinda again might be, making certain that Jenny's shop stayed open today took priority. And since my shop didn't open officially until ten o'clock, it made sense that I should go.

"But what about Marnie? We can't leave her by herself."

"Margaret, you go to Marnie's. It's only a five minute walk," I said. I turned to Jenny. "You'll have to mind both stores until I return."

"Let me make you a list of what I need." She picked up a pencil and a piece of paper. A minute later she handed it to me. I grabbed my purse and my keys and hurried off.

Melinda was behind the counter, handing out change to a customer. "Thank you," she said. "Come again." And then she turned to me. "I didn't expect to see you back so soon. What can I do for you? Are you looking for another recipe?"

"Marnie had an accident," I said. I hadn't been here two minutes and I was already feeling defensive. "She hasn't been able to fill Jenny's order for the coffee shop. I was hoping you might have most of what she needs." I handed her the list.

She perused it and raised her brows. "That's pretty much everything I have in the store. Let's see what I can do." As she counted muffins, transferring them to cardboard boxes, I asked, "Have you heard from Bruce Doherty by any chance?" I knew I was fishing, but it had occurred to me that if they had been flirting at the party, he might have followed up with a call.

"No, and I don't think I'm likely to." The way she said this, her eyes firing anger and her jaw set determinedly, gave me the impression that she was furious with him. This made no sense, unless . . . she had expected to hear from him but hadn't. I waited, hoping she'd continue without my probing. I had no way of knowing if my imagination was running rampant or if this meant nothing at all. "That's it for the muffins," she said, tying string around a box.

She gave me a stiff smile and handed me another box. "Here are the scones." She resumed counting pastries. Soon she had packaged everything. "Let me help you to your car." She grabbed a few boxes by the string and carried them out.

"Come again," she said as I closed the hatch.

"You're the second-best baker in the county," I said, giving her the friendliest smile I could muster. "And if Marnie doesn't make me those pecan rolls, I'll be coming over regularly." I walked around to the passenger seat and drove away.

Fifteen minutes later I parked in front of my shop. I stumbled in carrying a stack of parcels and almost dropped everything when Winston came galloping over. What a mess that would have been.

"Down, boy. Down."

Jenny appeared from the back, waving a manila envelope. "Matthew just came by. He sounded disappointed that you weren't here. He dropped this off for you and left. And then, just a couple of minutes ago, he phoned and asked that you call him the minute you get back."

I set the boxes on the counter and tore open the envelope. I was looking at a photo of an older man.

"They don't even look alike," I said, studying the scanned picture.

Jenny peeked over my shoulder for a closer look. "Oh, I don't know. It might be him if the man was about twenty years younger, fifty pounds thinner, and if his hair was dark brown instead of gray."

"Not funny."

"I've got to get back to work. I've got a shop full of customers," she said.

I waved her off and picked up the phone. Matthew answered on the second ring.

"I'm looking at the picture right now," I said.

"You were right. He's using a stolen identity. I'm going over to Marnie's this minute."

"Hold on. Not so fast. I just got an e-mail from the Investment Board. They said they forgot to mention that they also found a BJ Doherty registered as a financial advisor. This advisor also happens to be the new owner of the firm the older Bruce Doherty sold before retiring. It could be that the *B* in his name stands for Bruce. If he was working in the same firm along with his father, he might have used initials instead of his name to avoid confusion."

"You can't be serious. Now you're telling me that we don't know any more than we did yesterday?"

"I asked them to send me this BJ's pictures, and they promised to rush it. It shouldn't take terribly long. Probably no more than an hour or so. So, I hate to say this again, but you have to wait. Don't you dare say a word about any of this to Marnie until I get that picture."

My voice rose an octave. "Did Jenny happen to mention that he tried to kill Marnie last night?"

"She did," he said. "And first of all, we don't know that he tried to kill her. It could well have been an accident."

"You don't believe a word of that yourself."

"She also told me what you girls decided to do. I think it's a good idea. As long as one of you is by her side she won't be in any danger."

"Okay, fine," I muttered. "But, please, call me

the second you get that picture. I'll have my cell on."

I hurried over to Marnie's house, stopping along the way to pick up a newspaper. At least I'd have something to keep me occupied if she refused to speak to me. I had barely pressed the bell at her house, when the door was flung open and Margaret rushed out.

"Thank God you're here. She's as ornery as a bull at a rodeo. She keeps insisting she wants to be by herself. I thought she was about to call the cops to get me thrown out. Hope you have better luck than I did." She pulled on her sweater as she spoke, then took off at a jog.

"Who is that at the door?" Marnie called from the back of the house.

"It's me—Della," I said, crossing the living room. Marnie's decor was punctuated with the unusual and the just plain strange. A ruby red sofa in the shape of lips dominated the living room. On either side was a Hawaiian hula-dancing-girl lamp. The walls were covered with a mixture of framed posters—everything from a movie poster of Ingrid Bergman and Humphrey Bogart in *Casablanca*, to an Andy Warhol rendition of a can of Campbell's soup, to a reproduction of Leonardo da Vinci's *Last Supper*. To say the decor was eclectic was the understatement of the year.

"Who gave you permission to come in?" Marnie called from the bedroom. "I want you to leave right now." I ignored the comment and pushed the door open, finding myself in a frilly pink room. The white canopy bed had a pink coverlet and a pink tulle skirt. The bedside tables were undersized white Bombay chests with mirrored tops. The curtains were pink, and even the rug was pink—not what I had expected. Having said that, I shouldn't have been surprised. After all, Marnie had painted the outside of the house pink. And she certainly did like the unusual.

I cleared my throat. "Sorry, girlfriend, but I'm not going anywhere. So, here's your choice. You can be nice, or you can give me the silent treatment. It might be more pleasant for both of us if you play nice, but either way, I'm not going anywhere." She was lying on her back, wearing—what else—a pink bathrobe. She had one ice pack on her knee and a second one against her hip. Her arm was in a sling, and her left cheek was scraped and bruised.

"Oh, Marnie. I hate to say this, but you look awful." Her face fell and I added quickly, "I'm talking about your injuries."

"What is it with everybody? All I need is some peace and quiet, which I'm not going to get if you insist on jabbering. Now leave me alone. I'm perfectly all right."

"You call this perfectly all right?" I slipped off my sweater. "Now tell me how this happened."

"How do you think it happened? You don't imagine I threw myself down the stairs, do you? It was an accident."

"A bit touchy, aren't we?" She scowled and looked away. "Can I get you anything?"

There was a long pause, and then a smile quivered at the corner of her mouth. "Well, since you're already here, you might as well go get a couple of lava cakes out of the freezer and pop them in the oven. If I'm going to be laid up in bed, I might as well eat chocolate."

I grinned. "That's the best idea I've heard all day." I hurried to the kitchen and turned on the oven to 425 degrees.

"And you can add a scoop or two of ice cream while you're at it," she shouted. "By the way, the cakes are in the walk-in freezer."

I entered the new space, taking in the expanse of stainless-steel counters, the six-burner restaurant stove, and the wall of ovens. One, two, three . . . Wow. Four ovens. I looked around and spotted a metal door with a small window, almost like a porthole on a boat. That had to be the freezer. It looked huge. I pulled it open and almost jumped out of my skin when a loud beep sounded. An alarm on a freezer? I'd never heard of that. I looked inside. There were shelves upon shelves of frozen baked goods, enough to keep Jenny's coffee shop supplied for a busy week and still have some left over. I could have come here this morning instead of running out to Melinda's.

I located the tray of lava cakes, chose two, and carried them to the old kitchen, where I popped them in the oven and set the timer at eleven minutes, just long enough that the inside would warm but not cook. Deciding that a pot of coffee was definitely called for, I went in search of beans and a grinder. By the time the java was ready, the cakes were served, each with a scoop of ice cream. I put everything on a tray and carried it to the bedroom.

"What the heck is that beep on the freezer? It nearly gave me a heart attack."

"Oh, I had that put in. It's supposed to beep only when the door is left open longer than thirty seconds. But for some reason it also beeps when I open it. I never got around to having it fixed."

"Let me plump your pillows," I said, placing the tray on top of the dresser. I helped Marnie get comfortable and then handed her a plate.

"I had no idea you had so much food on reserve in the freezer. You wouldn't by any chance have reserves of handwoven goods too, would you?"

"Sorry, but I can't keep up with your demands. Weaving isn't exactly like making cupcakes, where all I have to do is double or triple a recipe."

"I wish," I said, sitting at the foot of the bed. Except for a few moans of satisfaction, we ate in silence.

Then Marnie put her plate on the bedside table and said, "So, tell me the truth now. Why are you here?"

"I told you why. I didn't want you to be by yourself when you can hardly move. By the way, you never told Jenny how this"—I gestured toward her injuries—"happened."

She studied me as if trying to read my mind, and then said, "You think Bruce had something to do with it. You think he shoved me down the stairs?" To my surprise, she sounded more resigned than upset. She sighed. "I guess that's the price that comes with having friends who care."

"That's the nicest thing you could have said." I went over to her and wrapped her in a bear hug.

"Ouch! Ouch!" she cried.

I jumped away. "I'm so sorry. I didn't mean to—"

She chuckled. "I'd always heard that love hurts, but I never thought to take it quite so literally." She continued in a more serious tone. "I think I overreacted a bit yesterday. I'm sorry."

"I'm sorry too. It was my fault as much as yours."

The phone on her bedside table rang and she gestured for me to get it. I handed it to her.

"Oh, hi, Liz," she said into the receiver. "No, I haven't spoken to my insurance agent yet, but I left him a message and I expect to hear from him today. Yes, I'll let you know the minute I have it settled." She chatted for a few more minutes, then said good-bye and handed the phone back to me. I nestled it back in its cradle.

"Just as I expected," she said. "She spoke to the mayor and he was very happy with her taking over the librarian's position until they hire someone."

"It was nice of her to offer."

Marnie nodded. "She's doing it for Helen, of course."

"Have you heard anything about her funeral arrangements?"

"Actually, her body was sent to Charlotte for the autopsy, and the police are still waiting for the medical examiner's report. I might organize a simple service for now, and then arrange for the burial later. Who knows how long they keep bodies in these cases."

"Good idea. It could take a long time. This is a murder investigation. They have to make certain they gather every last bit of evidence before they allow interment."

The phone rang again. This time it was the insurance agent.

"I'm so glad you called," Marnie said. She explained about her flag, and then, sounding shocked, she said, "How could you know about it? I just found out myself yesterday." She was quiet for a bit. "In today's *Belmont Daily*? Really?" She pointed at the newspaper I'd left at the foot of the bed.

I picked it up. To my surprise, right there, on the front page the headlines announced, LOCAL WOMAN LENDS VALUABLE PIECE OF HISTORY TO LIBRARY EXHIBIT. The article went on to explain how Marnie Potter owned a family heirloom, namely an antique flag valued at hundreds of thousands of dollars. Marnie was described as a generous patron of the library, lending this flag for a period of one week, beginning the following Monday. There was a general invitation to the public to come by, followed by a plea for donations to help repair the roof.

Marnie was still on the phone, looking none too pleased. "What do you mean, it's going to cost me more?" She listened for a moment and then snapped, "I have no idea who could have leaked this to the paper." After a sharp good-bye, she slammed the phone into the cradle.

"Can you believe this? He said that because of that article, people now know I own the flag, so I have to either get an alarm system installed or pay about ten times the normal amount of insurance." She grabbed the paper from my hands and perused it. "Who the hell could have blabbed to the newspaper?" she mumbled to herself.

"The only person I can imagine is Liz Carter. She's organizing that exhibit. The whole purpose is to attract as many visitors as they can. I'm sure she never thought that bringing attention to the flag might cause you a problem."

"That's the problem. She never thought," Marnie said. "I don't know why I agreed to let that woman borrow it. I have a good mind to call her right now and give her a word or two."

"Before you do that, why don't you call a security company and find out how much an alarm system might cost. It might be less than you expect. It wouldn't be a bad idea for you to take precautions. After all, you're a woman living alone."

"Do you have an alarm system?" she asked pointedly.

"Er, no. But now that we're talking about it, I think I'll get an estimate for my place too."

"Really?" Just as I'd hoped, my considering a system for my place suddenly convinced Marnie that she should do the same. "Maybe you're right. I'll look into it."

Now that she seemed calmer, I tried again. "So, tell me exactly how you fell down those stairs?"

"It was an accident. Honestly. We had dinner at the Loft in Belmont." I knew the restaurant. A trendy place, it was situated on the second floor of an old manufacturing plant and decorated in a modern industrial style, with stainless steel lamps hanging from a black-painted ceiling that was crisscrossed with rusty metal pipes. The tables and chairs were metal. The floor was worn wood. The kitchen was clearly visible in the back of the cavernous room behind a glass wall. And the menu was enormously expensive. "The staircase was dark, and I'd had a bit too much to drink."

"You don't normally drink much," I said.

"I know, but yesterday we were celebrating after finding out how much my flag is worth. If I sell it, I might have enough money to last me the rest of my life. I wouldn't even need the life insurance policy anymore."

"Did you say as much to Bruce?"

"Yes, but he thinks it would be silly to cancel the policy now—even though we're still within the cancellation period. We would get all our money back and have no penalties. But if we wait until next week, it'll be too late."

"So, you lost your balance?"

"I think so," she said, sounding uncertain. "All I know is one minute I was walking down, my hand on the railing, and the next thing I knew, I was bouncing down the stairs, bumping and banging every part of my body along the way."

There was one more question I had to ask, even knowing that it was likely to upset Marnie again. "Where was Bruce during this time?"

"He was right there with me. He was so worried, my poor sweetheart. He ran down the stairs, and when he saw how sore I was, I thought he was going to cry."

I'll bet he was. But not because she was sore.

My cell phone rang, interrupting my thoughts. I snatched it from my purse and glanced at the call display. Matthew, at last.

"I have the picture," he said without preamble. "And it's just as we feared. Bruce Doherty is an alias."

"I'm with Marnie right now," I said. "Are you bringing it over?"

"I'll be there in five." The line went dead.

"Who was that?" Marnie asked.

"Matthew. He's bringing something he wants to show you."

"What is it?"

"I'm going to let him tell you."

I picked up the plates and coffee cups. I carried them to the kitchen and rather than return and face Marnie's questioning, I hid there until the bell rang. I opened the door to a grim-looking Matthew who held a brown manila envelope in his hands.

"She's in her bedroom," I said and led the way through the living room.

I let him into the bedroom and stepped in after him.

"What's wrong?" Marnie asked. "Why does everybody look so glum? I'm not sick or dying. I'll be like new by tomorrow."

"I have something I'd like you to look at," he said, opening the envelope. He pulled out a couple of photocopies and handed them to her. Puzzled, she studied them.

"Am I supposed to know these men?"

"I contacted the Washington State Investment Board and this is the picture they sent me of the real Bruce Doherty. I'm afraid the person you know as Bruce Doherty has been using this man's identity." He pointed to the picture of the older man.

She frowned, staring at the photo in her hands. "But that can't be. I saw his business card. Last night he left his wallet on the table when he went to the washroom, and I peeked in," she said in a defeated tone.

I came closer and pulled a chair to the edge of the bed. "Does that mean what I think it means?" I asked. "You already had some suspicions?"

Her chin quivered, but she held on to her self-control. "Not exactly. But with all the grief you were giving me about him, I just—I don't know— wanted to check for myself." She stared down at her hands. "I guess that means Bruce is a con artist. What did he want from me? I don't have any money. Why didn't he go after some rich old woman? Why me?"

"I don't know," Matthew said.

"That life insurance policy he made me take. I named him as my beneficiary. You don't think—"

"I suggest you call your insurance provider and cancel that policy as soon as you can," he said.

"And let Bruce know you did it," I added. She blinked back tears and nodded.

"So what happens now?" she asked.

"There's nothing much we can do. I would like to report him to the police," Matthew told her, "but unfortunately, lying is not against the law. Neither is carrying other people's business cards."

"I don't ever want to see him again," Marnie said. All at once, her tears came bursting forth. I wrapped my arms around her, but she pushed me away. "I don't want anybody's pity. I should have known better. Imagine, a good-looking man like that, falling in love with a fat old lady like me. What was I thinking?"

"Marnie, don't talk like that. It could have happened to anybody," I said, handing her the box of tissues from the bedside table.

"Right," she said, dabbing at her eyes. "If you don't mind, I think I'd like to be by myself right now."

"Are you sure? I could stay, maybe prepare you some lunch?"

"No, you've already done enough. Just go. Both of you." She sounded angry as much as hurt. And I couldn't blame her. Matthew and I had been the bearers of the worst news.

"Sure," I said. "I'll give you a call later, see how you feel."

"Fine."

"But before I go," Matthew said, "let me ask you, does Bruce have a key to your house?"

She shook her head. "I was about to give him one, but I never got around to it."

"That's good," he said. "If anybody drops by, don't answer the door. Call Della or me."

She nodded. "He called a little while ago and said he was going to come check on me this afternoon. See how I was doing. He asked if he could borrow my key and make a copy of it, so he could drop in on me at any time and make sure I was safe." She harrumphed. "And I thought that was sweet." Her eyes filled with tears again. "Good grief, I can't believe how stupid I was."

"Don't talk like that, Marnie. His behavior has nothing to do with how smart you are. Con men are experts at manipulating people. And he's probably got years of experience at it."

"Promise me you won't let him come in," Matthew said.

"I promise," she said, and her gaze lowered to her hands again. Noticing her engagement ring, she suddenly tore it off and tossed it into a dish on her bedside table. "He can just drop dead, for all I care."

I wanted to tell her she'd get over it. I wanted to tell her there were plenty of nice men out there and that she would meet one someday. But my instincts told me that would only upset her more.

Matthew sat by the edge of the bed and took her hand in his. "All I have to say is, if I was just a few years older, and you were just a few years younger, I'd go for you myself."

My heart melted. If I hadn't already been in love with the man, I would have fallen for him right then and there.

"You don't really mean that," Marnie said, her face brightening. "You have a perfectly lovely woman, your own age. Forget about me and pay some attention to her."

I felt the red flow into my face. I signaled Matthew. "I think we should both get back to work and let Marnie get some sleep."

We let ourselves out, making sure the house was locked, and Matthew offered me a lift back to my shop. "Thanks, but I can use the walk. That was really nice of you," I said. "What you said back there. It made her feel better."

He smiled. "She needed a cheer-up." He dashed across the street, hopped into his car, and waved to me as I set off on foot.

I needed to be by myself too. My suspicion that Bruce was involved with Helen's murder was stronger than ever. And no matter what Matthew said, I didn't want to just sit back and leave well enough alone. That man was a killer. He'd planned on killing my friend, and if he wasn't stopped he would kill again. I knew that just as sure as my name was Della Wright.

All I had to do was figure out a way to prove it.

Chapter 11

"What are you doing back already?" Margaret asked as I walked in. Winston galloped over and threw himself at me, jubilant with excitement.

"Here you go," I said, fishing a dog biscuit from my pocket. He ran to his cushion and chewed contentedly.

"It's over," I said. "Matthew showed her the picture of the true Bruce Doherty. She never wants to see him again—whatever his real name is."

"Oh, my God. So he *was* using an alias. What do you suppose he was after?"

"I figure he's a con man. He was going to take her for everything she's got."

"Including her life," she added. "That's so scary. She could have been killed."

"What's important is that she's safe now."

"Amen." She tapped the sales book. "I've got to get back to Jenny, but on a brighter note, you'll be happy to know that I sold three items for you while you were gone."

I flipped it open to the last receipts. "One kitchen rug," I read, "and a set of fingertip towels."

"Oh, and I have an order for a handwoven shirt."

"Really? That's amazing." I had priced the shirts rather high, thinking I'd readjust if they didn't sell. But if I already had a sale so soon after making them available, maybe they weren't unreasonable after all.

I waited until Margaret left before turning on my laptop and searching the online telephone directory for Nancy Cutler's phone number. I punched the number in on my cell phone, got her voice mail, and left a message asking her to call me back. And then, since it was quiet, I settled at my loom and resumed working on Marnie's dish towels. I was nearing the three-quarter mark when the bell tinkled. I headed for the cash register, and to my surprise, when the customer turned away from the display, I saw it was none other than Nancy Cutler. As usual, she wore a dark suit and a striped shirt, but this time her hair was loose. No wonder I hadn't recognized her from behind.

"Hi, Della." She came forward. "I was just at Mercantile's and called home for my messages. Since I was only a few steps away, I thought I'd stop by. You wanted to talk to me?"

"Actually, I do." Maybe it was my imagination, but I thought she suddenly looked uncomfortable. "Since Helen's death, I've been wondering if there was anything that happened at the party the other night that might help the police discover why she died. I remembered the way you left so abruptly, and I can't help wondering if something happened to upset you."

Nancy blushed and stammered. "No, of course not. It was a lovely party. Nothing happened. I just remembered that I had to get up early the next morning."

That story was transparently false, but I didn't argue it. I just looked at her steadily. She squirmed under my unflinching gaze.

"Why would you think I noticed something?" she asked nervously.

"From what I gathered, you were seen speaking to Marnie's fiancé for a few minutes. Your conversation seemed to have started pleasantly enough, but something he said must have upset you because all of a sudden you turned and fled. Tell me what he said."

She blanched visibly and shifted from foot to foot as she seemed to struggle with her decision. "I'd heard he was a stockbroker," she said. "Or a financial advisor. And I thought that if he was marrying Marnie, he might be settling down here and opening an office. So I gave him my name and number in case he needed an assistant or a secretary." She stopped, and tightened her lips.

"And what happened?"

"I'd rather not say anything. I wouldn't want to start any rumors. What if I was wrong?"

"Wrong about what?"

She sighed heavily and seemed to struggle with herself. "You must promise not to repeat this. I feel silly for even saying it, but"—she hesitated again—"I thought I recognized him. But I've been thinking about it since, and I must have been mistaken. It was a long time ago, and I never met the man in person. All I ever saw was a photograph, and it wasn't even a clear one."

"What are you talking about?"

"Helen Dubois's younger sister, Sybille. She was my closest friend. Twenty years ago she vanished."

"I heard about that," I said.

"We lived in Chicago at the time—roommates. During our third year there, Sybille started dating a man named Brent Donaldson. My God, she was crazy about that man. He was all she ever talked about—how handsome he was, how smart he was. How they were going to get married."

"Were they engaged?"

She nodded. "She showed me her engagement ring. I wanted to meet him. After all, he was marrying my best friend. She tried to talk him into coming over for dinner, but he always had some excuse. One time she insisted until he finally agreed, but he called and canceled at the last minute."

"Maybe he was just busy."

"So busy he had no time for a whole year?" I had to agree that sounded suspicious. "One day, she came home all excited," she continued. "She had a picture of him. She'd taken it without him knowing, and made me swear to never tell him. It seems he had an aversion to being photographed."

I gasped. "He didn't want to be identified later."

She gave me a crooked smile. "Well, he had nothing to worry about because the shot was from far away, and he wasn't even looking at the camera. I couldn't have picked him out of a crowd if I'd tried." She scowled. "I didn't put it all together until after she disappeared. That was when I came to the same conclusion you just did. The man was up to no good. Why else would he be so adamantly set against having his picture taken, or meeting her friends?"

"I think we just hit the nail on the head."

"One day she just didn't come home from work. At first I wasn't really worried, but the next morning when she still hadn't returned, I called the police. The investigation went on for months. They tried to find Brent Donaldson, but it was as if the man had never existed. They questioned me about him for hours. I told them everything I knew about him. If I hadn't spoken to him on the phone a number of times, I might have thought she'd made him up."

The possibilities this story stirred up were so shocking that it was a moment before I could speak. Then I said, "Hold on a second. You said you couldn't have picked him out of a crowd. What made you think you recognized Bruce Doherty as Brent Donaldson now, twenty years later?"

"It was his voice. I was just chatting with him,

thinking that his voice reminded me of someone, but I couldn't figure out who. Brent used to call Sybille at the apartment all the time, and he'd chat with me when he did—ask me how my day was, that sort of thing. Once I knew who this Bruce sounded like, I started thinking he looked like him too. Bruce has the same body type, the same dark hair and strong nose. But as I said, the picture was taken from far away and it wasn't clear. I'm certain I was mistaken."

"Did you tell him he reminded you of Brent Donaldson?"

Her eyes grew wide. "Oh, my God, no. The first thing that went through my mind was that if Brent Donaldson is still alive and Sybille is still missing—legally dead, according to the courts—he probably killed her." A veil of fear descended over her eyes. "This is not the kind of thing I'd want to have get out. If I'm wrong, I could be sued for slander."

I reflected on all of this after she left. If Brent Donaldson and Bruce Doherty were one and the same, Nancy was probably right. Bruce was responsible for Sybille's disappearance, or murder. But why would he have killed her? Sybille had been declared dead only a few years ago, so there was no question of life insurance or inheritance in this case. Besides, Brent disappeared around the same time she had. He must have had another motive. But what?

Hmm. I wonder . . . Could Sybille have shown her sister a picture of Brent? If so, what if Helen had recognized him? She might have confronted him at the party. Even though Nancy insisted the picture was taken from too far away for her to recognize him, that didn't mean that was the only picture Sybille had taken. She might well have snapped more than one shot and sent the better one to her sister. The more I thought about it, the more convinced I became that Sybille had shown her sister a picture of her boyfriend. Unfortunately, the only two people who could answer that question were Helen and Sybille, and both were dead.

If I was right about this, then Bruce Doherty had one hell of a motive for killing Helen. I snatched up my phone and punched in Matthew's number.

"Wait till you hear what I just found out!" I said, my heart racing.

"Can it wait? I don't have time to talk right now. I spent most of the morning fiddling with my printer to get a clear picture of Bruce Doherty. If I allow any more interruptions I won't have done any writing all day."

"Oh." That was disappointing. "How about dinner then?" I asked, my hope surging.

"Sure, we can grab a bite. Say around six?"

"That works for me."

"Fine. I'll pick up pizza, and I'll leave Winston with you until then."

"Great. I'll provide the wine." We said good-bye, then I punched in Marnie's number. After the fourth ring, an answering machine picked up.

"Hi, Marnie, it's me, Della. I'm just calling

to"—I heard a click on the line and suddenly Marnie was on the phone.

"I'm here. Sorry. I'm screening my calls."

"How are you feeling?

"Much better," she said. "I took a few painkillers and I was able to get a couple of hours' sleep. I've been walking around this morning. I can even move my arm a bit. I'm thinking of coming in to work."

"Don't even think of it. And don't you dare take your arm out of the sling. Much as I'd love to have you here, I think you should stay in bed and get some rest. If you don't, it'll take you much longer to recover." And then I asked her what I really wanted to know. "Have you heard from Bruce?"

"No," she said, with an exasperated sigh. "He hasn't even called to find out how I am. What a jerk. I have a mind to give him a good talking-to."

"Not a good idea. It would only make things more difficult. Don't forget, he's been lying about his name, his career, and God knows what else. For all we know, the man could be dangerous. I wouldn't even take his calls if I were you."

"But . . . I have to give him back his engagement ring." I heard the hopefulness in her voice. One minute on the phone with him and she'd be putty in his hands.

"Tell you what. Matthew is coming over for a bite around six, but if you like I can go with you to Bruce's hotel later. That's something you shouldn't do on your own."

"That's a good idea." The tone of her voice told

me she did not think it was a good idea at all. This
was a bad sign. She was probably already second-
guessing her decision to stay away from him. If
she was left alone for too long, I had no doubt that
she'd give him a call. "Or, if you'd rather," she
said, "maybe we could do it tomorrow?"

"No," I said. "Tonight is good." She grudgingly
agreed that I pick her up around eight thirty. This
would give me ample time to bring Matthew up-
to-date and decide what our next move should be.

The rest of the day was slow, which in a way
was a relief since I was without help. This gave me
the chance to finish the second of Marnie's dishcloths and get through almost half the third. At
five o'clock, when Jenny closed her shop, I closed
mine too.

"I hope pepperoni is okay with you," Matthew
said, dropping the box on the table. "Because
that's what I got."

"Sounds great," I said, pouring the Chianti. I
handed him a glass and he sipped while I set the
table.

He eyed me over the rim. "You look good." I
flushed with pleasure. He had been paying me
way more compliments lately.

"You're looking mighty fine too," I said. *See,
Marnie? I can so flirt.* I was hoping for a bit more
pleasant banter, but Matthew tackled his slice of
pizza with enthusiasm.

"You won't believe what I found out," I said. "Nancy Cutler stopped by the store today." I told him about Nancy's behavior at the party, the way she had been chatting pleasantly with Bruce one minute and then running out in a panic the next. "She isn't one hundred percent sure, but she thinks she recognized Bruce as the same man who used to date Helen's sister before she disappeared. If it's him, he was using a different name back then. She knew him as Brent Donaldson."

"Are you serious?" he said. "Interesting—Bruce, Brent—both names start with the letter *B*."

"So do the family names," I pointed out. "Doherty and Donaldson. Is that supposed to mean something?"

"Maybe so. Don't ask me why, but people who use aliases frequently choose names with the same initials. If he turns out to be the man Helen's sister was dating, the name Brent is probably an alias too. He might have been using dozens of aliases over the years. If and when we find out his real name, I bet it starts with the same initials." He took another sip of wine and then said, "What doesn't make sense to me is why he would show up here, in a town where he knows he runs the risk of being recognized."

"I forgot to mention that Nancy and Helen's sister, Sybille, lived in Chicago at the time. And here's another interesting tidbit. Nancy never met Brent Donaldson in person. It seems that every time Sybille invited him to come and meet her roommate, he made some excuse to put it off. I get the feeling the man didn't want to be seen."

"By the way, if Nancy never saw him, how does she explain recognizing him?"

"She'd seen that one picture of him. And get this—when Sybille showed it to her, she made her promise never to mention it to him. It seems he wouldn't let her take his picture, so she had to take it secretly."

"Ah, that explains why he wasn't worried about coming out here. He probably didn't realize Sybille even took pictures of him." He thought for a second, then added, "But people change over the years. How can she be so sure it was him?"

"She recognized his voice. He used to call Sybille at the apartment, and Nancy and he talked lots of times."

His interest seemed to sharpen. "Now, that's a detail that sounds convincing." He put his fork down. "How long ago did Sybille disappear?"

"I'm not exactly sure, but I think it's been twenty years or so."

"People often change physically over time. After twenty years, most of us are hardly recognizable. But a person's voice, the inflections and accents, those are things that don't change."

"So you think there's something to Nancy's story?"

"Enough to make it worth looking into," he said. "If it's true, that would explain the argument between Bruce and Helen at the party. She must have recognized him and confronted him. And it gives him a hell of a motive for wanting her out of the way."

"Hold on a second. Helen was living out here. And she never met, and probably never even spoke to the man. So how could she have recognized him?" he asked.

I rolled my eyes. "I don't know. Maybe Sybille took another, clearer picture of her boyfriend and sent it to Helen. Or maybe she sent her an enlarged copy of the one she showed Nancy. The point is, this theory makes sense."

"Without proof, any theory makes sense."

I hated it when he talked like a defense attorney. "You're supposed to be helping, not hindering."

"The problem is, only two people could answer that question and they're both dead."

I drummed my fingers on the table. "I wonder if he made Sybille take out a life insurance policy too."

He gave me a lopsided grin. "Sorry, kiddo. I know how much you want to be right, but you said Sybille disappeared, right?" I nodded. "And they never found her body?"

I knew what he was about to say. I had already come to the same conclusion. "I know. I know."

"It's impossible to get an insurance company to fork over the face amount without proof of death. And that, my dear, is hard to do without a body."

"I said I know."

"All right," Matthew said, wiping his mouth with a napkin. "Let me add this: I agree with you that the man could potentially be very dangerous. You may be right and he could be a killer. One thing for sure, Marnie has to stay away from him."

"I sure hope she does. I had the impression she was wavering when I spoke to her earlier today. She wants to give him back his engagement ring. I'm afraid she wants to use that as an excuse to contact him."

"What? That is just plain crazy. Under no circumstances is she to go anywhere near that man."

"I promised to pick her up. If I'm with her, I don't see how—"

"Are you crazy? No way. I won't let you."

I looked at my watch. "But I'm supposed to be there in an hour."

He was still shaking his head. "Didn't you hear a word I just said? Call her right now. Tell her you can't make it and that she's absolutely not to go by herself."

I picked up the phone. After four rings, the answering machine came on.

"Hi, Marnie. It's me. Pick up." I waited until the dial tone. "I know she's screening her calls," I said to Matthew. I hung up and punched in her number again. Still no answer. "Now I'm getting really worried."

One look into Matthew's eyes told me he felt much the same. He pushed back his chair. "Let's go." Winston jumped to his feet and galloped to the door. "No, Winston. You stay." He slunk off with his head low.

I grabbed my sweater and scratched Winnie behind the ears. "Don't worry. We'll be back." I locked the door and raced down the stairs to keep up with Matthew's long legs. "We'll take my car," I said. "It'll be faster." Minutes later, we came to a screeching halt in front of Marnie's house. I scrambled out of the driver's seat, and got to the door just as Matthew was pressing the bell.

"Try again," I said. "She's got to be home."

"I've already tried three times. I don't care how sore she is, if she's home, she would have made it to the door by now."

"Unless she's . . ." I couldn't bring myself to say it out loud. "What if he came by? She's in love with him. He could have sweet-talked her into letting him in."

"Do you know if she keeps an emergency key anywhere?"

"I have no idea," I said, picking up one rock from the border of the flower bed. Soon Matthew and I had turned over all the rocks. We'd checked the mailbox and under the doormat.

"I found it," he said, slipping the key into the lock. "It was above the doorframe."

The door swung open and we ran inside. I raced to the bedroom. It was empty, the bed neatly made. "She's not here." I hurried back out and knocked on the bathroom door. "Marnie? Are you in there?" No answer. I pushed it open. Empty. My heart was pounding harder with every passing minute. I ran to the kitchen, and then to the professional kitchen. My eyes fell on the walk-in freezer and my heart almost stopped. *Oh, dear God, no.* I tore open the door, and almost collapsed with relief. The only thing in the freezer was food.

Marnie was not at home. I trudged back to the living room and let myself collapse onto the red-lips sofa.

"Where do you think she is? Actually, don't answer that." I dropped my face into my hands. "I should have stayed with her. If anything's happened to her, I'll never forgive myself."

Matthew sat down next to me, and wrapped an arm around my shoulders. "She's probably just gone to the store or something. It's way too soon to worry."

"No. She knew I was coming here at eight thirty. If she needed anything, she would have asked me to pick it up."

Matthew looked at his watch. "It's only a quarter to eight. You said she was expecting you at eight thirty? I bet she'll be back by then."

I wanted to believe him. "I don't know. I have a really bad feeling." His forehead furrowed. "What is it?" I asked.

"I have an idea where she might be. Come with me."

Chapter 12

I started the car and looked at him.

"Where, exactly are we going?"

"The Longview."

"I was afraid you'd say that." I put the car in gear and we took off.

The hotel was just a few blocks down Main Street, and it came into sight all lit up against the evening sky. I drove into the parking lot behind the hotel, pulled to a stop, and opened the door.

"Wait here," Matthew told me. "I don't think you should come with me." I didn't argue, but if he thought I was going to wait in the car, he had another think coming. I stepped out.

"Della," he said sharply, "this is something I want to do by myself."

"Fine. You do whatever it is you want to do. I'll watch." I threw up my hands. "No harm."

He shook his head in frustration. "You drive me crazy."

"Oh yeah? Well, it's a short drive," I said, grinning. He'd once said this to me, and it gave me tremendous satisfaction to give it back to him.

He walked to the hotel lobby, while I scampered to keep up. By the time I joined him at the front desk, Bunny had one ear pressed to a phone. "There's no answer," she said, putting the phone down. "Are you sure about this? What if he's in the shower?"

"Knock a couple of times, and if there's still no answer open the door. If he's inside, all you do is apologize and ask him if he wants the turndown service."

She grimaced. "It'll sound a bit weird, since he's been here for weeks and I've never offered him the turndown service till now." She disappeared behind a door, reappearing a moment later with a key card in hand. "He'll probably think I'm there to seduce him," she mumbled as she led the way.

"You don't think—" I started to ask, and then swallowed hard. I'd been worrying about this since Matthew had told me where we were going. "You think Bruce hurt Marnie?" I was near tears.

Ahead of us, Bunny paused at a door and knocked. She waited a second and then slipped in the card and pushed it open. "Management," she called out. No answer. She stepped aside, letting Matthew in first. She and I followed.

Matthew came to a sharp stop and gasped. As I reached him, the bloody scene came into view just as a sweet, metallic smell hit me. I reeled from the gruesome sight.

Next to me, Bunny shrieked. She looked as if she would faint.

"You ladies get out of here," Matthew ordered.

"That's okay," she said, and took a deep breath. "I'm fine. I'll go call the police." She turned and ran down the hall.

I turned my attention to the body on the floor. I felt faint from relief. It wasn't Marnie. It was Bruce Doherty, lying on his back next to the bed, with a deep and bloody gash along his forehead. Behind him, the wall was splattered with blood. Matthew took a step closer, leaning over him.

"Is he . . ."

"Dead as a doornail," he said. "Let's get out of here. We don't want to contaminate the crime scene."

He closed the door, making sure it was locked, and we walked back to the reception area, where Bunny was just putting the phone down. She was still pale, but when she spoke her voice was less shaky.

"The police are on their way." She brushed a hand through her blond hair. "This is going to be terrible for business. Damn it. First somebody breaks into my hotel and steals my most expensive painting, and then one of the guests gets murdered. How to drive customers away." She laughed, but it sounded more like a hiccup. "I invested a lot of money in this place. I can't afford it to go under." She gave us an apologetic smile. "I'm sorry. That was rather callous of me. That poor man is dead, and meanwhile here I am worrying about my business."

"It's a normal reaction," Matthew said.

"Do me a favor," she said. "Could you ask the cops to be discreet? Maybe they could use the back entrance and keep their cruisers farther away in the parking lot."

"I'll do what I can," he said.

He looked around and, spotting a couple of armchairs, he said, "We might as well sit while we wait."

"Yes, of course. In the meantime, can I get you something to drink?" Bunny asked.

"A glass of water, please," I said. My mouth had gone bone dry.

"Same here," he said. Bunny disappeared in the direction of the dining room. As soon as she was out of sight, I leaned over to him.

"You won't tell the police about Marnie, will you?" He took my hand, squeezing it gently. That simple gesture calmed my racing heart. It occurred to me again that lately Matthew had been openly affectionate with me—a shoulder hug here, an arm squeeze there. It wasn't much, but it gave me a warm feeling, and the hope that maybe, just maybe, he was beginning to . . . well . . . like me more.

"I'm sorry, Della. I know she's a friend of yours, but I can't withhold information from the police."

"What information? You don't know anything. You're only guessing. And I promise you, you're wrong. Marnie would never hurt a soul."

He gave me a lopsided smile. "Your loyalty to your friends is one of the things I like best about you. But let me point out one thing. The fact that you're asking me not to tell the police about Marnie proves that you jumped to the same conclusion I did." My eyes watered, and by the time the cop car arrived, tears were running down my cheeks. Next to me, Matthew said, "Damn it, Della. Don't use tears to try to control me. It's not fair."

I wiped my cheeks with my sleeve. "I'm not trying to make you do anything."

Two policemen walked in. The first one was Officer Lombard, and the second was her partner, Harrison. She nodded to Matthew, and then took one look at me and raised her eyebrows. "Della? Della Wright? I can't believe it. Are you the one who called in a dead body?"

Bunny returned with the water in time to hear the question. "No, Officer. That was me." She handed Matthew and me the glasses.

Relief washed over Officer Harrison's face. He took off his cap, brushed his dark hair back, and plopped the cap back on his head. "That would have been quite the coincidence," he said. "Two bodies in less than a week."

"Della and Matthew were with me," Bunny added. "Matthew thought we should check on the deceased because he was worried about his state of mind."

The officer turned to Matthew. "Did you already suspect he might be dead?"

"No. All I knew was that his fiancée had decided to end their relationship, and I worried he might be taking it badly."

"Does this deceased have a name?"

"Bruce Doherty," Bunny said. "He's been a guest at the hotel for about a month and a half."

The policewoman scribbled the name down and then slipped her notebook back into her shirt pocket. "All rightee, now. Can somebody here direct us to the body?"

"His room is down the hall, second from the end," Bunny said, looking nervous. "Officer, would you mind taking the back entrance? I would like to deal with all this as discreetly as possible." She waved vaguely toward the dining room. "You know—the guests."

"I'll go around with you," Matthew said, already heading to the door. "Della, you wait for me."

"No problem." This was one time I was more than happy not to be included.

"Should I come?" Bunny asked. "I don't have anybody to work reception."

"We can speak with you later," the policeman said, and the two officers and Matthew left.

A second later, a group of people walked through the lobby on their way out, and Bunny glanced nervously toward the door. Luckily the officers were already halfway through the parking lot. The guests stopped and congratulated Bunny on the delicious food and the quality of the service.

"Thank you. I hope you come again," she replied, just as another group walked through. Suddenly, I recognized one of them.

"Melinda? Is that you?"

The beautiful blonde had looked at me, then quickly glanced away, pretending not to see me. Now she feigned surprise.

"Why, Della. Fancy running into you here. I just had dinner in the restaurant. After hearing so many wonderful things about it, I simply had to experience the food." The rest of the people who were walking through with her, continued out, and I realized that she wasn't part of their group.

"All by yourself?" I asked.

She shrugged. "If a girl waits for invitations, she ends up never going anywhere." She opened her bag and pulled out a novel. "A good book is all the company I need."

"I hope you enjoyed the food," Bunny said.

"Oh, I did. It was wonderful," she gushed. She dropped the book back in her bag and made a big show of looking at her watch, her eyes wide with surprise. "Oh, it's getting late. I'd better run. I have some baking to do for tomorrow." And she was off like a shot.

Time went by. No more than ten or so minutes, but each one felt like hours. I startled every time the door opened, only to see more restaurant customers walk by. At long last, Matthew reappeared with Officer Lombard.

"We contacted the coroner," she told Bunny.

"He should be here momentarily. And don't worry. I told him to take the back entrance. My partner is waiting for him there." She looked around. "Is there any place private where I can ask you a few questions?"

"My office is in the back. We can go there."

"That will be perfect."

"Della, in the meantime, if anybody asks for me, can you tell them I won't be long?" They left the reception area. I waited until they had closed the door. I turned to Matthew.

"Did you find out anything?" I whispered.

"You mean, as in who killed him? I'm afraid not. There was a heavy glass vase on the bedside table, just a few feet away from where he was lying. It had a big crack along one side, and it was smudged with bloody fingerprints. I think that was the murder weapon."

My heart almost stopped. Bloody fingerprints. I prayed they weren't Marnie's. I hated myself for asking, but I needed to know.

"Did you see anything there that could tie Marnie to the murder?"

"There was one thing. When the police combed the room, they found an engagement ring near the entrance. It was deep in the pile of the carpet. They wouldn't have seen it if Lombard hadn't gotten on her hands and knees and felt around." My spirits took a nosedive.

"Maybe it wasn't Marnie's," I said, hearing the desperation in my voice.

"And maybe I'll be elected president of the United States," he said, giving me an incredulous look.

"What did you tell them?" I asked.

"I couldn't lie. You know that, don't you?" I nodded, and he continued. "I told them everything I'd found out about the man—including his being engaged to Marnie and his using an alias. I also mentioned that I stopped by her place this morning to show her the picture of the real Bruce Doherty and that I advised her to break off her engagement."

That wasn't so bad, I thought, exhaling.

"But," Matthew went on, "I'm afraid I let it slip that he'd talked Marnie into purchasing life insurance with a payout of one million bucks. And as soon as I mentioned that it was a joint life policy, they pounced on it as a possible motive for murder."

"Oh, no. I completely forgot about that. Now that he's dead, she gets to collect the face amount."

"Well, that's not guaranteed. Some companies have a waiting period before benefits can begin. I expect they'll be picking Marnie up for questioning." His eyes sought out mine and he held my gaze. "I'm sorry."

"It's not your fault. I know how bad it looks for Marnie right now, but even if that ring turns out to be hers, there'll be a logical explanation. You'll see." He didn't say anything. "You believe she's innocent, don't you?" I insisted.

"Della, I understand how much you want her to be innocent. But we aren't sure of anything right now."

Before I had a chance to say anything, Bunny stepped out of the office. "Your turn," she said, waving me in. "Have fun."

I pulled myself to my feet. Matthew followed suit and squeezed my shoulder reassuringly. "Don't worry. I'll wait for you." He gave me a peck on the forehead.

I walked into a tiny room, barely large enough to contain a desk, a file cabinet, and two chairs. Officer Lombard asked me to sit and then spoke. "Could you tell me, in your own words, what you witnessed when you walked into Mr. Doherty's room?"

"Matthew probably saw more than I did. I followed him in and I barely got a glimpse of the body before I left. He was lying on his back near the bed. He had a gash on his forehead, and there was some blood." I glanced nervously at the pad in which she was writing. "That's all. I didn't notice anything else."

"Did you see anybody touch anything?"

"You mean Bunny or Matthew? No. Actually, Matthew made a point of making us all leave the room right away so we wouldn't contaminate the crime scene. And he closed and locked the door behind us."

"How did you know Mr. Doherty was dead?"

"It was pretty obvious. First of all, we knocked

a few times before Bunny unlocked the door. When I saw him, his coloring was so pasty, and the way he lay there, with one arm twisted under him, not to mention all the blood. It was obvious he was dead."

She took notes. "Is there anything else you think the police should know?"

"I can't think of a thing."

And that was that. Officer Lombard thanked me and I left. Though I'd been so nervous about being interviewed, the entire thing had taken no more than a few minutes. No more sting than a mosquito bite.

"How was it?" Matthew asked when I returned to the reception area.

"Short and sweet."

"Listen," he said, looking at his watch, "it's getting late. How about I let Winston stay over at your place tonight?" I welcomed that idea. Spending the night alone after seeing a dead body was not something I'd been looking forward to.

We climbed back into my Jeep and I drove him home, detouring past Marnie's house. It was dark, all lights out.

"She must be asleep," I said.

"Or on the run," he countered. I could have clobbered him, but the same thought had occurred to me. I dropped him off and went home.

I let myself in and found poor Winnie whimpering and walking in tight circles at the door. He hadn't been outside in hours. I took him out for a

quick pee and then settled him on his cushion in the
corner of my room. He started snoring instantly—
lucky dog. *I wish I could fall asleep as easily,* I thought.
I climbed into bed, sure that I'd be counting sheep
all night. But surprisingly, the next thing I knew it
was eight o'clock the next morning. I'd slept right
through my alarm.

Winnie watched, fascinated, as I ran around, pulling on clothes and brushing my hair. Ten minutes
later I was downstairs at my counter, and he was
in his usual spot—on his cushion sleeping, again.

"You look like you could use a cup of coffee,"
Jenny said, bringing over a mug and a muffin.
Margaret followed.

"You have no idea," I said, and took a deep
gulp. "Did you hear about Marnie's fiancé?" I
asked, waving away the blueberry muffin. My
stomach was in no shape for food.

"No. What did the creep do now?" she said.

"It's not what he did, but what was done to
him. He was murdered last night."

Coffee splashed all over my counter as Jenny
jerked her cup. "I'm so sorry," she said, grabbing
a napkin and wiping, while I pushed sales book
and business cards away from the mess.

"There, all clean and no damage done," I said.

"Did you say he's . . . dead?"

"Stone-cold. Somebody hit him over the head
with a vase."

"Murdered—how awful," Margaret said. "I admit, I didn't like him much, but I certainly didn't wish him any harm, except for maybe a good hard slap in the face from Marnie." She picked up Jenny's empty cup and stopped. "Does Marnie know?"

I shrugged. "I'm not sure."

"Poor her," she said, and then looked down at the empty cup. "I'll get you a fresh one."

"You haven't spoken to her?" Jenny asked, tossing the sodden napkins into the wastebasket. "This is going to be really hard on her. You should give her a call."

"I'm not sure I should, at least not until the police have questioned her."

Jenny froze. "Why would they want to question Marnie?"

"They'll probably question everyone who knew him," I said discreetly.

Margaret reappeared with a full cup. "Here you go."

"Some people are going to think she's lucky," Jenny said, stirring absently. "At least he's out of her life now. But I think this is the worst thing that could have happened. His death will devastate her. Now she'll probably elevate him to sainthood. She won't believe that he was anything less than perfect."

"Oh, my God," Margaret said. "This is exactly what you predicted."

Jenny frowned. "What are you talking about?"

"Don't you remember? When you read Marnie's cards, you told her that a man she knew was surrounded by danger."

"So I did." She planted a hand on her hip and gave me the eyebrow. "Gee, imagine that. I made a prediction and it actually came true."

"Ha, ha," I said. "Trust me, she doesn't think of him as a saint. Matthew and I had a long talk with her yesterday. He showed her the picture of the real Bruce Doherty."

"So she already knows he was using an alias?"

I nodded. "She knows his entire background was fiction, and she suspects that the real reason he wanted her to take out life insurance naming him as beneficiary might have been part of a plan to kill her."

"You told her all that? Even though she was already angry with you? And she believed you?"

"Matthew showed her the real Bruce Doherty's picture. She knows we were telling her the truth. She made the other connections herself. The last thing she said before we left was that it was over with him and that she never wanted to set eyes on him again."

Jenny's mouth dropped open. "I would never have imagined."

"I guess you don't know everything that's going to happen." It was my turn to give her a knowing smile.

"Touché," she said, laughing. In that moment I knew that all the bad feelings between Jenny and me were gone. It had been silly of me to worry. Our friendship was solid.

"I have a favor to ask," she said. "Would you mind driving to Melinda's bakery again? We're all out of everything, and from what you told me, I doubt that Marnie did any baking last night."

"No problem," I said, grabbing my keys. "Keep an eye on my shop till I get back."

I climbed into my car, intending not to go to Belmont but to drive to Marnie's. She had a freezer full of baked goods. But what was more important was that this gave me the perfect excuse to stop by her house. If the police were there, my arrival wouldn't seem unusual. And if they weren't, it would give me a chance to prepare her.

Chapter 13

A disheveled Marnie swung the door open before I had even reached it. Her eyes were bloodshot and swollen, and her nose was red from crying. She grabbed my arm, glanced around outside, and pulled me in, panicked.

"Thank God you're here!" she exclaimed. "I'm going out of my mind. I just know the police are going to come and arrest me." The full impact of her words hit me. Not only did she know about Bruce's murder, but she expected to be arrested.

"Marnie, I think you should tell me where you were last night."

"I didn't kill him, if that's what you think." I remained quiet, and she continued. "Okay, I admit I went to see him." She looked at me with watery eyes.

"I don't know about you, but I could use a cup of coffee," I said, my voice shaking. I wasn't sure I was ready to hear the rest of the story.

"I just made a fresh pot," she said. I followed her to her kitchen and located the coffee.

"I didn't kill him. I swear I didn't."

"I believe you," I said, handing her a cup. *At least I want to.*

"I sure hope the cops do too," she said, walking back to the living room. "I went to his hotel to have it out with him. I wanted to face him alone—sorry," she added sheepishly. "To give him his ring back and tell him to his face exactly what I thought of him." She rubbed her temples. "I don't know what I was hoping to accomplish. I suppose I still had a tiny hope that he was going to somehow make all the bad go away, and that everything would turn out all right." She rubbed her naked ring finger. "But when I knocked on his door, it swung open. I was getting ready to throw his ring in his face, when I noticed he was lying on the floor. I walked another few steps inside, and that's when I saw his face covered in blood. He was . . . dead. I got out of there as fast as I could."

"Oh, Marnie."

"I know. It was stupid of me." Her eyes filled with tears again. "You believe me, don't you? That I didn't kill him."

"Of course I do." Even though I believed her, the fact that she'd run away, and didn't report his death, did not bode well.

She sighed, as if a great load had been lifted from her shoulders. The doorbell rang, interrupting us. Marnie jumped to her feet.

"It's the police," she whispered. "They're coming for me."

"You stay put. I'll see who it is."

"Or maybe it's Liz," she said, her voice full of hope. "She called earlier, begging that I let her take the flag right away. I didn't have the energy to say no. The flag is all ready to go. It's in the box on the coffee table." She darted to the kitchen and I made my way to the door. Sure enough, when I looked through the peephole, it was none other than Liz.

"Why, Della, what a surprise finding you here so early in the morning." I had the distinct impression she was dying to dive into a serious gossip session. I gave her no such satisfaction.

"I could say the same to you."

"Oh, Marnie called and said I could come over and pick up the flag." She stepped in and looked around. "My, this is quite the decor." I gathered from that comment that she'd never been here before.

"It's cheerful, isn't it?" I said.

"It certainly is. Where's Marnie?" She looked around.

"She can't come to the door at the moment. But I'll get you the flag." I went over to the coffee table and picked up the box. When I turned, she was right behind me. "Excuse me." I stepped past her and detoured past the small gold-leaf writing desk in the corner. I grabbed a sheet of paper and a pen. I set down the box. "I hope you don't mind writing her a receipt for the flag." A look of surprise flashed over her face, but she recovered.

"By all means. I don't mind at all."

I scribbled a few words, then read them out loud to her. "I hereby confirm that I am in the bor-rowed possession of one antique Betsy Ross flag and that I will return it to Marnie Potter by the last day of April of this year." I handed her the pen. "That gives you just about two weeks. Sign your name and date it, here."

I watched as she did so. She handed me the pa-per and took the box in exchange.

"I'll have it back in less than ten days," she said. "Thank Marnie for me, will you, dear?" She gave the room one last glance and left.

I returned to the kitchen with the receipt and gave it to Marnie, explaining what I'd done.

"Oh, I wouldn't worry about it. Liz is a good soul. She's always helping, donating her time and energy to charitable organizations. But thanks all the same."

My eyes fell on her hand, and I suddenly re-membered something Matthew had said. "Marnie, what did you do with your engagement ring?"

"I—I . . ." She scrunched her forehead, trying to remember, *or maybe coming up with an excuse.* I couldn't believe that thought had just crossed my mind. "I think I put it back in my jacket pocket."

"Could you go and check?"

"Sure," she said, pulling herself out of her chair. She left the kitchen, returning a few minutes later, her face looking nearly as pale as Bruce's had been on the floor of his hotel room. "I don't know what happened to it," she said. "I remember taking it out of my pocket when the door swung open. And I was sure I put it back, but now I can't find it. You don't think I—"

I nodded miserably. "The police found it near his body."

She collapsed into her chair. "Oh, my God. I am so screwed."

"Uh, Marnie, did you happen to touch anything else in the room while you were there?"

"No," she started to say, and then stopped. "Oh, I forgot. I did touch something. The glass vase was on the floor. I picked it up and put it on the bedside table." And then the full impact of her action hit her and her eyes filled with horror. "Now you're going to tell me that vase was the murder weapon, aren't you?" I nodded, and at that, what little color had remained in her cheeks drained away.

At the same moment the doorbell rang, and Marnie started to get up.

"Let me get the door. If it happens to be the police, I'll tell them I'm here to pick up some baked goods for Jenny."

She stood. "I'll start putting together some pastries," she said. I went to the front door.

I looked through the peephole and saw that, just as I'd feared, it was Lombard and Harrison. I took a deep breath and opened the door.

"Good morning, Officers," I said.

Surprise filled the police officers' eyes. "What are you doing here?" asked Harrison, looking suspicious.

"Marnie does all the baking for Coffee, Tea and Destiny," I said. "I came by to pick up the order."

"Did you discuss the murder of her fiancé with her?"

I might have been tempted to deny it, but I knew they wouldn't believe it. "I told her and offered my condolences," I said.

"Did Ms. Potter already know about his death, or did your news come as a shock?"

"I don't know," I said. "I'd just told her when you rang the bell. She didn't say anything. She just started to cry," I said, squashing the surge of guilt that followed. Lying, in general, was not something I did easily. But Marnie was my friend, and I'd be damned if I was going to say anything that got her into even deeper trouble. At that moment, a small movement at the edge of the kitchen entrance caught my eye, and I realized Marnie was hiding behind the doorway, listening in on the conversation. Good thing. Otherwise she might contradict everything I said. "Have a seat." I gestured toward the sofa. "I'll go get her."

I found her behind the door just as I'd expected. "You heard?" I whispered. She nodded. "It'll be okay," I mouthed. "Just tell them the truth." And then I called out loud, "Marnie, the police are here." We waited a few seconds and then stepped into the living room. Marnie's eyes were still swollen and red. The officers jumped to their feet.

"Good morning, Ms. Potter," Lombard said. "I'd like to extend our deepest sympathies."

Marnie nodded. "Thank you. I still can't believe it. He was so full of life, and now . . ." She squeezed her eyes shut.

"I'm sorry. I know this is a difficult time for you, but I'm going to have to ask you to come with us. We have some questions we need you to answer. Please get your coat."

"Are you taking me to the station?" she asked. "You want to ask me about Bruce's murder?"

"I'm afraid so," the older officer replied.

"But why would you want to question me? I don't know who killed him."

"Maybe not so much about his death as about his life—who he knew, who might have had it in for him—that sort of thing."

She picked up a sweater from the back of an armchair and followed the police officers out. At the door, she turned back to me. "I left my spare key in its usual hiding spot," she said. "If you don't mind—"

"Don't worry," I said. "I'll lock up."

I watched Lombard get into the driver's seat, while Officer Harrison opened the back door for Marnie, placing a hand on her head and helping her in. This was not good. They were treating her like a criminal. As much as they said otherwise, I was sure she was on her way to being arrested. The questioning was only a formality. And with her engagement ring being found near the body, it would be difficult for her to maintain her innocence. Not only did Marnie have a motive, but that ring put her in Bruce's room around the time he died. I wanted to help, but I had no idea what I could do.

I went back to the walk-in freezer. This time, when it beeped I was only slightly startled. I bagged everything Jenny might need.

Try as I might, at five foot nothing, there was no way I could reach the key above the doorframe. *Shit.* I snatched my phone from my bag and speed-dialed Matthew. He answered on the first ring. "I'm at Marnie's," I said. "She just left for the station with the police and she asked me to lock up, but I can't reach the key." I heard a chuckle at the other end. "Don't laugh. Marnie is probably being grilled as we speak. I don't see anything funny about the situation." I had always been sensitive when it came to my height.

"Sorry," he said. "I'm not laughing." But I could hear the smile in his voice. "I'll be right over."

Minutes later he drove up in an antique Corvette—his latest project. Since his teenage years, his favorite hobby had been restoring old cars. He hopped out and jogged over. He quickly glanced around to make sure no one was watching—the street was quiet—and then snatched the key from its hiding place. A second later the door was locked and the key back in its spot.

"I'm sorry I laughed," he said, "but I kept picturing you jumping, trying to grab the key."

"As you said," I snapped back. "Not funny." I

would have given anything to be six or even eight inches taller. That way, I'd at least be kissable height for Matthew. As it was, the top of my head didn't reach his shoulder.

He grew serious. "Tell me, do you have any idea whether the police read Marnie her rights?"

"They didn't. At least not while I was there. All they said was that they had some questions about her fiancé." I could almost hear him thinking in the silence that followed.

"How do you feel this morning? Still think she's innocent?"

"Of course I do."

"I hope you're right. And if they haven't given her the Miranda, that means they aren't arresting her—at least not yet," he added. "I really should be writing, but I'll see if there's anything I can do to help her case. I have a feeling she'll need a lot of help. I'll give you a call when I come up with an idea."

"Do you really think you can do something?"

He shrugged. "Not sure. It's sensitive. Usually I help the police *make* a case against a suspect, not the other way around. And I don't want to ruin my professional relationship with them. Leave it to me." He helped me load the bags of baked goods into the back of my Jeep, then hopped into his 'Vette and sped away in the direction of the police station. I drove to work, hoping he could find a way to prevent her from being arrested. But knowing about her engagement ring in the carpet and the vase with her prints on it—not to mention the insurance policy . . . I wondered again if Marnie stood to collect on Bruce's life insurance policy. Not much chance of that, especially if she was arrested for his murder.

I carried the first two bags through my store and into the back, setting them on the counter.

"Do you have many more to bring in?" Margaret asked, putting down her bar cloth.

"Three or four. Want to help?" She followed me out and we carried in the last of the bags. Jenny was sorting through, pulling out box after box. She held up a cupcake. "How come everything here is frozen?"

"That's because I didn't drive into Belmont," I said. "I went to Marnie's. When I was there yesterday, I saw she had a freezer full of baked goods. I didn't see the point of getting them from Melinda's. Besides, it was a good excuse to see how she's doing."

"Good idea." Jenny put the box down and continued putting away the food. "Did she already know about Bruce?"

I nodded.

"Poor her. How is she holding up?"

"As well as can be expected under the circumstances. But she's being questioned by the police right now."

"Questioned?"

"They got there just as I was about to leave."

"Oh, my God. Tell me Marnie didn't have anything to do with his death."

"You're her friend. You know her better than that," I said. "How can you even make such a suggestion?" It occurred to me that she didn't even know about Marnie's going to Bruce's hotel room and she had automatically jumped to that conclusion, which meant that as soon as it became public knowledge, Marnie would be as good as convicted. I felt sick.

At that moment Margaret set the last bag on the counter. "What suggestion?"

"I was just telling Jenny that the police picked Marnie up. And Jenny asked me if Marnie killed Bruce," I said, incensed.

"That's outrageous," Margaret sputtered.

"I didn't mean it that way," Jenny argued.

"What other way is there?" I asked. And then seeing the look on her face, I changed my tone. "I'm sorry. I guess I feel protective of her. Anybody who knows Marnie has to realize that she could never hurt anybody."

"That's right," Margaret said. "She couldn't hurt a fly."

"Hopefully that will be everybody's opinion," I said. "Starting with the police."

I heard the telephone ringing from my shop and raced over. "Dream Weaver, good morning. Della speaking."

"Della? It's me."

"Mom? Hi. How are you?"

"How I am is worried. I just heard about a second murder victim in Briar Hollow. Please tell me you didn't find that body too."

"Don't worry. I didn't. Matthew found him." It was better not to mention that I happened to be present. "You know, don't you, that the victim was Marnie's fiancé?"

"He was? Oh, how terrible. You never told me she was engaged."

"I didn't? It happened very recently," I said. "And very fast."

"What do you mean, fast? How long had she known him?"

"Not long at all. Only one month."

"Really." I could almost hear the gears in my mother's brain clicking. Any second now, she would question how Marnie could get a man to propose in such a short time when I couldn't even get Matthew to date me after years of knowing him.

"It was a terrible mistake on her part," I said quickly. "The police are looking into him. So far all we know is that he was using an alias, and he talked Marnie into buying one million dollars of life insurance with him as beneficiary."

There was a gasp at the other end. "Are you suggesting he was planning to kill her?"

"That's one possibility. At this point we just don't know."

"Oh, my. That poor woman. She must be devastated."

"She is. Totally devastated."

"I think I'll give her a call. What do you think? Or should I just send her some flowers?"

"I'm sure she'd like to hear from you, but give her a day or two. Right now she's pretty raw."

"You're right, of course. So how's Matthew?" she asked.

"He's well," I said, wondering how I could pre-empt an interrogation. The best way was probably just to tell her what she wanted to know without waiting for the questions. "We've been having dinner pretty regularly lately."

"Dinner . . . as in dinner dates?"

"I'm not sure. He seems friendlier these last few weeks. More affectionate too." And before she got the wrong impression, I added, "Not romantic or anything, just—I don't know—warmer."

"That's good. I hope you're responding in the same way?"

"I am, but I have to be careful. I want him to take the lead."

"Right. Good thinking. Oh, I'm so happy. That is such good news," she said, her voice rising an octave in her excitement. Before I knew it, we'd said good-bye and hung up. This was the first time in ages that I'd had a lovely conversation with my mother without feeling pressured. Maybe that was the trick—just tell her what she wanted to hear. The problem was that what she wanted to hear was not always what really happened.

I wandered over to my loom, thinking about what I'd just told my mother. It was true. Matthew had been behaving differently toward me lately.

For a long time we'd had a friendly but sparring relationship. Lately, the bickering gave way to gentleness, and the change had been so gradual that I'd hardly noticed. What could it mean? I stared at the shuttle in my hands.

There was no point in obsessing about this. I would simply have to keep my eyes open and encourage Matthew every chance I got. I loaded my shuttle with a fresh bobbin and returned to my weaving. Soon my worries for Marnie were replaced by more positive thoughts. With Matthew's help, Bruce's murder would be solved and Marnie's life would go on. I had no doubt about it.

Most days I could count on a few hours of weaving before business picked up sometime around midmorning. But today—probably because of the news of Bruce Doherty's murder—business was hopping right from the start. To my surprise, one of my first customers was Liz Carter. She came bursting through the door a few minutes after ten.

"I just heard," she said, her voice shaking with emotion. "It's such a tragedy." Her sadness seemed sincere. "Poor Marnie. How is she doing?"

"She'll recover," I said, not wanting to say too much. "It will take some time, but she'll get over it."

She nodded grimly. "I suppose," she said. "Can you think of anything I can do to help her?"

"Not at the moment, but if I do, I'll let you know."

"She wanted to take care of Helen's funeral arrangements. Maybe I could help her do that," she said.

"Do you have any idea when the medical examiner plans to release her body?"

"As a matter of fact, I called the police department as soon as I heard they'd picked Marnie up this morning." I wondered how that piece of news had gotten out so fast. As if reading my mind, she explained. "Mercedes Hanson saw her get into the police car his morning. She told me about it when she stopped at the library to drop off some books." Mercedes didn't have a malicious bone in her body. If she'd said anything, it would have been out of concern.

"What did the police say?" I asked, referring to the release of Helen's body.

"The medical examiner will soon be finished. And then they'll need someone to claim the body before releasing it. I don't mind doing that."

"The police weren't able to locate any living relatives?"

"Seems not," she continued in a gossipy tone. "Anyhow, I'd better get going. I'm on my way to church. I'm meeting with Father Jones to finalize the library fund-raiser. He promised me some volunteers. I'll ask him about organizing a funeral service at the same time. Helen would have wanted a religious ceremony."

"That's very nice of you," I said.

"The only problem is," she said, "I'll have to get into Helen's house and find something nice for her to wear." I must have looked surprised because she added, "For the viewing."

"Of course," I said.

"I'll let you know what Father Jones suggests regarding the funeral, and you can tell Marnie."

I watched the door close behind her, as questions crowded my mind.

Helen's body hadn't been released yet, so why did Liz need to get her a dress? Besides, she'd already been dead for nearly a week, and she'd been autopsied. Could an open-casket service even be held under the circumstances? Why did I have the feeling that this was just an excuse for Liz getting into Helen's house? *I'm definitely getting paranoid.*

The bell rang and I looked up to see Nancy Cutler walking in with two other friends of Marnie's who'd been at the party.

"Go ahead," she told them, waving them toward the coffee shop. "I'll join you in a minute." She came over to the counter. "Hi, Della. Can you believe what happened to Bruce Doherty?"

"It was quite the shock," I said, and then I changed the subject before she could get away. "I've been thinking about what you told me regarding Brent Donaldson, and I can't help wondering, do you have any idea whether Helen ever saw a picture of him?"

She puckered her brow, thinking. "I know Helen never met him. But whether she ever saw a picture of him, I couldn't be sure. I remember Sybille begging Brent to come to Briar Hollow with

her. She so wanted him to meet her sister. But
he never did. On the other hand, I wouldn't be
surprised if she sent Helen that same picture she
showed me."

"What makes you say that?"

"I don't know. It just makes sense. She was so
excited to show me, and even with the geograph-
ical distance, she and Helen always remained
close. I'd be shocked if she hadn't. On the other
hand, the police asked me for a picture of him
during the investigation of Sybille's disappearance. Surely they wouldn't have asked me if
they'd gotten one from Helen."

"Not necessarily," I said. "The more pictures
they have, the better."

"True," she agreed.

"Did you and Helen ever discuss the case?"

Her eyes widened. "Are you kidding? That was
all she ever talked about. The police never found
out anything, but that didn't stop her from carrying on her own investigations. For years, she
called me regularly, sometimes a couple of times a
week. She'd ask me the same questions over and
over again. 'Did Sybille ever mention meeting any
of Brent's friends or family?' 'Did I know where
he was born?' 'Did they have any special places
where they used to go?' 'Could they have run
away together?' It got to the point where I started
feeling as if I was a suspect. I finally stopped taking her calls. Then, when I moved back out here, I
got an apartment in Belmont rather than in Briar

Hollow, just so I wouldn't have to run into her every day. Eventually, of course, I did. And you know, Helen probably blamed me on some level for Sybille's disappearance, because whenever she saw me she'd just pretend she didn't see me."

"How awful for you," I said.

"To tell you the truth," she continued in a whisper, "I think Helen had sort of lost her grip on reality these last few years. I know it's not nice to speak ill of the dead, but honestly, she became as loony as a tune." She made a circling gesture around her ear.

"That's so sad," I said, wondering whether Nancy was making this up or not. It was possible. Helen had probably spent years obsessing about finding her sister. She'd fought to keep the police investigating long after the case had grown cold, putting up rewards. Had she continued until her mind had snapped? I suddenly remembered that Marnie had mentioned Helen falling apart after years of trying to find Sybille. That was when she'd turned to the courts to have her sister declared legally dead. Poor woman. It sounded as if she'd waited too long to turn the page. By then she'd already lost her mind.

"If only I could find out for sure whether Sybille ever sent Helen a picture of her boyfriend," I said.

"What difference would it make at this point? The case is closed." She looked at me incredulously. "Oh. I get it. You're looking for proof that Bruce and Brent are the same man. But even if she did see his picture, that was such a long time ago. She would have thrown it away by now."

"I'm not so sure about that," I said. "No matter how much she may have wanted to put the whole thing behind her, she would never have gotten rid of any pictures, any letters, or for that matter, any evidence she may have gathered. I bet if we searched, we'd find a box somewhere in her house, filled with every—" I stopped abruptly as an idea came to me. That was exactly what I would do. I would search Helen's house.

"Della?"

I startled. Nancy was staring at me strangely.

"Are you all right?"

"Yes, of course. I'm fine," I said. I couldn't remember what we'd been talking about and had to scramble for something to say. "I'm just worried for Marnie. This is devastating for her."

"Of course. It would be for anyone." I detected a note of condescension in her voice. She adjusted her sweater. "Well, I'd better get going. Got a lot to do today." She marched toward the door and left.

For the rest of the day, my mind kept going back to Helen. I hadn't told a soul about my idea of sneaking into her house. She'd been dead five days now, and the police had already moved on to a fresher case—Bruce's. I wondered how risky it might be to go in.

Chapter 14

The gossip train was running full tilt right through my shop, with a nonstop stream of customers, all intent on hearing the latest over a cup at Coffee, Tea and Destiny. At one o'clock, Margaret came up front and brought me a ham and cheese sandwich and a cup of java.

"I figured you'd be hungry. And seeing as you're on your own today, you wouldn't have time to get something to eat."

"Thanks. I'm famished."

She retreated back to the coffee shop and I was able to grab a few bites in between sales. At three thirty, the store became empty and I was just starting on the second half of my sandwich when Mercedes Hanson stopped by.

"Hi, Della," the teenager said as the door closed behind her. "I guess Marnie's not here?"

"She might be home," I said.

Mercedes slouched over to me, her eyes filled with worry. "No. I just went by. There's no answer.

I saw the cops picking her up this morning. I'm so scared for her."

"I know. I'm worried too. But Marnie did not kill Bruce. If you're worried about her going to jail, remember this: the truth will prevail in the end."

"You really think so?"

"I do," I said, with more confidence than I felt. "By the way, Liz Carter stopped by. She mentioned you went by the library this morning and told her."

"Is that what she said? That I told her?" Mercedes exclaimed. "It was more like she forced it out of me."

"What do you mean?"

"I was walking by the library on my way to school, and she called me in to help her move a heavy desk. That turned out to be a total lie. She just wanted to pump me for information about Marnie."

I planted my elbows on the counter. "I think you'd better tell me everything."

"Well, first of all, the desk was on wheels, so all I did was roll it over by about two feet. She pretended to be so surprised, said she never noticed the wheels. Yeah. Right. And then she started asking questions about Marnie. How was she doing? Did I know if the wedding was going on as scheduled? I feel so stupid for it now, but before I knew it, I just blurted out how worried I was, that I'd seen the cops take her away in the police car. And, you know, the weirdest part, is as soon as I said that, I got the feeling that this was good news to her. Of course she pretended to get all sad."

"Really," I muttered to myself.

"And then, at lunchtime, I found out that Marnie's fiancé was murdered." Her brow furrowed. "That's when it hit me. I bet she already knew Mr. Doherty was dead. She wanted to find out whether Marnie knew too."

I held back a gasp. If Mercedes was right, that would mean Liz had heard the news before anybody else. How could she have known, unless . . . *Ridiculous*, I thought. *But true that the gossip mill in this town traveled at the speed of light.*

I became aware that Mercedes was still talking. "Poor Marnie. Do you think I should stop by and offer her my condolences?"

"I think that's a very nice idea."

She nodded. "Maybe I can bring her some flowers or something. I'll ask my mom to come with me. Do you think she'll be coming back to work soon?"

"I don't know," I said. "I have an idea. How would you feel about helping out at the store until Marnie is feeling better?"

"Really? You would let me work here?" You would have thought I'd just invited her to a party. "That would be amazing. I'd love it. Maybe I can work on those napkins I'm making for her."

"Good idea. You've become so good with your own weaving that I think you could answer questions and help customers just about as well as I can."

We discussed payment and the number of hours she would come in, and by the time we came to an agreement, she was walking on sunshine.

And by then it was already after four. Matthew would be here to pick up Winston soon, and I was tempted to ask him to have dinner together. There was so much I wanted to tell him. But I also wanted to get into Helen's house before it got dark out. If I wanted to search without attracting undo attention, I'd have to do it without turning on the lights.

"How would you like to start right now?" I asked.

Her face lit up. "You mean, like, right this minute?"

"Like, right this second."

"Sure. What do you want me to do?"

"You can start by putting your bag behind the counter and minding the store for me while I go run a few errands."

"What do I do if somebody wants to buy something?"

I opened the drawer and pulled out a sales pad. "Here is the receipt book." I briefed her on how to process credit cards and how to operate the cash register. "Don't worry. I know you'll do fine," I assured her. Helen's house was only a few blocks away. The last thing I wanted was for anyone to notice my red Jeep parked in front of her house, so

I took off on foot. After making sure there was nobody on the street, I walked around to the back of her house. My fear that the door lock would have been repaired proved needless. It slid open effortlessly. The only obstacle was a yellow crime scene tape across the entrance. I stepped between the ropes of police tape, and a minute later I was inside. I left my purse on the kitchen counter and paused to think. It occurred to me that if I'd just had a nasty argument, the first thing I would have done after coming home would have been to call a friend and vent. I picked up the kitchen phone, the one I figured would have been the most likely one she would have used, and I pressed REDIAL. After a few rings it picked up. I was just about to hang up when I realized it was an answering system.

"Hi, I am not home right now, but—" It was Nancy Cutler's voice. I hung up before the end of the message.

My head was spinning. If Helen had called Nancy the night she'd died, why hadn't Nancy mentioned it? On the other hand, Helen's telephone was old. It had no call nor time display. There was no way I could prove exactly when that last call had been made. It could have been weeks ago. Or, for that matter, whether Helen had even reached Nancy or the answering system, or whether she'd hung up before it even started ringing. I spotted another telephone in the hallway and tried that one. To my horror, the police dispatcher picked up.

"Oh, eh, wrong number. Sorry," I said and put the receiver down. *Shit, shit, shit.* I prayed that the woman wouldn't automatically recognize the number as coming from the phone of a murder victim. Then I realized how silly that was. She probably answered hundreds of calls a day. There was no way she would take notice of one particular wrong number. I took a deep breath. *Why would Helen have called the police?* Or was it simply that the police had used her phone when they were here? If that was what had happened, there was no way of knowing whom she had last called from that phone. *Well, that was a waste of time.*

I started my search with Helen's bedroom. I opened the closet. It was full of staid dresses and skirts—grays, browns, beiges. Not a colorful garment anywhere in sight. It made me feel even sorrier for the woman. Her sister seemed to have been the only ray of sunshine in her life.

On the floor was a jumble of practical shoes. I reached for the shelf on top. Way too high. I went in search of a chair and carried one over from the kitchen. The only thing I found on the shelf was a stack of shoeboxes containing old tax returns, credit card statements, and IRA investments— money that she'd saved for her whole life and would never get to enjoy. I put the boxes back the way I'd found them and returned the chair to the kitchen. I went through the dresser drawers, then the bedside table. Nothing.

Next, I tackled the living room, looking under the sofa and inside the entertainment unit. I moved on to the hall closet and then to the bedroom. Still nothing. I was in the second bedroom, which Helen had used as a combination crafts and sewing room, when I heard a scraping noise. I froze. It sounded like the sliding door being opened. I listened, and sure enough, the next sound I heard was soft footsteps, like somebody tiptoeing through the kitchen. Somebody was in the house. I ducked down and slid under the bed.

My purse, I thought. I'd left it on the kitchen counter. Anyone who looked inside would know right away that I was here. If the intruder was the killer, I was as good as dead. A new sound sent my heart racing. Any faster and I'd be going into fibrillation. What if this was the police? I might not be murdered, but I'd be in deep trouble. At this point, I didn't care who it was, just as long as they didn't find me. I considered bargaining with God. I could promise never to play detective again. But I doubted I could keep such a promise. The footsteps came closer and I held my breath until I thought my lungs would explode. They continued down the hall, but just as I exhaled, the steps turned around. The door opened and the intruder walked in. All I could see, in the inch of space between the dust ruffle and the parquet floor, was a pair of high-heeled shoes—definitely not policemen's shoes. I allowed myself a small measure of relief. Whoever this woman was, at least she couldn't arrest me. *Could it be Liz?* And I was almost tempted to lift the dust ruffle and look. But if Liz had arranged to pick up a dress, she would have come in the front door. And she certainly wouldn't be searching the house. No. Whoever this was had no business being here. No more than I did, I reminded myself.

The intruder tiptoed across the room, stopping by the side of the bed, just a few inches from where I hid. There was the squeak of a tight drawer being pulled open, and then it slammed shut. The woman went through them all—the same drawers I'd just searched. But why? The high heels moved away, this time pausing at the closet. I heard a creak and the sound of shuffling.

All this time I fully expected to be discovered, but to my relief, after a while the woman moved on to another part of the house. Minutes went by. At long last I heard the sliding door open and shut, and then silence. I waited another few minutes before slipping out from under the bed. I dashed to the kitchen, grabbed my purse, and then ran to the living room window just in time to see a blue economy car speed away. I tried to remember what kind of car Liz Carter drove. Hadn't Marnie once joked about Liz's car being almost as old as she was? Yes. She'd talked about how proud Liz was of her old red Ford Mustang. So if the intruder hadn't been Liz, then who? And why?

I returned to Helen's bedroom and searched it all over again. This was the last room where the intruder had been. If she'd ended her search here, didn't that imply that this was where she had found whatever she had been looking for? I riffled through drawers, played checkers with the shoeboxes in the closet. This time I remembered to look under the bed. Still, nothing. If something had been taken, I couldn't for the life of me guess what it was. I stood there, hands on hips, wondering where else I should search, when my eye fell upon something peeking from under the bedside lamp. When I pulled it out, I found myself looking at two snapshots. The first was a picture of Sybille smiling widely at the camera. She was standing on a beach, wearing a bathing suit that showed off her perfect figure, her long blond hair blowing in the breeze. *The girl was a beauty. A real knockout.* I put it aside and picked up the second picture. My breath caught. *Well, what do you know?* I was studying the grainy snapshot of a twentysomething man. It was a close-up, and even though it was yellowed with age, I had no doubt that the man in the photo was Bruce Doherty, or Brent Donaldson, as he called himself back then. I wondered if this was an enlargement of the shot Nancy had seen two decades ago.

This brought up more questions. I hadn't looked under the lamp earlier, so for all I knew, these photos might have been here all along. Or the intruder might have planted them just now. If so, why?

Another possibility was that Helen had had this picture all along. But that didn't make much sense either. If she'd had it, she would have given it to the police. The only thing I knew for certain was that Bruce Doherty and Brent Donaldson were one and the same. And if Helen recognized him, this gave Bruce a motive for murder. I debated taking the pictures to show to Matthew, but decided against it. He would have my hide for tampering with evidence, and whatever warm feelings he had for me would be gone.

I snatched my cell phone from my bag and snapped a few shots of both photographs. And then I slid the pictures back under the lamp.

I returned to the sewing room, pulled the cardboard box out from under the bed, and lifted the cover. Inside was a mountain of old snapshots and letters. My eyes settled on the photograph on top—a young family: a mother, a father, a prepubescent girl I recognized as Helen, and a child, Sybille. I set the box on the bed and sat down next to it, sorting through the jumble of pictures. It was like seeing family members grow older before my eyes. There were old wedding photos. Helen's parents, I supposed. There were pictures of a baby girl, Helen at around two years old. Then shots of her being bounced on her father's knee. A few snaps later she became a schoolgirl with a homemade haircut complete with crooked bangs. I dug down a few inches and came across a picture of another child—pretty blond Sybille. Even back then the girl had been a looker. There were dozens more family photos, and then, suddenly, no more

of the parents and only a few of Helen. Sybille
grew from a beautiful child into a stunning ado-
lescent. I came across a picture of her taken at the
beach. In this one, another young woman stood
next to her. The brunette was rather plain. To my
surprise, I recognized her. It was Nancy. But what
really caught my eye was the way Nancy was staring at Sybille. Her expression was flat, as if she
had carefully erased any emotion from her face. I
studied it for a long time before dropping it back
into the pile. I dumped the rest on the bed. The
handful of remaining photos were all of Helen,
and she seemed to grow old before her time, mor-
phing into the image of her mother. The rest were
letters and greeting cards. I pulled out a letter. It
was from Sybille and was dated twenty-two years
earlier.

*Dear Sis, Sorry I haven't written in so long, but I've
been crazy busy with work.*

As I read, the love between the two sisters was
almost palpable. Sybille went on to describe her
recent promotion and the added responsibilities it
involved. She chatted about a recent splurge, a
new dress she had purchased for a date with a
new boyfriend—no mention of his name. I finished the letter and selected another. This one was
dated November of the same year. Here, Sybille
described a recent date she'd had with her boyfriend, and this time she named him—Brent. He
had taken her to dinner at a fancy restaurant and
then they had club-hopped until the wee hours of

the morning. She went on to admit that she was head over heels and that she expected a proposal by New Year's. I read a few more letters, learning more about the relationship. Brent was secretive, Sybille complained. He resented her asking questions, got moody whenever she asked him to meet her friends. And then I found one letter that had stirred even more questions. In this one Sybille talked about Nancy, mentioning that she seemed cold and distant lately, and wondering whether she might be jealous of her new success at work or perhaps of her romantic life. I put the letter down, staring at the blank wall.

I wondered if Nancy had been the good friend she professed to be, or if she resented her beautiful and successful roommate? Sometimes envy and jealousy could turn into hatred. I was beginning to wonder if Nancy might not have been so sad to see Sybille disappear.

With Sybille gone, she wouldn't have to keep comparing herself to someone who would always be more beautiful and more successful than she could ever hope to be.

When I picked up the letter to read it again, I noticed that it was growing dark. I looked at the time—seven thirty. I'd left the store more than three hours ago. Matthew would have picked up Winston, and was probably—I hoped—wondering where I'd disappeared to. And I'd completely forgotten about Mercedes. I'd told her I would be right back. Was she still waiting for me, or had

Jenny sent her home before locking up? I stuffed the letter in my pocket, threw the pile of paper into the box, and shoved it back under the bed. On my way back to the shop, the evening shadows disappeared into the night.

To my relief, the shop was dark and locked up. I turned and headed upstairs to my apartment.

"Where the hell have you been all this time?" The question, coming from the darkened hall, nearly startled me out of my skin. I flicked on the light.

"Matthew. What in the word are you doing here? You nearly scared me to death."

"Do you have any idea how worried I've been?"

"You were?" I said, smiling. "For me?"

"I got here at five thirty. Jenny was already gone. And Mercedes told me you should have returned an hour earlier. I waited with her for another hour until, finally, I sent her home and called Jenny to come lock up."

"Oh, no. Poor Mercedes. Was she very upset?"

"Poor Mercedes? Don't you even care that you had me out of my mind with worry?" he said.

I wasn't sure whether to be pleased or angry. I reached the landing and he stared at me, frowning. Suddenly he reached over and plucked something from my hair. "What is this? Dust bunnies?" His eyes narrowed with suspicion. "You've been snooping around again, haven't you?"

"I have not," I snapped back, my face burning. I shoved the key into the lock and pushed the door open. "If that's the kind of conversation we're going to have, you might as well leave."

"Sorry, but I haven't been waiting all this time to be sent home without at least some explanation of what you've been up to." He signaled to Winnie to follow him in. "Besides"—he brandished a bottle of wine and continued in a gentler tone—"you can't really expect me to drink this all by myself."

"Fine," I said, mellowing. "But only because of the wine. And because of Winnie," I added, patting him on the head. I led the way to the kitchen and pointed Matthew to the glasses while I looked for something to eat.

"I could make pasta," I said, pulling out a package of spaghetti and a can of tomato and basil sauce. "It'll only take a few minutes."

"Sounds perfect," he said, plucking another dust bunny from my hair. He gave me the eyebrow and tossed it into the wastebasket.

"Make yourself useful, won't you?" I said and handed him a couple of plates. He went off to set the table and I busied myself preparing the meal. While the water boiled, I plucked my cell phone from my purse and called Marnie. After four rings, I left a message.

"Hey, Marnie, I'm worried about you. Give me a call." I hung up. "Do you think she could still be at the police station?" I said, when Matthew returned to the kitchen.

"I stopped by the station on my way here. That

was two hours ago, and they had questioned and released her hours earlier."

"But she's not answering her phone. I'm getting worried."

"I expect she'll be sleeping right about now. I'm sure she stayed awake all night yesterday. Maybe she took a sleeping pill."

That made me feel a bit better. Still, I couldn't brush off my worry entirely. We settled in the dining room and dug into our food.

"Now tell me what you were really doing all this time," he said.

"Promise you won't be mad at me?"

"How about this? I promise not to yell at you no matter how angry I am."

"I guess that's the best I can expect," I said, sighing. "Well, I was thinking about Helen, and it occurred to me that if I'd just had an argument with someone at a party, the first thing I'd do when I got home would be to pick up the phone and call a friend, somebody I could really vent to." Matthew's eyes narrowed. "Before you freak out, I swear I didn't tamper with evidence. I didn't take anything. All I did was look . . . and maybe touch a few things."

He paled. "Are you telling me you broke into her house? And you did what? Check her phone?"

"I, er . . . yes. Then I went to search for a picture of Brent Donaldson."

"You broke in? How?"

"You promised you wouldn't yell."

He fell against the back of his chair and dragged a hand over his face wearily. "I swear, woman, you are going to be the death of me. I can't believe this. You trespassed onto a police-protected crime scene."

"I wanted to know for certain whether Brent Donaldson and Bruce Doherty were the same person. Besides, I didn't exactly break in. The lock to the sliding door in the back is broken. All I had to do was slip in between the crime scene tape."

He wiped his face again. "You illegally entered a crime scene."

"How else was I supposed to find out whether Helen had a picture of Brent Donaldson?"

"You let the police investigate. That's how."

"I only wanted to take a quick look around. I was planning to tell you about anything I found, and let you decide what to do about it."

He closed his eyes, and for a moment he looked as if he was praying. His mouth was moving, but all I could make out was, "Blah, blah, blah, grant me the patience."

"Honestly, I don't know why you're so upset."

"Where did you get this brilliant idea?" he said.

"It was something Nancy Cutler told me." I repeated what she'd said about the photograph of Brent that the police searched for after her roommate's disappearance. "I thought if Sybille had sent a copy to Helen, it would explain the argument she had with him. It would even support my theory that she recognized Bruce as Brent that night. And it would also give Bruce one hell of a motive for wanting Helen dead."

"And did you find any pictures?"

I nodded eagerly, and hurried to the kitchen for my purse. "Wait till I show you." I returned a moment later to find Matthew looking much the way Helen had in death. His face was beet red, as if he was about to explode.

"Please don't tell me you stole a photograph."

"Don't be silly. All I did was take a picture of it." I turned on my cell phone and scrolled through the file of pictures until I got to one of Brent. I handed it to him. "See?"

"I never met Marnie's fiancé, so I have no idea whether he's the same man," he said, his coloring returning to normal.

"Trust me, he is. And that means Bruce Doherty must have killed Helen Dubois."

"Except for one small detail," he said, crossing his arms.

"This, I can't wait to hear."

"I heard from the ME in Charlotte this afternoon. As it turns out, Helen Dubois did not die from manual strangulation."

"What! But—I'm the one who found her body. She was all purple and bloated. Her tongue was protruding from her mouth. Even the police officers could tell she was strangled."

"The bloating and discoloration you describe can also be a side effect of cyanide poisoning."

"Poison? But—"

"Let me explain. When a person swallows or inhales cyanide, it interferes with the red cells' ability to extract oxygen. So the victim literally suffocates to death—thus the bloated face, the protruding tongue, the pitikia of the eyes, just as in strangulation. But in cases of cyanide poisoning, there is usually considerable foaming at the mouth. In Helen's case, there was no evidence of foaming, and this is possibly what led to the original confusion."

"Foaming at the mouth?" I'd never heard of that except in animals with rabies.

He nodded. "According to the medical examiner, there should have been foaming as she gasped for breath. The only explanation he offered was that somebody must have cleaned her up after she died."

"That means whoever killed her not only administered the poison but then stood by and watched her die. That would take nerves of steel." I tried to imagine Bruce Doherty being that cold, and shivered.

"Whoever killed her must have wanted to cover up the poisoning, and try to pass the cause of Helen's death off as strangulation. And if Dr. Cook had signed the death certificate instead of her body being sent to the medical examiner, the true cause of death might never have been discovered."

"Cyanide poisoning," I repeated, still trying to

get my mind around this sudden turn of events. "How easy is it to get cyanide? Is it something you can pick up like rat poison?"

"Because it is so deadly and acts fast, it used to be the poison of choice. Now, it's more difficult to find, but not impossible. That's one of the things the police are looking into—who has access to cyanide."

"Who *would* have access to it?"

"Mostly people who use it for their work, like metal polishers, photographers, jewelers, and probably a dozen others. But there are also people who have some left over from years ago. There was a recent case, an artist had over a hundred pounds of it stored in his basement. He went down to investigate a strange smell and accidentally tipped over a five-gallon bucket of it. By the time the fire department came, he had stopped breathing."

"All he did was smell it and he died?"

"Any sodium cyanide can produce deadly gas when exposed to acid. That's what they use in gas chambers."

"If Helen was poisoned, does that mean Bruce is innocent?"

"It doesn't clear him. However, poisoning is usually a woman's crime. Also, if the poisoning was made to look like a strangulation, it suggests that the killer was trying to make the murder appear to be the work of a man."

I felt a pang of guilt. I'd spent the last few days

trying to find a way to turn Marnie against her fiancé because I was sure he was a killer. As it was looking now, he might not be guilty after all.

As if he read my mind, Matthew said, "Bruce may not have killed Helen, but he was up to something. Why else would he have been using an alias?"

I shook my head in bewilderment. "I'm still trying to figure this out. Whoever killed Helen might have also killed him?"

"That's a possibility," he said. "It isn't as if Briar Hollow is teeming with criminals."

"Thank God that intruder didn't see me," I mumbled without thinking. "Or else I might be dead right now."

"What are you talking about? What intruder?"

"Somebody broke into Helen's house while I was there."

"Somebody— What?"

I said to him. "Now you're definitely yelling."

He dropped his head. "I'm probably going to regret this," he said, then raised his eyes and glared at me. "Tell me everything."

So I did. I told him about checking Helen's phone and getting Nancy Cutler's number. And then I repeated as best I could the conversation I'd had with her, in which she'd insisted that the police never found Brent's picture after Sybille disappeared. And then I told him about how I'd hidden under the bed when I'd heard the intruder come in.

"That explains the dust bunnies. And you never saw her face?" I shook my head. "Do you know what she was looking for?" he asked.

"All I know is that she searched the whole house."

"And you have no idea who she was."

"None," I said. "When I finally got out from under the bed, I raced to the window just in time to see a small blue car driving away."

"Did you think of taking the license plate number?"

"It was too far away."

"What kind of a car was it?"

I shrugged. "It was small. That's all I know." He rolled his eyes. "What do you want from me?" I said, exasperated. "You're the car buff. Not me."

"I'm not asking you what year or model. Surely you can at least tell the make."

"I don't know what make. But it was lighter than navy, more of a royal blue, okay?" I quickly went on to tell him how I searched the house a second time after the woman left, and how I came across the picture of Brent. "I didn't look under the lamp the first time I searched that room. So for all I know it could have already been there."

"And you didn't notice anything else that looked different or out of place."

"Sorry."

"So, if we look at all the evidence we've uncovered today," he said, and I couldn't help noticing how he said "we." "We know that A, the killer poisoned Helen; B, he or she remained in Helen's house long enough to make certain she was dead; and C, he or she then cleaned up some of the evidence—the foam—perhaps hoping that her death would be attributed to manual strangulation. We also know that this killer is likely to be a woman, but we still don't know who or why."

"I've been thinking about it," I said. "And even though I have no proof, I bet the intruder was Nancy Cutler." I pulled the letter from my pocket. "Wait till you read this." I handed it over.

"What is it?"

"It's one of the last letters Sybille wrote to Helen before she disappeared."

He pulled his hands back as if I was holding out a venomous snake. "Are you crazy? That's evidence. You shouldn't even be touching it."

"This is not evidence. It has nothing to do with Helen's murder. It was written more than twenty years ago." I read it out loud to him.

"I hate to tell you this," he said when I finished, "but if Nancy Cutler killed Helen, that letter would most definitely be classified as evidence. You have to give this to the police."

"I can't do that," I said. "I'd have to explain how I got it."

"You either give it to the police or you put it back where you found it."

"Fine. I'll put it back. But why would it be evidence?"

"Think about it. That letter is in Sybille's own words. She talks about Nancy becoming cold and distant. The first conclusion you came to when you read that was that Nancy was jealous."

"It makes sense," I said. "Sybille was gorgeous, *and* successful, *and* she had a boyfriend."

"That makes me wonder if Helen and the police could have had it wrong all these years."

"What are you saying?"

"I'm beginning to think that Brent might have had nothing to do with Sybille's disappearance."

"You think Nancy killed Sybille?" All at once it hit me. "Of course. That's totally logical. But there's one thing I don't understand. If Brent, or Bruce, was innocent, why did he take off when Sybille disappeared? Nancy said the police searched high and low for him and never found so much as a trace of the man."

"I suspect he was using an alias even back then. Even if he had nothing to do with Sybille's disappearance, he probably figured, and rightfully so, that as soon as the police found out he was using a false name, they'd think he was guilty. And let's not fool ourselves. He may not have been responsible for Sybille's disappearance, but he was guilty of something. Otherwise, why use an alias?"

"Hmm, I just remembered something," I said. "Nancy told me that at one point after Sybille's disappearance, Helen was calling her, asking the same questions over and over again. She began to wonder if Helen considered her a suspect."

"Could be," he said thoughtfully. "I wonder . . ."

"What? Tell me."

"Let's suppose for a moment that Nancy killed Sybille twenty years ago. And somehow she managed to make everybody believe that Brent did it. That would have been easy, considering that there was never a body and that Brent disappeared around the same time she did. Now, we move forward twenty years, and Nancy recognizes Bruce at a party. What do you think her first reaction would be?"

I gasped. "No wonder she ran out in a panic. Bruce was the only person in the world who knew what had really happened, and if he said anything she could be charged for murder."

"Then," he continued, "she's home wondering how she can keep him from talking, and the phone rings. When she answers, it's not Bruce—even worse, it's Helen. She's recognized him as Brent and she wants to call the police." Matthew picked up his glass and raised it. "And that, my dear, gives us a recipe for not only one but two murders."

"You're right. The only thing she could have done to stay safe was kill both Helen and Bruce." I raised my own glass to him. "Damn. You're good at this." I took a sip of wine and put my glass down. "So what do we do now? Do we call the police and tell them?"

"I don't think so."

"Why not?"

"Because as likely as this scenario may sound, it isn't the only possibility. The only thing on which we can agree on right now is that Sybille was probably right. Nancy was envious of her. She may have secretly been in love with Brent."

"That's ridiculous. Nancy said they never even met."

"So she says. But, even then, a lot of women fall for men they've never met—movie stars, the man they see every day at the bus stop, the model in the aftershave ad. It happens all the time. There are even cases of women falling in love with convicted murderers who are in prison for life."

I could imagine how that might have happened in Nancy's case. "Sybille was crazy about Brent, so she probably gushed about him all the time—how wonderful he was, how handsome he was. Even if Nancy never met him, Sybille fed her a continuous stream of fantasy about him. Nancy did tell me that they spoke on the phone a few times when he called for Sybille. If he was flirtatious during their conversations, Nancy may have given those chats a lot of importance."

"Or," he said, "they could have been having an affair."

"He and Nancy?" I said, laughing. "I'm sorry. That's just ridiculous. You have no idea how gorgeous Sybille used to be." I pulled out my cell phone again and showed him. "Look at her."

"She certainly was," he said, handing me back my phone.

"Next to her, nobody would have looked twice at Nancy."

"You'd be surprised how many men will fool

around with unattractive women even when they have beautiful wives at home," he said. "Some men are cads."

"So I'm told," I said.

"Present company excluded," he said with a wink.

"But of course."

"So let's say Nancy was infatuated with Brent. When Sybille vanished, she might have thought that she now had a chance to get him for herself. She probably never imagined he had anything to do with Sybille's disappearance, but even if she did, she would have wanted to protect him. Who knows what kind of excuses she made for him in her mind? *Sybille was a bitch. She ran off with another man. If he did something to her, she deserved it.*"

"That's awful."

"It's called denial. People do it all the time when they don't want to look at the truth. When the police showed up, she might even have given them a wrong description of Brent."

"And hidden his picture," I added. I could see where he was going, and this scenario sounded as plausible as the first.

He continued. "Except, of course, that for all her hopes and fantasies, once Brent Donaldson fled, she never saw or heard from him again. Then, suddenly, years later, she runs into him." He shrugged. "There are dozens of other possibilities. Maybe Nancy took one look at him at the party and all her dreams came flooding back. Even though he was engaged to somebody else, she thought this was destiny. He had just landed right in the town where she lived. If she tried, she could probably get him. That same night she gets a call from Helen, who tells her she recognized him and that she knows he killed Sybille. Nancy may have rushed over to Helen's to stop her from calling the police."

"Or," I said, seeing where he was going with this, "Nancy could have called him at the hotel and warned him that Helen recognized him. And then he went to Helen's house and killed her." I paused. "But if he killed Helen, who killed him?" I opened my hands. "We're back at square one."

He didn't answer. He just stared at me. And then it hit me.

"You still think Marnie killed him, don't you?"

Up until that moment, the evening had been surprisingly pleasant. After Matthew's initial reaction to my news, he had mellowed and become warm and amiable. But try as I might not to let his opinion of Marnie affect me, I couldn't help but be hurt.

"How can you even imagine that Marnie could be guilty? She would never hurt another person."

"I'm not saying I'm convinced she's guilty," he said.

"But you're also not sure she isn't," I snapped back.

He leaned forward, placing a hand over mine. "Della, I just want you to prepare yourself for the worst. You know as well as I do that sometimes good people do bad things. When emotions get involved, control can just as easily fly out the window. The moment I saw the crime scene, I knew this murder was not planned. Nobody plans to kill someone by hitting them over the head with a vase. The way I see it, Bruce knew his killer. He let her"—seeing the look in my eyes, he added, "or him—into his room. There was no sign of forced entry, and except for the victim's body and the cracked vase, no sign of a violent argument. I imagine he and the killer were having a conversation. At some point Bruce said something that angered his visitor. She picked up the vase without even realizing it, and before she could stop herself, he was lying on the floor with his skull bashed in."

"You keep saying 'she,' as if you are certain the killer is Marnie." The truth was I wasn't entirely convinced of her innocence either. After listening to Matthew's description of how the crime might have happened, I could imagine Marnie doing it. Hell, the truth was, given the right circumstances, I could imagine anybody committing murder—even me.

Matthew pushed away his empty plate. "That was delicious, but I'd better be getting home. It's already nine thirty." It wasn't late, but I could feel the tension in the air, and he could too. I declined his offer to help me clean up, and I walked him and Winston to the door. He gave me a quick peck on the cheek and left. So much for friendly and warm.

Like Scarlett said. Tomorrow is another day.

Chapter 15

I was in no mood to do anything but sulk. I left the dishes to soak and contemplated going straight to bed. But what was the point of that? I wouldn't sleep a wink all night.

And instead of having a better idea of who had killed Helen and Bruce, I was more confused than ever. I was even beginning to think that Matthew was right and that maybe, just maybe, Marnie had killed Bruce in the heat of the moment. I was worried sick about her. I hadn't heard from her all day, and that was beyond strange. Was she avoiding friends out of grief? Or guilt? Or maybe a combination of both? I imagined her lying prostrate in bed. I pictured her holding a knife in her hands and considering suicide. That horrible image took anchor in my mind until a typhoon wouldn't have shaken it.

I grabbed the letter from Sybille, snatched my car keys, and raced down the stairs. Minutes later I was in front of Marnie's house, traipsing through her infant garden beds and peering through windows. The rooms were too dark to make out any more than faint outlines of furniture. But when I got to the end of the house I noticed a dim light—probably a night-light in the bedroom. Surely she was just sleeping. She had once confessed to me that she hated the dark and couldn't go to bed without a night-light. I trudged to the window and peeked inside. Sure enough. I could make out the shape of Marnie's body in her bed. At that moment she shifted her weight, and I felt a tidal wave of relief. Matthew was right. Marnie was all right. She must have been exhausted from her insomnia of the night before and simply taken a sleeping pill. I hastened back to my car before some neighbor mistook me for a thief and called the police. I drove to within a block of Helen's house and made my way over to it, sticking to the shadows. I went around back, feeling my way along the clapboard wall. Soon I was inside again. I tiptoed in the dark to the second bedroom, felt around until I found the box under the bed, and dropped the letter in. The second I was out of the house, I ran all the way to my car, with my heart beating a staccato in my chest.

I shoved the gear stick back into drive and pulled away from the curb. I was half a block away when an idea occurred to me. Nancy Cutler owned a small house on the outskirts of town. All I had to do was drive by and take one quick look at her car. Then I would know instantly if she'd been the intruder.

I took Main Street all the way out of town, which sounds like a longer distance than it is. A few minutes later I reached the edge of Briar Hollow, passed the city limits, and turned right at the first road. Soon I saw half a dozen bungalows. I slowed to a crawl and peered out in the dark. One of these, I knew, was Nancy's house. But which, I wasn't sure. In the moonlight all the houses looked the same. I tried to remember the one time I'd been to her home, what distinguishing feature it might have had. But the houses, like Nancy, were all as plain as unpainted clapboard. I was halfway down the street when I noticed the white curtains in the windows of one house, and it came back to me in a flash. I recognized them. I'd made them for Nancy myself. I slowed to a stop and tried to see the color and make of the car in the driveway. But in the dark of the night, it could have been any color. I couldn't have said what color it was if my life had depended on it. I put the car into reverse and backed up until the headlights of my Jeep lit up the driveway like a pair of searchlights. The car was a red midsized sedan—so different from the car that I'd seen speed away from Helen's house that even a total car ignoramus like me could tell them apart.

Whatever crimes Nancy might be guilty of, breaking and entering into Helen's house is not one of them.

I was at my loom the next morning, working on Marnie's gift, when Jenny showed up. "There you are," I said, putting down my shuttle. "I was getting worried. It's almost eight thirty. Are you all right?"

"I'm fine. I overslept, that's all. Where's Margaret?"

"She's in the back, making coffee."

"Oh, good. Have you heard from Marnie? Do you know if she's done any baking?"

"I'd be surprised if she did," I said, making my way to the counter. I didn't mention that I'd spied her in bed last night. "I know she was exhausted. She's been going through hell. I wouldn't be surprised if she was still sleeping. If you like, I can drive into Belmont and pick up whatever you need."

"Really? You don't mind? I'd owe you huge," she said.

"A cup of coffee will do." I picked up my bag from behind the counter and fished out my car keys. "Just keep an eye on the store till I get back."

"Will do. Here's the list of everything I need. Anything else that looks too scrumptious to pass up, you have my permission to buy," she said, handing me a piece of paper. "Hold on. Let me give you some money."

"You can give it to me later," I said and walked out. I could have gone to Marnie's, but I didn't want to wake her up. Besides, I had an ulterior motive for going to Melinda's.

Soon I was in my Jeep, driving toward Belmont. I liked driving. Like weaving, it was an activity I especially enjoyed when I was preoccupied. Until I'd climbed into bed last night, I hadn't realized just how much I hoped Nancy Cutler would turn out to be the owner of the blue car. Because at this point I was pretty sure the intruder who'd snuck through Helen's home was the killer and most likely the owner of that car too. Now I was certain that Nancy had nothing to do with the blue car, or anything else to do with the murder after all.

As for Marnie, I knew she didn't own that blue car. And I knew she hadn't been the intruder. For one thing, her choice of shoes ran toward the comfortable rather than the fashionable. Besides, Marnie was my friend. She and Jenny were the first two friends I'd made when I'd moved to Briar Hollow. I would have trusted them with my life. Matthew's point, that sometimes good people did bad things, was a valid one, and for a moment I wasn't convinced of Marnie's innocence. But after going to bed, I'd turned it over in my mind until I was sure again. I had to look for others with a motive for wanting Helen and Bruce dead.

I passed the Belmont city limits and turned onto Main Street, and maybe because I was on my way to her bakery, my mind wandered to Melinda.

My instincts led me to think that the story she had told me about her interaction with Bruce at my party was a fabrication. But at this moment, I knew I could be wrong about that too. I had no idea who to trust anymore. My instincts were about as reliable as Jenny's predictions. What could I ask her, I wondered, that might help me uncover the truth? And then, as if by magic, the answer appeared right before my eyes. I was pulling into a parking spot in front of Melinda's bakery when I noticed the car in front. It was a royal blue economy car.

"Well," Melinda said, tossing her hair, "if it isn't my new best customer. I take it Marnie is still not feeling well?"

"Unfortunately not," I said, noticing that she looked a little peaked herself. Her eyes were bloodshot and underlined with dark shadows. She'd either been doing a fair amount of weeping or hadn't slept in a few days—possibly both.

She put on a jaundiced smile and said, "Please give her my condolences. I was completely floored when I heard."

As she said this, I couldn't help but note that her appearance, red eyes and dark shadows, was much the same as Marnie's yesterday. Could her sleepless night, like Marnie's, have also been caused by grief? I wondered again whether something had been going on between Marnie's fiancé and the beautiful blonde.

She wiped her hands on her baker's jacket and came forward. "So what will it be? Everything in the shop? Next time, maybe you could do me a favor and let me know ahead of time that you're planning on buying me out? I'd double my batches."

"I'll do my best, I promise," I said and handed her the list.

"It's not that I don't appreciate the business, but having to turn away regulars is not a great way to instill loyalty." She picked up a stack of cardboard boxes and began filling them. "Two dozen assorted muffins," she read, moving on from one counter display to the next.

"By the way," I said, "would you happen to know whose car that is out front? I hate to admit it, but I bumped it when I was pulling in."

She stared out the window, looking worried. "Which car did you say?"

"The little blue one across the street. The one in front of the red Jeep." A flash of something went through her eyes. Suspicion? Fear? Whatever it was, it had been no more than a flicker. If I hadn't been watching for it, I would never have seen it.

"For a minute I was afraid you'd dented my new Honda. That's Nick's car. And boy, does he love it. He'll kill you if you so much as scratched it." I guessed that Nick was the pimply-faced teenager who worked for her.

"Hold on," I said. "I didn't say I damaged it. At least not that I could tell. I just felt bad that I'd bumped it."

She crossed her arms and stared at me. "Why would you even bring it up, unless you wanted to give somebody a heart attack?"

"You're right, of course. I'm sorry."

She went back to filling the boxes with pastries,

running an ongoing monologue as she did. "One dozen lemon tarts. One dozen brioches. Ten scones." Soon she had packaged everything on the list, and the top of her counter was cluttered with bags and parcels. "Let me help you carry all these to your car." We darted through a sudden surge in traffic. "There you go," she said, her smile more sincere this time. "And don't forget to give me some warning the next time you plan on emptying my shelves."

As I headed back to Briar Hollow, I couldn't help but wonder. Had I imagined the wary look in Melinda's eyes when I mentioned the blue car? I had the impression she had lied. The only way I would know for certain was if I did a bit of sleuthing.

"That didn't take long," Jenny said as I walked in, loaded down with parcels. "How much do I owe you?"

I handed her the bill and while she wrote the check, I went back out for the second load. When I returned, Liz Carter was at the counter, chatting with Margaret.

"Hey, Della," she said. "How's Marnie doing? I still can't believe it. Such a tragedy. At least she wasn't left standing at the altar."

It was an odd comment, and totally inappropriate. Thankfully, Marnie wasn't around to hear it. "I haven't spoken to her today," I said. "I didn't want to wake her up this morning. I imagine she needs all the sleep she can get. But I'm sure she'll be all right."

"Of course. But so soon after poor Helen. Marnie just lost two people in less than a week. I'd hate to call myself a good friend of hers right about now. It might be bad for my health."

"How is your exhibit coming along? It's starting in a day or two, isn't it?"

"Actually, it's starting tomorrow morning." She stopped short and said, "I had such a fright this morning. When I got to the library, I found the door unlocked. I don't understand how that could have happened. I know I locked it last night, but there it was—not only unlocked, but open." She shook her head. "Thank goodness nothing was missing. I think I would have died if something had happened to Marnie's flag. Anyhow. The reason I'm here is this." She made a big production of opening her handbag and pulling out a few small white envelopes. "These are invitations," she said. "Admission is free. But a donation is welcome. There's one for you, one for Jenny, and one for Marnie. I promised to be back in"—she glanced at her watch—"oh, fifteen minutes. So I'd better get going."

"You're not doing all the work by yourself, are you?"

"No. Thank goodness. I found a few volunteers—ladies from the church group. There are two of them at the library right now. They're helping set up the registration line." She lit up again. "You should see the number of people who already pledged to donate. If everyone gives generously, I bet we'll make enough money to pay for the new roof we need."

"That would be great."

"When can you come? I'd like you to be one of the first to come through. The exhibit opens at nine tomorrow."

"Well, then, that's what we'll do. That way, I can be at the store by ten o'clock, and the rest of the day I'll remind all my customers to stop by."

"Brilliant!" she exclaimed. She blew me a kiss and almost waltzed out. Jenny popped in from the back, carrying a fresh cup of coffee.

"Who was that?" she asked, setting the cup on the counter.

"Liz Carter. She dropped off a bunch of invitations to the exhibit. Here's one for you," I said, handing her one of the white envelopes. "It's opening tomorrow at nine. That's when I think I'll go, before the crowds."

Jenny raised her brows. "Crowds? How many people do you imagine will show up?"

I shrugged. "I don't know. She seems very optimistic. She hopes to make enough to repair the roof."

"Maybe if all it needs is a small patch," she said. The phone rang and she went back to the coffee shop.

"Dream Weaver," I answered. "Della speaking."

"Della? It's me." It was Marnie and she sounded terrible.

"Marnie? Are you all right? Do you have a cold or something?"

"I'm fine," she said, and I realized she was hoarse from sleeping. "I went to bed about fourteen hours ago. I just woke up."

"You obviously needed it."

"Would you mind if I came in? I know I'm a murder suspect and all, but—"

The door opened and a few women walked toward the coffee shop. I waved and waited until they had disappeared behind the curtain.

"Don't even say such a thing. You know you're welcome here as often and as long as you like. In fact, I think you should move in with me for a little while. Just until you feel better."

"Don't be silly. I'm fine. It's just that I hate being by myself all the time."

"And we miss you," I said. "So that's settled. How soon can you get here?"

"I didn't do any baking. I hope Jenny won't mind if I make up her order out of my frozen pastries."

"Don't worry. I drove out to Melinda's and stocked her up for the day. Her baking isn't as good as yours, but I figured you needed your sleep. If you're not up to baking tonight, maybe you can bring in your frozen goods tomorrow."

"Thanks," she said without argument. She must be feeling even worse than I thought. "I'll be there in an hour or so. I thought I might drop by the library and see how the exhibit is coming along. It would be nice if you could come with me."

"It's not open yet."

"I know. All I wanted was a quick peek."

"I can't leave the store right now. But I was planning to go tomorrow. Why don't you come with me then?"

"That's an idea. "

"Great. See you soon," I said, and we hung up.

"Was that Marnie?" Margaret asked. She had come up behind me. "You know people are saying she killed her fiancé," she said in a low voice as she poured me a cup of coffee.

I'd been afraid that would happen. "Like who?"

She nodded toward the back. "Nancy Cutler is in there right now with some of her friends. I overheard them talking."

"She said that, did she?" My blood boiled. I marched around the counter and headed to the coffee shop.

"Wait," Margaret called out. "Please don't make a scene. I shouldn't have said anything. This is a small town. You know how people around here like to gossip. Tomorrow they'll be on to something else."

I paused and took a steadying breath. "Still, this is Marnie they're talking about."

"It will only make matters worse if you say anything."

Margaret was right. But, damn it, I couldn't let people talk that way about my friend. I had to do something. I returned to the counter. A few minutes later the beaded curtains parted, and Nancy, along with a trio of her friends, came through.

"Hi, Della," Nancy called out.

"Nancy," I said, "I've been dying to tell you." From the corner of my eye, I saw Margaret blanch. I threw her an innocent smile. "I've heard the most amazing gossip." The four women scampered over eagerly.

"Pray tell," the oldest one said. She was tall and skinny. She must have fed on nothing but gossip.

"Well, this may not come as a complete surprise to you," I said to Nancy, "but it looks like Bruce Doherty was using an alias, and that he was, in reality, Brent Donaldson, the same man Sybille Dubois was seeing when she disappeared."

"Really?" the middle woman said. She was a chubby redhead with too many teeth for her mouth. She turned to Nancy, who was noticeably silent. "You were Sybille's roommate back then, weren't you?"

"She was," I said, and continued sympathetically, "That must have been such a difficult time for you. Especially since Helen suspected that you might have had something to do with her sister's disappearance."

"She did?" the tall woman said. She turned to Nancy. "You never told me this."

Nancy's eyes narrowed. "That's ridiculous." I didn't point out that she'd said as much to me herself.

"It seems that Sybille was convinced you were jealous of her. She wrote to Helen about it."

Her voice rose an octave. "Where did you hear

that?" I noticed with satisfaction that her friends were watching her with growing interest.

"You know, what really surprises me is that you didn't recognize Bruce as Brent at my party."

The blood drained from her face, and for a second I thought I'd gone too far. But then she seemed to pull herself together, and even managed a weak laugh. "Good grief. You should know better than to repeat stories like that. That kind of talk could get all over town in a flash. Anybody who doesn't know me will start imagining all sorts of crazy things."

"That's true," I said, pretending sheepishness. "I should watch what I say. After all, by the time this investigation is over, the police will probably have suspected half the people in town. If we went around gossiping about everything we hear, there'd be no end to the trouble we could cause."

"That's right," she said. "And gossip can ruin a person's life."

The tall, skinny woman's eyes lit up with sudden understanding. "I guess we should be careful what we say about others too, shouldn't we?"

I smiled. "I'm sorry, ladies. I hope you'll forgive me. I only wanted you all to think twice before you said anything more about Marnie."

"So, none of what you said was true?" the skinny woman said.

"If you mean did I hear this from anybody?" I shook my head. "Not one word." Nancy had the grace to blush. And the relief in her eyes was so plain I was surprised the other ladies didn't see it.

"You made it all up?" one of her friends said.

I didn't answer.

"You really had me going."

She didn't look angry, but as the women walked toward the door, I couldn't help but wonder if I would ever see any of them again. Of course I would. No matter what they thought of me, they would never stop going to Coffee, Tea and Destiny.

Margaret came over and planted a kiss on my cheek. "That's for Marnie," she said. "I only hope the day I need it, I'll have a good friend like you to stand up for me."

Half an hour later, when Marnie walked in, I was just cutting the second purple-on-white dishcloth off my loom.

"Did you go to the exhibit?" I asked, bringing the dishcloth to the counter.

"I decided it will be more fun to go with you."

"I'm glad we'll be going early," I said. "I hate waiting in line."

"I'll get myself a coffee and be right back," she said, and disappeared into the coffee shop. She reappeared a moment later with a mug and a scone. "Jenny says Melinda's baking isn't as good as mine. I think she's wrong." She bit into it and chewed, giving it her full attention. "I hate to say this, but these are delicious."

"They may be, but yours are better."

She brightened up. "Maybe I should give her a few tips."

I raised a brow. "If you give her too many, she *will* get as good as you."

"I guess we can't have that," she said good-naturedly, and took another bite.

"So, how are you feeling, really?"

She froze, and her eyes welled with tears. "I'm okay as long as I don't think about it."

"If you need to talk, I'm here. You know that, don't you?"

She nodded. "I'm just finding it difficult to believe that everything that came out of his mouth was a lie, even his name. I was so sure he loved me." Her voice broke. "Meanwhile, he was planning to kill me."

"We don't know that for sure," I said. "I'm sorry. I shouldn't have brought it up. Try to put it out of your mind. Thinking about it will only make you feel worse."

"Believe me, I couldn't feel worse than I already do." She stared at me. "You've found out more, haven't you? Tell me." I hesitated. "You know I'll find out eventually."

"Two things. It turns out that Bruce used to be known as Brent Donaldson, about twenty years ago."

"Brent Donaldson." She played the name over her tongue. "Why does that name sound so familiar?"

"He was the man Sybille Dubois was involved with when she disappeared twenty years ago."

If somebody had hit her over the head with a rolling pin, she wouldn't have looked more stunned. "Bruce and Brent? They're the same person?"

"So it seems."

"How did you find out? Did Matthew tell you?"

"I discovered it," I said. "I decided to search Helen's house." I described how I'd sneaked in, and she listened, entranced, as I told her about the intruder showing up while I was there. "I hid under the bed."

"No wonder Matthew was so upset with you. What if that woman killed Helen? If she'd found you there, she could have killed you."

"I know. I know." I snatched my cell phone from my bag and scrolled through my pictures until I found the ones I'd taken of Brent Donaldson's snapshot.

She stared at it for a long time, holding her breath. "It's him, all right," she said, handing me the phone. She blinked back the moisture in her eyes. "I didn't want to believe it, but you're right. Brent Donaldson and Bruce are the same person. Does that mean he killed Helen's sister?"

"That was my impression at first, but the more I thought about it, the less sense it made. The fact that he was using an alias makes me pretty certain he was up to something illegal. But I don't know if it had anything to do with Helen's death, at least not directly."

"What do you mean, 'not directly'?"

"This is just an idea I discussed with Matthew," I said. "Maybe Helen recognized Bruce as the same man who used to date her sister." Marnie opened her mouth as if to argue, but I put up my hand. "Hear me out. Since her disappearance, the number one suspect has always been Brent Donaldson. But what if he was innocent, and meanwhile, somebody in this town was responsible? Then, out of the blue, twenty years later, Brent Donaldson shows up. Except he's calling himself Bruce Doherty these days. This local person knows that if Bruce is recognized by anybody else, he'll probably be brought in for questioning, and who knows where his answers will lead the police? The only way to make sure Bruce remains the number one suspect in Sybille's disappearance is to kill him."

Marnie's mouth dropped open. "Are you saying the killer is Nancy Cutler?"

"I didn't say that."

She nodded, her red hair bouncing on her shoulders. "You might as well have. Who else could it be but Nancy? She lived with Sybille back then, didn't she? They were roommates."

"That's true, but that doesn't mean anything. For all we know, somebody from Briar Hollow could have traveled to Chicago and killed her."

I could see from the look in her eyes that she didn't believe a word of it. I had pretty much discounted it too, but I'd been curious to know what she thought. Now I knew. I decided to change the subject before she began obsessing about it. "Did

Bruce ever say or do anything to make you suspect that he wasn't everything he pretended to be?"

She shook her head. "Never. But then, I wasn't really watching for it."

"Think back. Did you ever get a niggling feeling over something he said? Something you told yourself you were being silly about?"

"Maybe," she said, but she clearly had no intention of expanding on that. "What else?"

I looked at her blankly.

"You said you found out two things," she said.

"Oh, right. It turns out that Helen wasn't strangled. She died of cyanide poisoning."

"Cyanide? But isn't that impossible to get these days?"

"Not according to Matthew. It's still used industrially. So that means anybody who works with it would have access to it."

"We have to look into this," she said. "Find out every possible job where people would have access to it. That's how we'll find out who killed Helen."

"Let me pull out my laptop. I'll Google it." Five minutes later I had a short list. Marnie and I looked it over.

"Do you know anybody who works in mining, gold or silver plating, medical research, pest control, or who fumigates ships?" Marnie said.

"No. But listen to this. You can actually make cyanide at home, out of apple seeds."

"You're kidding. Let me look at that." I moved over and Marnie took my place at the laptop. "That's awful," she said. "That means anybody could have done it. How are we ever going to find out who killed her?" She picked up her cup and went to her loom. Soon she was walking the pedals at a brisk rhythm, and the set of place mats on which she was working grew at an astounding pace. Unlike me, when Marnie was upset, her output increased.

Some time later, the doorbell jingled and Matthew walked in. Winston came bounding behind him, covering me with slobbery kisses.

"Sit, Winnie." His butt hit the floor with a thud, and I dug through the drawer for a liver treat. He caught it in midair and scrambled to his cushion.

I mouthed to Matthew, "Marnie's here."

He glanced across the room. "Hi, Marnie. It's nice to have you back."

She waved and returned to her weaving.

He lowered his voice. "How's she holding up?"

"As well as can be expected." My eyes fell onto the invitation to the library exhibition. "By the way, how would you like to go by the library with me tomorrow morning? Marnie's flag will be on display. I was thinking of stopping by at nine. Marnie's coming too."

"Sure. How much are the tickets?"

"There's no fee. Visitors are invited to make a donation."

"I'll meet you here at nine." He leaned in a bit closer. "I'm just back from the police station. I told them about Bruce Doherty and Brent Donaldson being the same person. That just blew the old case wide open. By the time I left, they were already getting organized to search Helen Dubois's house."

"How did you explain knowing?"

"I didn't. I offered it as a theory only. I told them that the idea came to me because of something Nancy Cutler said—that she thought she recognized Bruce at our party. And I suggested that Helen might have had a picture of the man her sister was dating when she disappeared. I said I'd looked into Bruce Doherty's background, and I showed them the picture of the real Bruce Doherty. Turns out they already knew. They looked into him as part of the investigation into his murder. Then I told them about the argument Helen had with Bruce at your party, and suggested that she might have recognized him as the man her sister was dating when she disappeared. They jumped on that like fleas on a dog."

"So they'll search Helen's house and find the pictures."

"And the letter. You did put it back like I told you to, right?"

"Of course."

"I still can't believe—" He shook his head. "What am I saying? Why wouldn't I believe? You do this sort of thing all the time."

"You're beginning to sound like my mother."

He laughed. "God forbid." He gave me a peck on the cheek and left.

*   *   *

Half the morning had gone by and still only a handful of customers had come in, all of whom had gone straight to the coffee shop.

"It's my fault," Marnie said, putting away her shuttle. "I shouldn't be here. As long as people think I killed Bruce, nobody's going to set foot in this place."

"Don't be ridiculous," I said. "It's just a quiet day. We get them all the time." As I said this, the door opened and Melinda Wilson came in.

"Marnie," she said, walking over to the counter, "I came as soon as I heard. I am so, so sorry. Is there anything I can do?" Marnie's eyes watered. Melinda put her bag down and threw her arms around her. "I know you're hurting. I'm hurting for you." She stepped back and I was surprised to see that she looked as if she'd spent the night crying too.

"Why don't we go sit down for a minute?" Melinda said, guiding her toward the coffee shop.

They had just disappeared behind the curtain when I noticed that Melinda had left her purse behind. I picked it up, starting to call after her, and then I stopped. If Melinda was like me, she carried her car registration in her purse. All I had to do was take a quick peek and I would know for sure what kind of car she drove. I pulled out her wallet and flicked it open. A driver's license with a bad picture of Melinda, a few credit cards—I flipped through the cards quickly. But no car registration.

I was just about to put the wallet away when I came across a photo. It was a wedding picture, Melinda and her husband on their special day. I felt a twinge of guilt. Here I was, going through her personal things. What was wrong with me? I was replacing the photo when I focused on the husband—and froze.

This couldn't be. I stared at it in disbelief. I must have stood there for a full minute trying to make sense out of what I was looking at, until the sound of footsteps jarred me back to reality. I slipped the picture back in the wallet and closed the purse— and not a minute too soon. Melinda was approaching, her hand extended.

"You forgot your purse," I said.

"What were you doing?" she asked. "Were you going through it?"

"I didn't know whose it was. I was just looking for some ID." She studied me, and I gave her my most innocent smile. "Your driver's license hardly looks like you."

She seemed relieved. "I've never been photogenic," she said. "I always end up looking like a criminal."

Maybe that's because you are.

Chapter 16

As soon as she was out of the room I snatched the phone and pressed speed dial for Matthew's number.

"You won't believe what I just found," I said the second he picked up.

"I can't talk right now. I'm writing."

"This is important. Guess who used to be married to Bruce?" Without waiting for an answer, I blurted out, "Melinda Wilson."

"What?"

"It's true. I just came across a snapshot of them at their wedding. She's in a wedding dress and it's him standing next to her wearing a tux," I said.

"Where did you find this?" he said, and I knew from his voice that he thought I'd broken into Melinda's house.

"Melinda's here, in the shop. She just took Marnie to the back for a cup of coffee and left her purse at my counter. All I did was peek inside her wallet. Honest. I was only looking for her car registration. What was I supposed to do? Don't you

see? It all makes sense. Melinda was at the
Longview the night Bruce was killed. Judging by
the fact that she still carries around her wedding
picture, she's probably still in love with him. She
probably killed him in a jealous rage." And then a
new thought hit me. "Oh, my God. She's having
coffee with Marnie. What if she puts poison in her
cup?"

"Get Marnie out of there now," he said, his tone
urgent. "And then call the police."

I slammed the phone down and ran to the back,
arriving just as Marnie finished stirring sugar into
her coffee. She raised it to her lips.

"Marnie!" I screamed. Everyone in the shop
stopped and stared at me. "Uh, I'm sorry. I don't
feel so well." I doubled over, pretending to be in
pain. Marnie jumped up and rushed over.

"Do you want me to call an ambulance?" Behind her, Melinda watched me intently.

"Just help me upstairs. I need to lie down."

"Of course. Here, hold on to my arm," Marnie
said. "Would you mind keeping an eye on the
shop?" she called to Margaret. We stopped at the
counter, picked up our purses, and made our way
out of the shop and to the private entrance. I ran up
the stairs and made a beeline for the living room.

"What are you doing? You need to lie down,"
Marnie said. "You shouldn't be exerting yourself
like this."

"I have to call the police," I said, snatching my
cell phone from my bag.

"What are you talking a—"

I shushed her as the phone was answered. Under Marnie's confused stare, I asked the dispatcher to connect me to Officer Lombard.

"I have some information about Bruce Doherty's murder." Marnie's eyes widened. I gave the woman my name, address, and phone number.

"I'll get her to call you right back," the woman said.

"What information?" Marnie asked as soon as I put the telephone down.

"I think I know who killed him."

"Who?"

"Melinda Wilson. She used to be married to him."

"What? But that doesn't make any sense. Melinda is a widow. Her husband was killed in Afghanistan eight years ago."

"Marnie," I said, taking her hands in mine, "I just saw her wedding picture." I told her how I'd looked through the woman's wallet. "It was him, all right. He was standing next to her, wearing a tux. She was wearing a white wedding dress. From the hair and makeup, I'd say it was taken about ten years ago."

The doorbell rang, and I jumped up.

"It's Officer Lombard," the voice said through the intercom. I buzzed her up and soon she and Officer Harrison were sitting with us in the living room. "We were just driving by when we got the call from dispatch."

I repeated what I'd just told Marnie.

"And you're certain the man in the photo was Bruce Doherty?" Harrison questioned.

"Absolutely. The picture wasn't big, but it showed him from the waist up and cropped very closely. It was him—no question about it."

"Are you going to arrest her?" Marnie asked. She sounded more worried than relieved. "I can't believe she could have killed him."

"We don't know that yet," the policewoman said. "This is just another piece of the puzzle. But we'll question her." She and her partner stood. "Thank you for reporting this," she said, heading for the door. "Please let us know if you learn anything else."

"I will," I said, and closed the door behind them.

I returned to the living room, where Marnie sat in shocked silence.

"Are you all right?" I asked. "Would you like a glass of water?"

"I'm fine," she said. "Tell me something. Why did you rush in screaming my name? Did you think I was in danger?"

"I wasn't about to take any chances. Helen was poisoned. If Melinda murdered her, who knows what's going through her mind?"

"You think she might have poisoned me?" she asked, shaking her head in disbelief. "I always considered Melinda a friend. After everything I did for her, you think she was Bruce's accomplice? She wanted to murder me?"

"We don't know that," I said, hearing the uncertainty in my own voice. I picked up the phone.

"Who are you calling now?"

"Matthew. I phoned him after finding Melinda's wedding picture. He's the reason I got you out of there and called the police. He's probably sitting on pins and needles, waiting to find out what happened."

Marnie got to her feet. "I'll be downstairs," she said. "I could use a cup of coffee. One without poison."

When I rejoined her a little while later, Jenny and Margaret were standing around the counter, listening in fascination to Marnie's retelling of the events.

"I was really worried about you," Jenny said.

"I'll have to remember what a good actress you are," Margaret added.

"You really think Melinda could have . . ." Jenny shook her head. "I can't believe it."

"Please, nobody repeat this to anyone. If I'm wrong about this, I could be slapped with a slander suit. I just spoke to Matthew and he pointed out something: for all we know, she could have been divorced from him for years."

"Didn't you tell me that she and Bruce were having a clandestine conversation at your party?" said Jenny. "To me, that suggests something was afoot."

"That's how it sounds," I admitted. "But I know Matthew will say that doesn't prove a thing."

The shop remained quiet for the next couple of hours, then shortly after lunch, droves of people started coming in. Marnie joined me at the counter.

"Something's happened," she said, sounding uneasy.

"I think you're right." The atmosphere had changed. One could almost hear the drums beating. We watched as one after another, women were carving a path to Jenny's coffee shop.

Soon Margaret came scurrying over from the back. "I just heard. The police questioned Melinda and then released her."

"Who told you she was released?"

"Everybody is talking about it," she said. "One of her customers happened to be in her shop when the police came to pick her up. And then a few hours later somebody saw the police drop her off." She leaned in. "What if she comes after Marnie?"

Marnie paled. "Do you really think she might?"

"Of course not," I said. "But if you're worried, why don't you stay over at my place tonight? You'll feel safer if you're not alone."

"I wish I could, but I have some baking to do. You could come stay with me. Please?"

Margaret's and Marnie's panic was beginning to influence me. "All right. I'll ask Matthew if I can keep Winston overnight. I'll bring him along," I added. "We'll be fine. If anybody tries to come after you, I'll sic Winston on them. He'll lick them to death."

"Scary," Margaret said, with a roll of her eyes.

By the end of the day, none of Jenny's clients had so much as glanced at my displays. They had all walked straight through to Coffee, Tea and Destiny, leaving me with the lowest sales I'd had in a long time. There wasn't even enough money to warrant making a bank deposit.

Jenny and Margaret took off, and Marnie, Winston, and I left a few minutes later. I ran up to my apartment for a pair of pajamas and a container of Winnie's food.

"Let's walk," I said, returning downstairs. "Winnie needs the exercise."

"It won't hurt me a bit either," she said. "So Matthew didn't mind you keeping him?"

"He wasn't there when I called, so I left him a message. He won't mind."

Once at her place, we went straight to the kitchen. I pulled up a stool and watched as she prepared one of my favorite dishes, veal scaloppine.

"No, Winnie, this is people food," I said. He hung his head and plodded away, sulking.

"You know," Marnie said as she heated up a cast-iron frying pan, "I never mentioned it, but I couldn't help but notice the way Melinda was glaring at me at the party."

"Maybe she wasn't very happy at seeing Bruce in a relationship with you."

"Ha. Some relationship. She had nothing to be unhappy about. We never even slept together," she said. "He wanted to wait, out of respect for me." She slapped the veal into the flour. "And I thought that was so sweet." She shook her head, muttering something under her breath.

I was quiet for a few minutes, thinking over the events on the night of the party. "I wonder if she knew Brent would be there." Another thought occurred to me. "Maybe she didn't know that your fiancé was the same man she used to be married to. If that was the case, seeing him there must have come as quite a shock."

"If you're right, that means she had nothing to do with this plot," Marnie said, looking hopeful.

"I think I should go over and have a bit of a talk with her."

"If she's guilty she'll invite you in and then put cyanide in your coffee."

"Ha, ha. Maybe I'll stop by her shop tomorrow instead."

"Hand me those, will you?" She pointed to the jar of capers. "Thanks. I'd think twice before doing that. If Melinda knows you called the police on her, you'd better be ready for fireworks." She had a good point.

We had a quiet dinner, over which Marnie told me about being questioned at the police station.

"Now that they found out about Melinda's history with Bruce, I'm probably not the main suspect anymore," she said.

"How did you explain your ring being in Bruce's room?"

"I told them the truth. I figured they'd either believe me or they wouldn't. Besides, if I lied and they later found out, then I'd be as good as convicted."

"I'm glad you decided not to lie."

"They put me in a small room and made me sit there by myself for over an hour before they even started. I had plenty of time to think about it. If that was their goal, it worked. By the time they came in, I was singing like a canary."

I laughed, picturing Marnie trembling under the light shining in her eyes. "You would make a terrible spy."

"I'd spill the beans at the very sight of thumb screws." She giggled.

"There's something I never asked you," I said. "Why did you wait so long to introduce him to all your friends?"

Marnie blushed. Squirming, she said, "The truth is I couldn't believe he was really interested in me. I kept expecting him to stop calling. But then, when he asked me to marry him, I believed he was being sincere. That's when I told you. The night you threw me the surprise party, I'd just asked Bruce if he'd like to meet everyone." Her eyes barely watered, and giving a self-conscious laugh she blinked the tears away, making me believe that she would recover sooner than anybody expected her to. Marnie was a resilient person.

After cleaning up, I suggested we make it an early night and Marnie agreed.

"I'll take the sofa," I said.

"Are you sure?"

I bounced on it, testing its comfort. "Absolutely," I said. "This is fine. And Winnie can sleep on the floor right next to me." I flapped a sheet, spreading it over the sofa, then added another sheet and blankets.

"Hold on a minute," she said, hurrying away. She reappeared carrying a pillow and a folded bathrobe. "Here. I know it might be a bit big for you, but it's the smallest one I have." It was a pink chenille robe, a few sizes too large for my five-foot-nothing frame. "Just tie the belt tight and it'll be okay. And this is for Winnie." She placed a folded blanket at the foot of the sofa. "You'll be nice and cozy here." She patted Winnie on the head and he stretched out on his makeshift bed.

I climbed in. "Not bad," I said. "Almost as comfortable as my own bed."

Marnie said good night and turned off the lights. I must have fallen asleep within minutes because the next thing I knew, I woke up with a start. Winston was growling, a low, menacing rumbling deep in his throat. I'd caught him making that sound only once before, seconds before he attacked an intruder brandishing a gun. I sat up, glancing around the room nervously, but the darkness was so dense a prowler could have been inches away and I wouldn't have seen him. From the direction of Marnie's bedroom came the sound of snoring. Whatever had alerted the dog, it wasn't her.

"What is it, Winnie?" I whispered. And then I heard it, a metallic clang that seemed to come from the kitchen area. I threw back my blankets and felt around for Marnie's bathrobe. I slipped it on. "Quiet, Winnie," I said. By now, my eyes were growing accustomed to the dark. I could make out shadows well enough to avoid bumping into furniture. I tiptoed to the kitchen, barely breathing, I was so nervous. I'd made it to her old kitchen, when I heard the second clang. The noise seemed to come from the professional kitchen, just beyond this one. I slid my hand along the Formica countertop until I felt the knife block. I grabbed the chef's knife and stepped forward.

I had just reached the doorway of the professional kitchen when I heard footsteps outside, moving along the side of the house. Winston growled.

"Quiet, Winnie."

Whoever had been here was leaving. Next came the slam of a car door, and then a motor roared to life. I ran through the house to the living room window in time to see a car drive away. In the dark, I couldn't even make out the color.

Damn it. I flicked on the lights and returned to the kitchen, determined to find out what that intruder had been up to.

"What the hell is going on?" Marnie's voice startled me. I dropped the knife, and it stuck into the linoleum floor, barely half an inch from my big toe.

"Marnie! For God's sake, don't sneak up on me that way. I almost sliced off my big toe."

"You're the one who was sneaking around, not me. What are you doing snooping through my kitchen in the middle of the night? If you're looking for a midnight snack, come with me. I was just about to start my baking."

"I heard somebody back here. I came to investigate."

She stopped. "Are you sure?"

"Absolutely. Winnie heard it first, and his growling woke me up."

"I can't believe you were going to confront him. You should know better than that. Confronting an intruder is a good way to get yourself killed."

"By the time I got here, whoever it was was already on his way out. I got a glimpse of the car as he drove away. And before you ask, no, I couldn't see the color or the make. But I suspect it might have been a royal blue economy car."

"What makes you say that?"

"I guess I never told you. Remember the intruder who broke into Helen's house while I was there? I got a peek at that car as it drove away. It was a small royal blue car. Then, earlier, when I got you out of the coffee shop, I noticed that the car Melinda was driving was also royal blue, though I couldn't swear that it was the same one."

"You think Melinda broke into my house? That's ridiculous. How would she have gotten in?"

"Beats me, but I heard a noise coming from back here. A loud metallic clang."

"I have nothing in here that would make that sound." She marched over to the massive freezer. "Do you think she might have put poison in my food?" That was a frightening thought. She grabbed the handle and pulled it open. There was a loud beep. *Ah, the freezer alarm.*

"I would have heard that," I said. "Whatever she did, she didn't do it in the freezer."

She closed it and looked around. "Something that clanged," she said under her breath. She walked around the kitchen, picking up a frying pan here, a pot there, and banging them on the stainless steel counter.

"No, that sounds flat," I said. "What I heard had more resonance."

She paused, thinking. "The garbage can," she said, her eyes lighting up. She ran to the back door. "It's the lid. I bought a heavy metal bin because I'm always throwing out leftovers and I wanted something that would keep rodents from getting in. And the lid clangs." She went to grab it.

"Wait," I said. "Don't touch it." I snatched the wall phone.

"Who are you calling?"

"The police," I said. "I suspect somebody just planted evidence in your garbage. You, my dear, are being framed."

*   *   *

This time the police officers who showed up were two men, Barkley and Jones. Barkley, a big guy with more hair above his lip than on top of his head, looked at me as if I'd lost my mind.

"You're telling me that somebody just put something in your garbage can, and you want us to go look for it?"

Luckily his younger partner was more open-minded. "Where is this garbage can?" he asked.

Marnie led the way through the kitchen and opened the back door. "That's it, there." She pointed to the metal bin.

"You go ahead if you want," Barkley said. "But I'd be surprised if there was anything in there but trash."

Jones hesitated. "You wouldn't happen to have rubber gloves, would you?"

"I do," Marnie said. "I'll get them right away." She left, returning a minute later with an unused pair of gloves and a garbage bag. "For transferring the trash."

"Thanks. If you're right about this, I wouldn't want to destroy any prints," he said, struggling to put the gloves on. He raised the lid, took a deep breath, and plunged in. Piece by piece he picked out eggshells, empty sugar bags and milk cartons, a glob of hardened dough. He transferred it all into the garbage bag Jones was holding.

"Hold on," he said. "What's this?" He raised a metal container with a twist top. The label read PRO METAL RESTORE.

The officer studied the smaller print. "Cyanide," he read. "Guess you two were right after all." He threw his partner a look. "Sometimes it helps to listen."

"I'll call it in," Barkley said, oblivious to the dig. "They'll want to send a team." He stepped away, pulling out his cell phone.

"Let me get you another bag for that container," Marnie said, rushing off again.

"Make that a paper bag, if you don't mind." To me, Barkley explained, "Paper preserves prints better."

Jones returned, scowling. "Looks like the team is you and me. I'll just zip over to the station and pick up a fingerprint kit. You stay here and make sure nothing is disturbed." He gave Marnie and me a stern look as he said this. I wanted to point out that *we* had called *them*, so why would we want to destroy evidence? He took off.

Marnie tapped me on the shoulder. "I might as well get dressed and put on a pot of coffee. It's going to be a long night."

I looked at my watch. "I hate to tell you, but it's almost morning already."

She plodded away with a loud sigh.

Officer Barkley returned and set to work with Jones, brushing sooty black powder all over the garbage can. After taking dozens of photographs of the resulting prints, they lifted them using adhesive tape and then glued them onto white cardboard cards.

"This is fascinating," Marnie said. "I've never seen it done before." She had changed into an orange sweater, which was almost the same color as her hair, and a pair of black stretch pants. It was a subdued outfit compared to her usual garb. It made her look less pale.

"I'd better make up Jenny's order out of some frozen stuff again." She swung open the freezer door.

"At least you're cleaning out your freezer this way."

"I have a bad habit of making too much. And then what I don't use immediately, I freeze. Twice a month, I just throw out whatever is older than three weeks."

"Don't do that," I said, shocked. "Send it to one of the soup kitchens in the city."

"Now, why didn't I think of that?"

"You might even be able to get tax receipts for your donations." That was the business analyst in me speaking.

The policemen came in again, closing the back door behind them. Barkley walked on through, mumbling something about his job being done.

"Sorry, ladies," Jones said. "I'm going to need to fingerprint you, just to eliminate your prints from the ones we got off the garbage." He produced an inkpad and two white pieces of cardboard pre-stamped with the outline of five fingers.

Starting with me, he held each finger one at a time, rolled the tip over the pad, and then pressed it onto the card in the appropriate space for that digit. He moved on to Marnie and I went to scrub my ink-stained fingers at the sink.

"How fast can you fingerprint your suspects?" I said.

"Sounds to me like you're more informed than I am," Jones said. "I didn't know we had any."

"It's obviously linked to the two murders," Marnie said, exasperated. "Helen was poisoned—with cyanide."

Jones laughed. "I was just being sarcastic. We'll bring in everyone who hasn't already been printed as soon as we can. It shouldn't take more than a day or so. But I wouldn't get my hopes up if I were you. Anybody devious enough to plant evidence won't likely have left any prints. The only ones we'll get will be yours, and maybe the garbage man's."

"Great," Marnie said. "So we're still no further ahead."

Chapter 17

"Talk about making a person feel like a criminal," Marnie said later, as we loaded the bags of frozen pastries into her car. "This was the first time I've ever been fingerprinted." I knew exactly how she felt.

"Come on, Winnie. Let's go." He hopped into the backseat and planted his front paws on the console between the front seats.

"Look at him," Marnie said. "He looks like he's grinning."

"I'm glad somebody around here is having fun," I said.

We climbed in and took off. Moments later we were at the shop. To my surprise, the lights were on.

"Do you think Jenny is already here? It's only seven thirty," Marnie said.

We carried the bags in, Winnie trotting behind us.

"Matthew," I said, "what are you doing here?" He was sitting behind the counter, holding his head in his hands. He pulled away his hands and

I was shocked by how haggard he looked—deep dark circles under bloodshot eyes.

"I've been worried half to death," he said, jumping to his feet. He took two giant strides toward me and gathered me in a bear hug. *Matthew had been worried about me?*

"There you are," Jenny said, running in from the back. "Where were you? You don't just disappear like that. You had everyone worried sick."

"I slept at Marnie's," I said as Matthew released me.

"If you can call it sleeping," Marnie said. "We had an unexpected visitor in the middle of the night."

"Why didn't you answer your cell phone?" Matthew said. He looked as if he was ready for a rant. "I must have called a dozen times," he continued. "And left you just as many messages."

"You called? That's strange. I never heard it ring." I snatched my phone from my purse. "It's out of juice. Sorry. I never thought to check. Didn't you get my message? I called around five thirty to let you know I wanted to keep Winnie for the night."

"I never got that message. And I never thought of checking with Marnie," he said.

Margaret appeared in the doorway of the coffee shop. "Oh, thank God you're all right. What happened? Where were you?"

"You're here too? Who else did you call? The whole town?" I said.

"She was at my place," Marnie said. "And we had a bit of an eventful night. We had an intruder and called the police."

Margaret's eyes widened. "Someone broke into your place?"

"They didn't break in," Marnie said. "They planted evidence in my garbage can to frame me for Helen's murder."

"Come on over to the coffee shop," Jenny said. "I won't be open for another half hour. You might as well give us the details over breakfast."

"Stay," I said to Winnie. I fished through my drawer, gave him a treat, and he settled onto his cushion.

Marnie picked up the bag she'd just put down and marched to the back. "Breakfast is a damn good idea. I've been up half the night and I haven't had a bite to eat since dinner."

We pulled two small tables together and gathered around. Marnie popped a dozen muffins into the oven while Jenny served coffee to everyone.

"Why were you so worried about me?" I asked Matthew.

"I got some information from the police that I knew you'd want to hear. I called and called. Finally, I came over and knocked so loudly that I got Margaret out of bed. When I told her I couldn't reach you, she called Jenny."

Jenny picked up from there. "I used the key you gave me and checked your apartment."

"We waited inside for a few hours," Margaret

said. "And then we all came down here a little while ago and were just about to contact the police."

"Please tell me you didn't call my mother," I said.

"I was just about to," Matthew said. "And then you showed up."

"Thank God for small favors."

Marnie placed a tray of muffins on the table and soon I was retelling the events of the night between bites.

"You went after him with a butcher knife?" Matthew said. "Are you crazy? That's how people end up dead."

"Well, I'm fine, as you can see. Besides, I didn't exactly go after him. By the time I got there, he was already gone."

"You never saw him?" Matthew said, more calmly.

"No. We couldn't even tell you if it was a woman or a man," I said.

"It might be Melinda Wilson," Marnie said. "Or it could be Nancy Cutler."

"Enough theories," I said, wanting to end this conversation before it turned into a long-winded review of every possibility we'd examined. "I want to hear facts, not suppositions. What did you learn from the police?"

"I stopped by the station last night," Matthew said. He was sitting right next to me, our knees practically touching, and he kept glancing at me, as if to reassure himself that I was all right. "I found out that Melinda and Bruce were indeed married," he continued.

"Aha. I knew it."

"They were together for a little over two years. Her story is that she had no idea when they married that Bruce earned his living conning women out of their life savings."

Marnie scowled. "Of course she would say that. She's probably worried about being charged as an accessory."

Matthew continued. "According to her, that was the reason she left him. She found out about six years ago and moved out here. She admits that she was still in love with him at the time, which is why she never reported him to the police. She hoped he would change his ways and come back to her. She made up her story about being a widow because it was easier than having to explain why she divorced. She said she almost passed out when he walked into your party."

"It makes sense," Jenny said. "That could be what all the whispering between them was about."

"She told the police that she was furious when she saw him," Matthew said. "She was certain he was planning to bilk Marnie out of every dime she had, and she warned him that if he didn't leave Briar Hollow right away, she would call the authorities and let them know what he was up to."

"So she wasn't trying to kill me?" Marnie said.

"According to her, she was trying to protect you."

"Yeah. Right." She smirked. "I wasn't born yesterday."

"What about Sybille Dubois?" I asked. "Did she say anything about her?"

"Only that she heard about her over the years through local gossip, but she never made the link that the man Sybille had been seeing at the time was her ex-husband. When she found out that Bruce and Brent were the same man, she was shocked."

"Did she tell the police what his real name was?" I asked.

"His name was Barry Donnelly."

My eyes met Matthew's. "Initials BD again."

He continued. "He was born in a small fishing village in Maine. He moved to New York when he was in his early twenties, was hired as a chauffeur for a rich couple, and soon began an affair with the wife. Her husband died of a heart attack, leaving her a fortune, and then she died some years later, leaving Barry half a million dollars."

"Barry," Marnie said to herself. "I'll never be able to think of him as Barry."

"Half a million dollars?" Margaret interjected. "That's a fortune."

"It might be for most people," Matthew said. "But Barry blew through it in less than a year. That's when he started his life as a grifter."

"Do you think he might have killed the husband to get him out of the way, and then killed the wife some time later?"

"Maybe, but I rather doubt it. If Melinda is telling the truth, the man was a con artist, not a killer."

"What about the life insurance policy he made me buy?" Marnie asked. "Don't you think he was planning to kill me?"

Matthew avoided Marnie's eyes. "We'll never know," he replied, giving me the impression he did know, but preferred to spare her feelings.

"Probably not," Marnie said, sounding relieved. "Maybe he was really planning to marry me. I'm older than he was, and he probably thought I might predecease him. In that case, there was nothing wrong with him wanting me to make him my beneficiary. Still, maybe he really did care for me." Believing this seemed to make her feel better. I threw Matthew a grateful look.

"You're probably right," I told her, and to Matthew, "But hold on. If what Melinda told the police is true, why is she still carrying that snapshot of their wedding?"

"The police asked her that. She said that she normally didn't, but she had fished it out after deciding to tell them everything she knew. She only wanted to show the police that Bruce and Brent were the same man."

"Ri-i-ight," Marnie said. "Come on. She knew the police would be looking into his background. It was only a matter of time before they found out she'd been married to him. Her only chance was to give them the information before they came to her."

"I happen to believe her," Jenny said without hesitation. "Her story makes sense. Every last bit of it."

"What about the snapshot of Bruce—I mean Brent—er, Barry, in Helen's house?" I said. "Why would she have planted that?" Jenny and Margaret looked at me, confused. *Oops. I didn't tell them that part.*

"We don't know that she did," Matthew said. "You told me yourself, that picture could have been there all along."

"If you ask me, I'm convinced she was the woman who sneaked in while Della was hiding under the bed," Marnie said. Jenny and Margaret looked at me as if I'd just grown a second head. "Oh, Della never told you about her little detecting expedition, did she?" They shook their heads in perfect unison.

I glared at Marnie. "Have I ever told you you have a big mouth?"

"Sorry," she said, looking not nearly sorry enough.

I turned to Jenny and Margaret. "If I tell you, do you promise never to repeat this?" They nodded.

"I didn't tell the police about your 'expedition,' as you call it," Matthew said. "So they didn't question Melinda about the picture. They don't even know you or I know about it."

"I think she planted it there," Marnie insisted.

The bell above the door tinkled, announcing Jenny's first customers, so we put the tables and chairs back in place. Matthew and I returned to the front, and Marnie went straight to her loom, winking at me as she walked by. "Now, for God's sake, flirt with the man," she whispered.

I glanced at Matthew. He seemed not to have heard, thank goodness. That would have been embarrassing.

"It's sweet that you were so worried about me," I said. "Maybe I should disappear more often."

"Only if you want to see me really angry." He was only teasing. I wasn't sure where to go from there, so I said the first thing that went through my mind. "That must mean you like me a little bit."

His grin widened. "Just a tiny bit," he said, bringing his thumb and forefinger a fraction of an inch from each other. As he bent down I was certain he was about to kiss me, but he kept bending down, until he was on one knee. My heart skipped a beat, and then he tied his shoelace. And then he turned around and walked out, leaving me swaying on my feet.

"Wait," I yelled. "Don't go! We have a date to go to the library exhibit in"—I glanced at my watch—"half an hour."

He paused in the doorway. "Sorry, kiddo. I'd like to, but after yet another sleepless night— thanks to you—I'd rather go home and shower. I'll see it some other time." The door closed.

Marnie left her loom and made her way over to me, swaying her hips and grinning. "Well, what do you know? The minute Prince Charming thought his damsel was in distress, he came charging to the

rescue." A blush crept over my face. She continued. "If you play your cards right, you could land
that man. I'd say he's ripe for the picking." That
was exactly what I'd needed to hear. "And before
you ask me how to go about doing that . . ." She
planted her hands on her hips. "First thing you do
is go upstairs and change, and I'll tell you on the
way to the library. You'd better get moving if we
want to be there when it opens."

I ran upstairs and changed into a pair of casual
beige pants and a coordinating cashmere V-neck
sweater, adding a pair of gold hoop earring to
dress it up—just in case Matthew changed his
mind and appeared after all. I rejoined Marnie.

"Sorry, Winnie, but you have to stay here. You
guard the shop until we're back." He watched us
leave with big mournful eyes.

"Some guard," Marnie said. "He'd probably
roll over on his back, hoping the robbers would
rub his tummy."

It was a lovely spring morning. The sun was
bright and the temperature warm, so we decided
to walk over.

"When was the last time you cooked for Matthew?" she asked.

"A while ago," I said. "It's been maybe a month
or so."

"Well, it's high time you invited him to a nice
home-cooked meal."

"Good idea. I have a recipe for chicken Parmesan from my mother. He always loved that dish."

"Great. If you need help, I can come over and make sure you prepare it right. You concentrate on looking good and, remember, get him to talk about himself. Don't hog the conversation."

"Gee. What is it with everybody? I do *not* hog the conversation." She gave me the eyebrow, which I ignored. "I always let him talk." She looked at me with an expression that screamed skepticism.

We arrived at the library a few minutes after nine. Across the street I noticed Bunny Boyd getting into a car and driving off.

"Have you heard anything about Bunny's painting?" Marnie asked.

"Nothing," I said. "I wish we had time to stop by the hotel after this event. See how she's doing. I'll have to remember to give her a call when we get back."

We walked up the steps of the building and as we entered, I ran right into Melinda. Literally. One minute I was on my feet, the next I was on the ground. Melinda had dropped her large handbag, but rather than help me to my feet, she snatched it up and scampered off.

Marnie helped pull me up. "Talk about rude. You could have tumbled down those stairs and really hurt yourself," she said. "Did you see the way she grabbed her bag? As if she was afraid we'd steal it from her."

"Considering I did report her to the police, I'm just glad she didn't throw me down the stairs."

Seeing the look on her face, I added, "It was an accident, Marnie. Trust me."

We made our way to the registration desk and I took some bills from my wallet and dropped them into the donations box.

"Welcome to the exhibit," the girl behind the table said, handing us a couple of cards. "If you wouldn't mind filling these out."

"Marnie. Della. There you are." I looked around to see Liz approaching, all gussied up in a red skirt and jacket and pearls.

"Good grief, she looks like she's dressed for Christmas," Marnie whispered, and then giggling, she added, "But, who am I to talk?"

"I was afraid you wouldn't come," Liz said, throwing her arms wide. "I can't wait for you to see your flag on display. Look at all the people!" Her excitement seemed rather exaggerated, since there were no more than half a dozen visitors waiting in line to go in. Liz continued. "We usually only allow four or five guests in at a time because we don't want the displays to be too crowded. But since Marnie so generously lent us her flag, that makes you two very special visitors. Come with me. I'll bring you directly in."

She escorted us into the first area, called the fiction room. There, in the center between rows of bookshelves, stood an antique printing press, complete with dozens of metal stamps.

Marnie approached it. "Imagine how long it must have taken to typeset an entire book."

"That's why books were so expensive. Only the rich could afford them," Liz said. "Now, with modern printing, not to mention public libraries, reading is for everyone."

We moved on to the next exhibit, a group of local photos from the early twentieth century that were taken inside the Belmont newspaper printing plant. They were grainy black-and-white shots of workers in an industrial room. The next one presented century-old newspapers. The paper in the center was dated 1912 and featured an article about the sinking of the *Titanic*, complete with photos of the great ship.

"You've done an excellent job, Liz," I said. "This is fascinating."

"Thank you, but Helen had already planned most of it. All I had to do was finish what she'd started." We moved on from one display to the next until at last we reached the one featuring Marnie's flag.

"So what do you think?" Liz asked.

Marnie looked at it, frowning. "Did you send it out to be cleaned or something?"

I came in for a closer look. "What are you talking about?" Liz asked.

"Look. It used to be yellowed with age, but now it looks—I don't know—brighter."

"That's because it's under a neon light," Liz said. "I would never send a fragile piece of antique linen to be cleaned. The process could destroy it."

Marnie looked relieved, but only for a moment. She leaned closer. "That can't be my flag," she said suddenly. "Look. The top edge with the stars was worn, and now it looks perfect."

She was right. This flag looked very similar. It was also made of slubbed linen. It had the same circle of stars in the top left corner, but the fabric was brighter and less damaged. Now that I was looking at it more closely, it seemed like some-body had attempted to fray one of the corners, but it was the wrong corner.

"This is not my flag," Marnie said, her voice ris-ing with every word. "What happened to my flag?"

"Are . . . are you completely certain?" Liz asked, shocked.

"Completely," Marnie replied.

"She's right," I added.

"Oh, my." She looked around desperately. And then she ran to the entrance, where she whispered something to the girl behind the counter. Then she faced the room and made an announcement.

"Ladies and gentlemen, I have to ask everyone to please proceed to the exit. We have a small emergency. We'll reopen in a few hours. I'm sorry for the inconvenience."

People looked at one another, more curious than upset, and then slowly migrated to the door. As soon as the last person had left, Liz came run-ning back.

"I got one of the staff to call the police." I turned

around, and sure enough, the girl behind the table was on the phone, speaking excitedly.

"What happened to my flag?" Marnie asked again. "You said it would be safe, that nobody could get to it. But look." She pointed to the display, a glass box with a hinged door. "There isn't even a lock on this thing. Anybody could have opened it."

"I—I . . ." She shook her head, at a loss for words.

"You said that you only allowed a few people in at a time," I said. "Maybe somebody was able to take it out without being noticed."

"Well, we did have a power outage for about two minutes, just before you came in."

"Two minutes? That's not very long, but maybe long enough for an experienced thief to make the switch," I said.

"It must have been Melinda," Marnie mumbled. I stared at her, hoping she would get the message and keep her mouth shut. She caught my look. "She was leaving when we got here," she added defensively, and described the scene at the entrance. "She didn't even make sure Della was all right. She just grabbed her bag and ran away. I bet my flag was inside. And to think I walked right by her, never imagining—"

I cut her off. "We don't know who took it."

Liz started to say something, but then stopped.

"What were you going to say?" I asked.

She hesitated. "I really shouldn't say this, but . . .

Melinda was in this room when the power went out. I can't be one hundred percent sure, but I think she might have been standing right where you are," she said to Marnie. "Right near the door to the display."

"Listen, ladies," I said. "We don't know anything for sure. She could have had anything in that bag. So let's not get ahead of ourselves. I suggest we tell the police the facts, not what we think or imagine."

Marnie and Liz must have agreed, because neither of them made another comment about Melinda.

Chapter 18

When the police arrived, I was not surprised to find it was Officer Lombard and her partner, Harrison, again.

"This is turning out to be a bad habit," she said. "Every time I get a call, I wonder if it'll be you."

"This time it's me," Marnie said. "Somebody stole my flag." She explained about her flag, its provenance, and the approximate value attributed by the museum curator. "And now it's been stolen."

Officer Lombard turned to Liz. "Can you tell me who had access to the flag?"

Liz looked as if she was about to burst into tears. "I was the one who picked it up from Marnie. I brought it here and I kept it locked in my office until this morning. I came in at seven to prepare for the opening. That's when I put the finishing touches on all the displays. Nobody had access to it but me." Her eyes moistened. "I feel so awful. This is all my fault."

"Did anybody else have a key to the office?"

asked Officer Harrison. He had taken out his notebook and was ready to jot down the details.

"No, only me." And then her eyes lit up. "I just remembered something. The front door was open when I got here yesterday morning. Do you think they could have stolen it during the night?"

"Could be. But we'll have to consider all possibilities," Lombard answered. "Where do you keep the key?"

"At the counter." Her eyes widened. "Oh, no. It didn't occur to me before, but I guess any of the volunteers could have taken it. I can't believe any of them . . ." She shook her head. "It must have been during the night."

"I'm going to need a list of all the volunteers."

"Liz said there was a power outage earlier," I said. "Somebody might have taken it during that time."

"When was this?" the officer said.

"About forty minutes ago," Liz said, glancing at her watch.

"Where is the electric panel?" asked Officer Lombard.

"It's right over here," Liz said, leading the officers to the counter, a few steps away. She pointed at the wall. Right below the panel was a book cart.

As if reading my mind, Officer Lombard said, "Somebody could have been hiding behind the book cart and pulled the master switch at just the right moment. And then it would have taken only seconds to get to the display, remove the flag, and put in the replacement."

"But how could they do that in the dark?" Marnie asked. "Look at that display. It looks professionally done. The flag is perfectly fanned out. All the folds expertly done."

"Night goggles," I said. "While everybody else was in the dark. Whoever did this would have been able to walk around and see what they were doing. This was no amateur. Whoever did this was experienced." *And Melinda's bag would have been big enough to carry those.*

"You're telling me a professional thief took my flag?" Marnie said. "But how did it come to their attention?"

Liz covered her mouth. "Oh, no. That was my fault too. I gave the *Belmont Daily* an interview. I wanted word to get around about the exhibit, so I mentioned your flag and how valuable it is." For a moment I thought Marnie was going to burst into tears, but instead she turned on her heel and stormed out.

"If you don't need me, I'd better catch up with her."

The officers nodded their approval. "We'll give you a call if we have any other questions," Lombard said, and I darted after Marnie.

"Wait," I called out on the library steps. She was wearing her granite face. We walked in silence until we reached the store.

"We both know who did this," she said.

"You mean Melinda?"

"Yes. I'm sure she stole my flag. But you're

right. We'd better keep this to ourselves. It would be just my luck to get sued for defamation of character and have to pay a huge fine—on top of losing my flag."

"I don't know that she actually stole it herself," I said. "But I think she was involved. Furthermore, I think she had something to do with Bunny's stolen painting, too."

Marnie froze with her hand on the doorknob. "I swear I'll get my flag back if it's the last thing I do."

"I hope you do." Through the glass, I could see Winston wiggling his butt excitedly at our return.

As we walked in, he threw himself at me, delirious with joy.

"Down, boy." I patted him until he became calmer. And then I went directly to the coffee shop and picked up two coffees and a couple of muffins.

"How was the exhibit?" asked Jenny from behind her counter.

"It would have been better if Marnie's flag hadn't been stolen."

"What!"

"You heard me." I looked around. There were half a dozen customers in various stages of breakfast. I whispered, "Come over when you have a break. I'll tell you all about it." I returned to the front, where Marnie had settled at her loom. She was walking those pedals with a fury.

"Thanks," she said, as I set the coffee and muffins down. I went to the counter, picked up the phone, and punched in Matthew's number.

"Hi," I said, when he answered. "How are you feeling?"

"All right," he said. "I'll do some writing soon and then maybe take a nap before I pick up Winston."

"How would you like to come over for dinner tonight? I'm planning to make my mother's chicken Parmesan."

"It's a date," he said.

"It's a date," I repeated. I was on the verge of telling him about Marnie's flag, but decided to end the conversation on a personal note. Marnie had often pointed out that all I seemed to ever talk about with Matthew was crime. Not this time.

After hanging up, I went to my own loom, next to Marnie's.

"You haven't even touched your coffee," I said.

"I'm not thirsty."

I pulled my chair next to hers and sat. "Marnie, I have a feeling they'll find it. Now that we told them everything we know, they'd be crazy not to suspect Melinda. It's just a question of time before they find enough evidence to search her place."

"It's driving me crazy that there's nothing I can do but wait. I want to break into her place right now and get my flag myself."

"The police will arrest her, and when they do, they'll find your flag and Bunny's painting. I wouldn't be surprised if you got it back before the end of the day."

Her sigh was long and heartfelt. "I wish I could believe that, but it's not even guaranteed that they'll search her house—a judge would want some strong evidence before authorizing a search warrant. So what are the cops going to do if they don't search? Place her under surveillance? This small town has no budget for stuff like that." She shrugged. "And for all we know, she's probably got a warehouse or a locker someplace where she stores all her stolen stuff."

I was very much afraid Marnie was right. "Worse comes to worst, at least you had it insured."

She spun around in her chair and faced me. "Oh. I called the insurance broker, all right. But the insurance was only taking effect after the value of my flag was confirmed by an independent appraiser. Until then the insurance was in a waiver period."

My jaw dropped. "Oh, Marnie. Why did you let Liz borrow it? You should have said no."

"Shoulda, woulda, coulda. I know. It was stupid. I mean, nothing ever works out for me—not when it comes to money, and obviously not when it comes to love."

I put down my shuttle. "You can't say friendships never work out for you."

Winnie must have sensed how she was feeling, because he came lumbering over and rested his head in her lap. His big innocent eyes worked their usual magic.

This time her sigh was more sorrowful than angry. "I love you too, Winnie," she said, picking up her coffee cup and breaking off a piece of muffin.

Good boy, Winnie.

I brushed the muffin crumbs off my lap and gathered the empty cups. "What you said earlier got me thinking." Marnie gave me a bleary look. "Maybe we shouldn't wait for the police to prove Melinda's guilt," I continued. "Maybe we should prove it ourselves."

"And how do you propose we do that?"

"If she stole your flag this morning, she wouldn't have had time to take it anywhere. If she has a storage place, it's probably some distance away. I bet that flag is still in her house, or maybe in the back of her bakery."

"What are you suggesting?"

"I think we should catch her in the act."

She smirked. "That might work if we had something of value we could use to entice her."

"I think you should spread the word about the valuable gold-and-diamond brooch your grandmother also gave you," I said, winking.

She gave me a puzzled look, and then understanding lit her eyes. "Of course," she said, playing along. "Except it wasn't diamonds. It was rubies. And it's been in the family for generations."

"Better not make the story too fascinating or nobody will believe it."

"You're right. So instead of a piece of jewelry,

why don't I make it something like a complete set of some very expensive sterling flatware?"

"Yes. That's way more believable." At that moment, the door flew open, sending the bell into a frenzy of jingling. Nancy Cutler stepped in and looked around. She spotted us and came over.

"Hi, Marnie, Della," she said, moving closer to Marnie's loom. "What are you working on?"

"Place mats," Marnie said. "Della keeps selling out of them. I can't make them fast enough." I sensed that Nancy was gathering her courage. She cleared her voice.

"Marnie, I came in to apologize. I was sure you had killed Bruce, and now I know I was wrong."

I turned and stared. "What convinced you?"

"I found out that Melinda was married to him," she said. "And then, thinking back, I remembered the way they were behaving at your party, having that cloak-and-dagger conversation. I noticed it at the time, but for some reason I'd forgotten all about it. I guess it was the shock of recognizing him."

"So you admit you recognized him?" Marnie asked. I already knew this, but I kept quiet, wondering if her story might change in this telling.

"Yes. At first I didn't," she said. "Don't forget, twenty years had gone by, and I'd only seen him in one picture, and not a very clear one at that. But his voice . . . I recognized him in the middle of our conversation. I never left a party so quickly in my life. I was afraid that if he'd killed Sybille and realized I knew who he really was, he'd come after me. I had nightmares about him for days. I should have gone straight to the police. I'm sorry I didn't."

"He didn't threaten you, did he?" Marnie asked.

"No. He probably didn't know who I was. I only introduced myself as Nancy. I doubt he would have remembered me as the roommate of a girl he used to date twenty years ago, especially a roommate he'd never met. But I was afraid that if Sybille had shown him a picture of me, he might come after me to keep me from talking. I know that was cowardly of me. I should have said something right away."

"Don't feel too bad," Marnie said. "I might have done the same thing."

"That's nice of you to say. By the way, I heard about your flag too. I'm so sorry."

Marnie nodded. "Thank goodness I didn't lend Liz my Paul Revere flatware as well. At least I still have that."

"It might be worth even more than the flag," I added.

"Paul Revere," she said. "Is that just the name of the company? It wasn't actually made by him, right?"

"Yes, this set was," Marnie said with a straight face. "That's why it's so valuable."

"Oh! I'd love to see it sometime," Nancy said.

"I keep it locked away in a closet. I don't think I've used it in over ten years."

"You should use it," I said. "It's a shame to have something so special and not enjoy it."

"You're right. I'm just so afraid something might happen to it. I think I'd die if I accidentally mangled a fork in the garbage disposal."

"I have a feeling you'd be very careful, and you'd keep it in perfect shape." Nancy looked at her watch. "I should really be going. I just wanted to stop by and apologize."

"That was sweet of you," Marnie said, walking her to the door. As soon as Nancy had left, Marnie came hurrying back. "Do you think she fell for it?"

"We should find out soon enough. If she did, it shouldn't take more than a couple of days for the whole town to have heard."

"A couple of days. When do you think Melinda will try to break in?"

I thought this over. "She'd probably have to get organized somehow, so maybe tomorrow night, or the night after?"

"And we'll be ready for her when she shows up," Marnie said, rubbing her hands together in anticipation.

Chapter 19

At noon Marnie shooed me out, insisting I go buy the ingredients for the chicken Parmesan.

"Otherwise, you'll be serving him frozen pizza again," she said. I grabbed my sweater and headed for the grocery store. I was at the poultry counter when I heard a familiar voice behind me and turned around. Nancy Cutler was about ten feet away, talking with a silver-haired lady.

"I feel so awful," she was saying. "Poor Marnie. It isn't enough that her fiancé turned out to be a con artist, but now her flag was stolen."

"I read about that flag. Wasn't it a family heirloom worth a small fortune?"

"Worth a *large* fortune," Nancy said. "Thank God she hadn't also lent the library her family's collection of Paul Revere flatware. Otherwise that probably would be gone too."

"I didn't know she had such valuable heirlooms," the older woman said.

"Oh, yes. I hear that flatware is magnificent. It should be in a museum."

I walked away before Nancy noticed me. The trap was set. By the end of the day, the news of Marnie's valuable collection would be all over Briar Hollow and Belmont. This meant that I had to come up with a plan sooner than I'd expected. I should be ready to put it into action tonight. I quickly got in line to check out. Minutes later, when I returned to the shop, I already had an idea of how we could go about it.

"There's no way you can sleep at your place tonight," I told Marnie. "What we'll do is sit in the car and watch the house."

"All night long?" she said, grimacing. "How do you propose to stay awake all that time?"

"I thought you suffered from insomnia."

"Sure, but it's not like I don't sleep at all. It's just that I wake up around three or so and then can't get back to sleep."

"What we need is something to let us know when somebody is going in."

"I know," Marnie said. "My neighbor across the street has a three-year-old. I remember her having one of those baby monitors. She doesn't use it anymore and I bet she wouldn't mind me borrowing it." She marched over to the telephone and picked it up. "You go on upstairs and start assembling all the ingredients for your recipe. Once you have everything measured and lined up on the counter ready to start, give me a call. In the meantime, I'll call her."

"Thanks, Marnie. You're a doll." I planted a kiss

on her cheek and ran up to my apartment. I set my
mother's recipe on the counter and lined up all the
ingredients—thyme, oregano, basil, eggs, milk, garlic, olive oil, breadcrumbs, tomato sauce, grated
cheese, and parsley, leaving the chicken in the refrigerator until the last minute.

I pulled out my cell phone and called Marnie.
"Marnie? I'm ready to start."

"I spoke to my neighbor as she was about to
leave the house. She offered to stop by and drop
off the baby monitor."

"That's great."

"Okay. Now, come back down. You shouldn't
start preparing the recipe until about half an hour
before Matthew gets there."

Marnie's neighbor got to the door just as I did.
She was a tall brunette with intelligent eyes. In the
stroller she was pushing a beautiful little girl.

"Oh, my God. She looks just like you," I said,
holding the door open.

"Thanks," she said. "Emma, say hello to Della."
The child looked away.

"She's shy," the mother said. "I've been mean-
ing to come in and see your shop. Here I am at
last. Hi, Marnie." She opened her bag and produced the baby monitor. "I just put in a fresh bat-
tery. It's got really good range." She turned it on,
demonstrating how it worked. "But why in the
world would you need this?"

"You know me," Marnie said. "I get up in the

middle of the night to bake and sometimes I go back to bed and don't hear the oven timer."

"Oh. What a great idea." The little girl grabbed her doll and threw it to the floor. "Don't do that, honey," her mother said, picking it up.

"I'll have it back to you in a few days," Marnie said. "Just as soon as I find the time to go shopping for one."

"No rush. It's not like I'm likely to ever use it again. *My* oven is closed for business," she said, patting her flat stomach. "By the way, I heard about your flag. I feel so bad for you. Thank goodness you didn't lend the library your silverware too."

Marnie's jaw dropped. "How did you hear about my silverware?" she asked.

"Judy Mitchell told me. I think she heard it from the kid who works at Melinda's bakery." She glanced at Emma, who was trying to climb out of her stroller. "Well, we'd better get going." She said good-bye and left.

"You were right," Marnie said. "It's already all over town. Let's hope Melinda decides to get it tonight. Otherwise, God only knows how long we'll have to keep the lookout."

"You know, I realized we can't use my Jeep," I said. "She'd recognize it right away."

"And we can't use my car either," she said. "We'll have to go to Belmont and rent a car."

"Why don't you do that right now?" I opened

the cash drawer and pulled out a few bills. "You'll probably need to use your credit card, but here's some cash to cover the cost."

"Why would you have to pay for it? It's my flag that's missing."

"That's exactly why. Losing your flag is a high enough cost as far as I'm concerned. But I'll tell you what: you can repay me the minute you get it back."

"Deal." She grabbed her coat and the baby monitor. A minute later she was gone.

The rest of the afternoon went by in a sudden flurry of activity. Customers dropping by the coffee shop stopped to commiserate about Marnie's flag, her silverware, her fiancé, and to share their opinions about who the murderer and the thief might be.

"I've heard everything," I told Marnie when she returned. "From how the police should set up roadblocks and search all the vehicles leaving town, to organizing a neighborhood watch."

"I like our plan better," she said, dropping the keys to the rental on the desk.

"Did anybody see you driving it?"

"No. I drove it to my place and parked it across the street, one house over. And I already set up the monitor in my bedroom. I left the radio on and went back to the car. I could hear it as clearly as if I'd been standing two feet away." She rubbed her hands together. "We are so gonna get that bitch. The nerve of her," she added. "Stealing my flag."

"Why don't you let me close up?" Marnie offered at five thirty. "You go on up and get dinner started." She came closer. "Now, listen to me. Matthew has been showing serious signs of interest lately, so it's time you reciprocated, and I don't mean just a smile here and there. I mean flirt, for God's sake."

"I will. I promise."

She harrumphed. "I know what your idea of flirting is, and it's not good enough. You're going to dress sexy, right?"

"Of course. I always do when he comes for dinner."

She nodded, as if granting me at least that. "When he shows up, kiss him."

"What? I can't just—"

"You can and you will. You don't have to wrap yourself around him like a clinging vine, but you can give him a nice warm kiss on the mouth."

I nodded, my eyes darting nervously as I tried to imagine myself wrapping my arms around his neck and . . . and . . . "Oh, God, what if he pushes me away?"

She planted her hands on her hips and glared at me. "There you go again, making up excuses for not following through. Are you sure you want that man?" I glared back at her. "Then, for God's sake, get him."

"All I have to do is give him a little kiss on the mouth," I told myself as I climbed the steps to my apartment. "That's not so difficult. And I'll pull away fast, before he can push me away." I was being silly and I knew it. Winnie galloped up the stairs behind me and followed me to the kitchen.

All my ingredients were premeasured and lined up neatly. Marnie was right. Following the recipe was easy this way. I beat the eggs in a bowl, and chopped the herbs and garlic into the bread crumbs. Then I dipped the chicken breast into the egg mixture and dredged them in the flour. Then I fried them up in the pan for two minutes per side, placed them on a baking sheet, dropping a few tablespoons of crispy croutons and some ready-made tomato sauce on top, and finished with a generous layer of grated cheese.

I stepped back, admiring my efforts. With Marnie's instructions, I'd completed the recipe in less than half an hour. Hopefully, she was right about the kissing-Matthew part too. After checking the oven temperature, I placed the chicken inside and then put a large pot of water on to boil for the pasta. I checked the time. I still had half an hour before Matthew arrived.

"Time to make ourselves beautiful, Winnie," I said. He looked at me as if I was a lost cause. "Come on. You can help me choose a dress."

I settled on a short little black number that Winnie approved. I smoked up my eyes with makeup and reddened my mouth with lipstick. I checked my reflection in the mirror. This was as good as I could expect, I decided, and went to the dining room to set the table. At six thirty the phone rang.

"It's me. I hope you don't mind, but I'm going to be late," Matthew said.

"How late?"

"Eight o'clock?"

"No problem. I'll have dinner ready by the time you get here."

"Thanks for being so understanding," he said, and hung up.

I put the phone down. "How do you like that?" Winnie looked at me and yawned. "You couldn't care less, could you?"

I lowered the oven temperature and poured myself a glass of wine.

At eight o'clock sharp, Matthew arrived. "Wow, you look amazing," he said, handing me a bouquet of red roses. Red roses meant passion. Matthew had brought me flowers a few times, but they were always pink or yellow, symbolizing friendship. I hoped he had chosen red on purpose.

"Oh. Roses. That's so nice of you." I placed them in a vase. It was only after I'd set them in the center of the table and was returning to the kitchen that I realized I hadn't kissed him yet. *Damn it.*

"Nice music," he said.

"It's Andrea Bocelli."

"Very romantic."

"That's why I picked it," I said.

Our eyes locked. In his, I read surprise. He took a step closer, and I did too. There was a moment's hesitation, then, all at once, I chickened out and said, "Dinner's ready."

The lovely atmosphere gave way to an uncomfortable tension.

"Mm, mm," he said, lightening the mood. "Smells good."

It did smell good. But under the foil, the dish looked a bit peaked. "I suppose it's not too bad, considering it's been baking for so long."

"It looks perfect," he said. "If it's a bit over-cooked, I won't hold it against you. It was my fault for showing up late." He picked up the bottle of wine and followed me to the kitchen with a running commentary about his day. "I was totally wiped out from so many sleepless nights, but I still managed to put in a good day's work. I'm not too far behind schedule after all. I might be able to make my deadline—unless you decide to give me another sleepless night." Luckily, he didn't know what I was planning to do a few hours from now.

"You don't really expect me to answer that, do you?" I said.

We dug in.

"By the way, thanks for repairing the table. It's as good as new."

"Nothing to it. I put in a few screws, that's all." He raised his glass. "To you."

"To us," I corrected, and again I saw surprise in his eyes. This time I didn't change the subject. I like to think that he would have said something equally romantic at that moment, but the telephone rang, interrupting our conversation. "I'd better get that." I raced to the kitchen and looked at the caller display.

"What's up, Marnie?" I said, picking up. She

whispered something I couldn't quite make out. "What? You'll have to speak louder. I can't hear you."

"I'm locked in the bathroom," she said faintly. "And somebody's trying to break into the house. I think it's Melinda."

I gasped. "Where is she now?"

"She's at the back door. At first she rang the doorbell. I would have answered, but I was in the washroom. I was on my way to the door when she started rattling the knob and I realized she was trying to break in. Then she walked around the side. That's when I grabbed the phone and locked myself in the bathroom. She probably thinks there's nobody home."

"We'll be right over." I slammed the phone down and ran back to the dining room. "Marnie's in trouble. Somebody's trying to break into her house." Matthew had overheard and was already pulling on his jacket. In the next minute we ran down the stairs, Winston in tow, and hopped into his car.

We came to a rubber-burning stop in front of her house and were racing up her walk when Bunny Boyd came strolling around the corner of the house.

"Oh, Della," she said, slapping a hand over her heart. "You scared me half to death!" I couldn't swear to it, but I had the impression she looked guilty. "By the way, nice dress," she added.

"Bunny! What are you doing here?" I asked.

"I'm worried about Marnie," she said. "I came over to make sure she's all right. I rang and rang and there's no answer. I know she's in there because I can hear the television. I just tried the back door. I hoped it was unlocked, but no such luck."

At that moment, the front door opened and Marnie peeked out. Bunny planted her hands on her hips. "You mean you were home? Why didn't you answer the door? My knuckles are sore from all that banging."

"That was you? I thought you were a robber, trying to break in." Her eyes traveled to me. "Wow. You're all dressed up." My Briar Hollow friends weren't used to seeing me dressed city-style.

Bunny rolled her eyes. "And that's exactly why I'm here, you silly woman. Why did you have to go and blab about your valuable silverware? Everyone is talking about it. Don't you know there's a thief in town? That was like inviting him to come over and rob you."

"What silverware?" Matthew asked.

"Er, Marnie has an antique set of Paul Revere sterling silver flatware," I said. "It's worth a fortune."

"You should have kept that a secret," Bunny continued. "You just got your flag stolen, and now you might lose your silverware too."

Matthew frowned. "What is she talking about? Your flag was stolen?"

I'd been so intent on having a romantic evening that I'd forgotten to tell him. I quickly updated him on this morning's events.

"I know damn well who took it," Marnie concluded. I elbowed her. "Ouch." She glared at me, rubbing her arm. "It was Melinda."

"We don't know that," I said.

"Of course we do. It had to be someone who was inside the library when the electricity went out. And she was there."

"Whether it was Melinda or not," Bunny cut in, "you can't just keep that silverware in your closet. What you need is a safety-deposit box at the bank. That's where you should keep it. What if someone broke in and hit you over the head?"

"Bunny's right," Matthew said. "It would be bad enough to get your silverware stolen, but you could end up dead."

Marnie gave her an epic eye roll. "Oh, for God's sake, Bunny. I don't have anything worth more than a hundred bucks in there." She nodded toward the open door. "I only said that to trap the thief."

I slapped my forehead. "So much for that plan," I said. "It's not going to work if you tell everyone it's a trap."

"Hey," Bunny said, "I take offense at that. I'm not just 'everyone.'"

"Of all the stupid ideas," Matthew said, throwing his hands in the air. "Why did I have to fall for a woman who's hell-bent on getting herself killed?"

Bunny and Marnie froze on the spot, and turned to look at him.

Marnie's eyes lit up. "Did I just hear you say you're—"

"You fell for me?" I said, cutting her off.

He looked embarrassed for a moment. "All I mean is I care for you, as a friend."

"Oh, for God's sake," Marnie exclaimed. "Will you two quit beating around the bush. You love her and she loves you. There. I said it. Now, can we get back to business? I want to catch myself a thief and get my flag back."

Bunny looked from Matthew to me, and back again.

I rolled my eyes. "Honestly, Marnie, stop your kidding." And the discomfort in the room dissipated.

"Let's all go home," Bunny said. "Tomorrow we'll do our utmost to squash those rumors."

"That's the only intelligent thing I've heard since I got here," Matthew said. "The only problem with that is the thief might be planning to rob you tonight. Here's what we'll do. You all go home. I don't want anybody getting into trouble." He gave me a meaningful look as he said this. "I'll stay and watch the house."

"But this is my house," Marnie said. "And my flag. I should be doing the stakeout."

"And my painting," Bunny added. "I think we should all stay."

"I agree with Matthew," I said. "If anybody shows up, it'll probably be earlier during the night rather than later. The robbery at the Longview was around one o'clock in the morning. Marnie, you come and stay at my place for tonight."

"If nothing happens by two or three o'clock, call me," Marnie said. "I'll come and take over."

"I'll do that," he replied. His tone told me he had no such intention. He came closer. "I guess that's one more sleepless night for me. Thank goodness I have my buddy here with me." He scratched Winston's head.

"Sorry," I said.

"Now go."

"I walked over," Bunny said.

"Come on, we'll give you a ride." We piled into Marnie's rental car.

As soon as the doors were closed, I said, "Does anybody know where Melinda lives?"

"I do," Marnie said. "It's only a couple of blocks from her shop. Why?"

"I think we should stake out her place too. If we're right and she's planning to rob Marnie, we should be there and warn Matthew when she leaves."

"Brilliant," Bunny said. "Let's go. I wouldn't miss this for the world. The minute the bitch leaves, I'm going in to look for my painting."

"That's breaking and entering," I said. "You can't do that."

Marnie gave me a sideways look. "Get serious, will ya? As if you've never sneaked into somebody's house before." There was no point in denying it.

Soon we were on the highway, heading for Belmont. Marnie turned right after we passed the city limits, and then came to a stop across the street from a white clapboard house with navy trim. It was set on a large lot with gorgeous landscaping. "This is where she lives," she said, as she turned off the headlights.

"It looks expensive," Bunny said, voicing my thoughts.

"Is that her car?" I pointed to the small red car in the driveway. "If it is, then she's not the driver of the blue car that belonged to the intruder."

"If it is, it must be new. She used to have a blue car," Marnie replied.

"If she's stealing expensive paintings and antiques, and selling them on the black market, she can afford a fancier car than that," Bunny said.

"If she's the thief, she probably wouldn't want to attract attention to herself by driving an expensive car," I said. "We'd better park a bit farther down the street."

Marnie turned on the motor and backed up. Just as she switched it off again, the front door opened and a woman stepped out. It was Melinda. Marnie grabbed my hand and squeezed it.

"Look, she's going to the trunk of her car."

We watched as Melinda carried groceries into the house.

"So much for catching her carrying stolen goods," Marnie said. "Unless she stole that baguette that was sticking out of the bag."

"The evening is young."

Time went by, and soon we'd been sitting in the car for more than an hour. "I don't know about you two, but I'm getting bored here," Bunny complained. "I think I'll go home."

"You'll have to take a cab," Marnie said, "because I'm not moving from here until we catch her in the act. I have a feeling something is going to happen tonight."

Bunny sighed. "Fine. But whatever it is better happen soon. I don't know how much more I can take of this." She snapped her fingers. "Let me out. I'll go look through the windows. Maybe I can see something."

"Don't be silly. I'm sure she's got everything safely hidden."

"In that case I'll see if I can get in." Before anybody could comment, she swung the car door open and hopped out.

"What is she doing? Is she crazy?" Marnie said. "She's going to get caught."

A moment later, a small blue car turned the corner and came to a stop in front of Melinda's house. Bunny dove behind a bush. The driver's door opened and Liz Carter stepped out, dressed like a cat burglar.

We watched in silence as Liz threw a satchel over her shoulder and made her way to the front door. Seconds later Melinda let her in.

"Are you thinking what I'm thinking?" Marnie said. "Melinda and Liz are working together."

"It's possible. But it could also be totally innocent."

"Innocent, my behind," she said. Before I could

think of what we should do, the front door opened again, and suddenly Liz Carter strode over to the bush where we'd last seen Bunny. Bunny stood up and went with Liz back into the house.

"Oh, shit," I said. This looked like trouble. "You stay here and call the police. Or better yet, call Matthew." I opened the door and jogged across the road to the house, slipping along the side of it. I tiptoed to a window and peeked inside. It looked into the living room.

Melinda was seated on the sofa with her back to me. Across from her, Bunny sat on a love seat, facing the window where I was. Liz was nowhere to be seen. After a minute of frantic waving, I realized that with the living room lights turned on, Bunny would never see me. I half crawled, half crouched along farther toward the back of the house, ruining my lovely dress in the process. I peered through one window after another until I spotted Liz, making coffee in the kitchen. And the domestic little scene shifted to one that made my heart race. She was fishing through her shoulder bag, pulling out a container—the same type of container the police had retrieved from Marnie's garbage can. *Cyanide!* She dropped a spoonful into the pot and stirred. *They're going to poison Bunny!* I snatched my cell phone from my pocket and pressed speed dial for Marnie.

"Where's Matthew? Shouldn't he be here by now?" I whispered.

"I only called him a few seconds ago. He's probably still at least ten minutes away."

"When he gets here, tell him that Liz just put cyanide into a pot of coffee. They're planning to poison Bunny." At that moment, Liz picked up the tray and left the kitchen. "Gotta go," I said. I kept my phone turned on and slipped it into my pocket. With any luck Marnie would still be able to hear everything that was said. I ran around to the front and sneaked a peek through the living room window.

"She's pouring the coffee. Shit. I have to do something."

Through the glass, I faintly heard Liz tell them the coffee was decaf. "So you don't have to worry about insomnia."

"I sure hope you can hear me, Marnie," I muttered. "And that you'll step in to save me if I need it." I scrambled for the front door, took a deep breath, and rang the bell. The door swung open and Melinda appeared.

"Della." She leaned out and scanned the area—*looking for witnesses*? "What in the world are you doing here? It's late."

I pushed past her and went straight to the living room. "Bunny," I said, trying to sound cheerful, "I've been waiting forever. You were supposed to come right back. What's taking you so long?" Bunny stared at me wordlessly.

Standing next to her, Liz was staring at my feet. "What happened to your shoes?"

I looked down. They were muddy from traipsing through garden beds. "Now, how could that have happened?" I said. "I'm so ditzy sometimes. Come on, Bunny. Maybe you can afford staff, but I have to get up for work tomorrow." Bunny started getting up, but Liz placed a firm hand on her shoulder and pushed her back into the sofa.

"Not so fast." She turned to me. "Do you know what I caught your friend here doing?"

Melinda answered. "She was casing my house. I think she was going to come back and rob me later."

"That's ridiculous," I said.

"I'm not making this up," she said, incensed. "Liz caught her spying through the window."

"Let's go, Bunny. We don't have time for this."

Before she could move, Liz reached inside her bag and pulled out a gun. She trained it on me. "Go sit by your friend."

Whoa. When somebody points a gun at me, I do as told.

Melinda gasped. "Liz, what are you do—"

"Quiet, all of you. Let me think." She seemed stuck in some terrible mental struggle. She swung to face Bunny. "I asked if you were by yourself, and you said yes. Now, is there anybody else out there?"

"She wasn't lying," I said, avoiding a direct answer. "I told her I was leaving, and I did. She didn't know I would come back." Liz hesitated, still in turmoil.

Melinda took a step toward her. "Calm down, Liz. Let's not do anything we'll regret. Put your gun away and let's talk about this."

Liz looked pensive for a moment, and then nodded. "You're right," she said, slipping her gun into her pocket. I would have felt better if she'd put it back in her bag. As it was, it would take her no more than a split second to pull it out again. "I don't know what came over me," she continued, sounding remorseful. "I've never overreacted this way. I guess I'm just paranoid because a killer is on the loose. I should know that you and Bunny wouldn't harm a fly. I'm so sorry." For all her seeming contrition, I felt certain she would pull the gun back out in a nanosecond if cornered.

"Let's all just sit down and have a cup of coffee," Melinda continued in a placating tone. "Della, why don't you pour for everyone?" I picked up the pot with shaky hands. From Melinda's reaction I guessed she wasn't a part of this, whatever *this* was. I wondered if she was adding one and one and coming up with two, the way I had. I poured and offered the first cup to Liz.

"Why don't you start with Bunny?" Liz said. I handed the cup to Bunny, sending meaningful glances at the cup and shaking my head imperceptibly. Panic flashed through her eyes and I knew she'd understood.

"So, if you weren't reconnoitering in order to come back and steal from me," Melinda said in a conversational tone as I offered her the next cup, "what were you doing?" Bunny threw Liz a worried look. Liz's eyes narrowed.

"Maybe I'm wrong," Bunny said, sending another nervous glance toward Liz, "but I thought Melinda was the thief who took my painting. I just wanted to look and see if I could figure out where she might be hiding it."

"You thought I was the robber? Why would you think I had anything to do with that? I'm a baker, not an art thief!" Melinda exclaimed. She sounded so shocked that I began to think she was innocent of the robberies too. *That would mean . . .*

"But you were standing right next to the display when Marnie's flag was stolen when the power went out," Bunny said.

"Oh, so now you're accusing me of stealing that too. For your information, I was nowhere near that display when the lights went out. I was clear across the room by the printing press."

"Drink up, everyone," Liz said. "Don't let your coffee get cold."

"Liz, you tell them," Melinda said.

"Liz is the one who told me," I said. I looked at her. "Didn't you?"

Melinda was utterly confused. "Is that true? You said that? But don't you remember? You were standing right next to me. You told everyone not to move while you tried to find the electric panel. I was still in the same spot when the lights came back on."

"Let's not get all excited over a misunderstanding," Liz said. "Why don't you sit down, Melinda? Drink your coffee before it gets cold. You too, Bunny, Della." Melinda's face fell, but she went back to the sofa and brought the cup to her mouth.

"Stop!" I screamed. "The coffee is laced with cyanide. She wants to poison us."

Melinda looked stunned. She stared down at the cup in her hands, hesitating. "That's ridiculous. Why would Liz want to poison me? She and I are old friends. Liz? What's going on?"

"Don't pay any attention to her. She's just trying to make trouble."

Melinda eyed the coffeepot. "Why didn't you want a cup of coffee too?" she asked. She picked up her cup, handing it to Liz. "Here. If Della is lying, prove it. Take a sip."

Liz slapped the cup out of her hand and coffee went flying everywhere. She snatched her gun from her pocket. "I didn't want to have to do this, but you're leaving me no choice." Her smile was more of a snarl. "You and I were never friends. You only moved here to be close to me, because of my brother. You were always obsessed with him. Never once did you ever spend time with me, without pumping me for information about him. What he was up to. If he was seeing anyone. So pathetic."

Melinda's eyes widened. "Oh, my God. It was you. You killed him, didn't you? You killed your own brother. But why?" Tears were now running down her cheeks. "Whatever Barry did, he didn't deserve to die. You killed Helen too, didn't you?"

"Helen should have minded her own damn business. When I was talking to her at the party, she was sure she recognized Barry. Turns out her sister had taken some pictures of Barry and sent them to Helen. Luckily, at the time Helen had misplaced those pictures, so she was never able to give them to the police. But after she got home, she called me and told me she had found them a few weeks earlier and was about to go to the police with them. I managed to calm her down and told her I was coming right over. As soon as I got there, I suggested we have tea, and then while she went to get the pictures to show them to me, I put cyanide in her cup."

"So you took the pictures with you when you left," I said, more to keep her talking than out of curiosity.

"Yes. But instead of being grateful, Barry was furious with me. I swear that man was getting soft in the head in his old age. He moved here to be close to me, his big sister," she added in a singsong voice. "Of course, I'd never told him that Melinda lived in the next town. And then even when he got here and found out, he refused to move away."

"Why did he want to stay?" Melinda asked with something like hope in her eyes. Did she imagine that he'd wanted to rekindle their romance?

Liz probably read her the same way because she said, "It wasn't for you, if that's what you're thinking. It was for Marnie. Don't ask me why, but he was crazy about the woman. I think he had a mother fixation. What an idiot. Didn't he realize it was only a matter of time before it came out that Bruce wasn't his real name? That he was a con artist."

"But what you didn't know," I said, trying to keep her talking, "was that you left one picture behind at Helen's house."

"I know. She told me she had six pictures, but after I got home I realized I had only five. I went back later to search the house, but I never found the sixth one. But it doesn't matter because Barry is dead. And now nobody can link him to me. Helen didn't live to tell the tale and neither will you."

"Why did you kill him?" Melinda asked again.

"He confronted me at the hotel that night, kept telling me I was a murderess and that he was going to turn me in. And then he figured out that I killed Sybille."

"You killed Sybille?" Bunny said. "But why?"

"I think I know why," I said. "Sybille used to work at the Art Institute of Chicago, in the human resources department. She gave you a job, didn't she? And then what happened? Did she catch you trying to steal something?"

Liz laughed. "Close, but not quite—Barry talked her into hiring me as a night janitor. One day she stayed late for work and happened to catch me toying with the alarm system. As you can see, the girl had to go."

It occurred to me that Nancy Cutler was a very lucky lady. If she had told anyone that she'd recognized Bruce as Brent, chances were she'd be dead too.

"You've been robbing museums all these years?" Bunny said.

"And jewelry stores, and private residences," Liz said. She seemed to be enjoying herself. "Anywhere I find something worthwhile. That's how I came across some containers of cyanide. Museums use it all the time in restorations."

"You must be very good," I said, hoping flattery might get her to keep talking. Surely Matthew would show up soon.

"Enough with the chitchat," she said. "Now drink your coffee." She waved the gun. "Or would you rather get a bullet in the gut and bleed out slowly?"

"You can't shoot us," I said. "You know the police will work this case until they figure out what really happened."

She gave me a haughty smile. "Oh, they'll figure it out all right. They'll know that Melinda stole the flag and Bunny's painting."

"I did no such thing," Melinda said.

Liz widened her eyes. "Oh, but you did. The proof is in the hall closet."

Melinda gasped. "You planted something in there. What is it? Bunny's painting? But, how—how did you get in?"

"Oh, sweetheart. Give me a little credit, please.

I can get into museums with advanced security systems. Do you really think one little lock would be an obstacle to me?" She smirked. "The police will think that little miss sleuth, Della, and her buddy, Bunny here, came over and confronted you. So you pulled out your gun and shot them, and then, realizing what you'd done, you decided the only way out was an exit by cyanide. Good plan—don't you think?"

"There are three of us and one of you. You can't shoot us all at the same time," Melinda said desperately.

"Don't worry. I can work this scenario a few different ways." She raised her gun.

Suddenly there was loud banging at the front door. "Police. Open up!"

In one swift movement, Liz grabbed me by the wrist, pulling me to my feet, and swung me around so that I became her shield. She pressed the barrel against my temple.

"Tell them if they don't get away from the door, you're dead."

And then everything happened at once. Melinda dashed over, knocking me out of the way. The gun went off, and she and I collapsed to the floor. The front door flew open and Winston raced in, teeth bared and snarling. He leapt onto Liz, knocking her to the floor. Matthew appeared in the doorway, followed by Marnie, who was brandishing her purse like a weapon.

I was still on the floor when I noticed Liz's gun

a few feet away. I scrambled for it and jumped to my feet, pointing it at Liz. But I needn't have worried. Winston was standing on her chest, his face inches from hers, and growling.

"Get him off me," she screamed. "He's going to kill me."

"Winston, you stay right where you are," Matthew ordered. "Liz, you move so much as an inch and if he doesn't kill you, I swear I will. Della, you all right?"

"I'm fine," I said, and then he noticed the blood all over my torn dress.

"Shit! You're bleeding." He grabbed my arms, as if to prevent me from collapsing, his eyes filled with panic.

"It's not me. It's Melinda." I had crawled through the blood as I'd reached for the gun. She was lying on her back, her face a ghostly white, a pool of blood spreading around her.

"Call an ambulance, and the police," he said to Marnie, who was already on the phone, giving the address. I rushed to the kitchen and picked up a stack of dish towels.

Back in the living room, Matthew was inspecting Melinda's injury. "The good news is the bullet went clear through one side and out the other. Hopefully it didn't touch any vital organs." He sounded worried. He rolled her on her side and I stuffed a bunch of towels against the bleeding, while he did the same on the exit wound.

"When will that damn ambulance get here?"

Marnie said. "I called them ages ago." In reality it hadn't been five minutes, and I could already hear sirens in the distance. Moments later, the ambulance arrived, followed by three police cars. Uniforms kept appearing in the doorway until the small room was crawling with cops.

"It's okay, Winnie. You can get off now," Matthew said. Liz looked almost relieved when the police pulled her to her feet and snapped the cuffs onto her wrists. As they escorted her out the door, she was yelling about knowing her rights and demanding her lawyer, until she was unceremoniously shoved into the back of the police cruiser. Meanwhile the ambulance attendants were working on Melinda.

"Blood pressure eighty over fifty," yelled one of them. "Pulse, one hundred and twenty. Respirations, twenty-two. Get an IV going and get me an EKG. We're losing her."

They rushed about, trying to save her life, and finally one of them said, "She's stabilizing. Let's get her to the hospital." They lifted the stretcher and hurried out.

"Will she be all right?" I asked.

"She's young and strong," Marnie said. "I'm sure she'll be fine."

"Della?" I tore my eyes away from Melinda. Standing in front of me was Officer Lombard. "How did I know you'd be involved?"

From the hallway, her partner called out, "Looks like Melinda was the museum robber. I just found the evidence."

"No, she wasn't," I said angrily. "It was Liz. She admitted everything to Bunny and me."

"In that case, how do you explain this?" He was standing by the open closet, pointing at a large primitive painting—Bunny's painting. On the floor was a package I recognized as the one that had contained Marnie's flag.

My eyes sought out Matthew's. He was looking at me with such relief. That's when it hit me and my eyes watered.

"Are you all right?" he asked.

"I'm fine, because of you. If you hadn't come in right when you did, Bunny, Melinda, and I would be dead." As I said this, tears rolled down my cheeks.

"Don't cry, sweetheart," he said, gathering me in his arms. "You know I couldn't let anything happen to you. I need you in my life."

I pulled away and looked up at him. "You need me?"

He wiped a tear away with his thumb. "Who else am I going to worry about if I can't worry about you?"

"Does that mean you . . . you . . ." I couldn't bring myself to say the word.

"Love you?" he said. He brought his thumb and index finger close together. "Maybe just a little bit." And then he kissed me.

Weaving Tips

An Easy Beginner Project

Of all the possible weaving projects a beginner can choose from, my favorite is place mats. Not only are they easy to make and fast to complete, but a place mat is an item everyone can enjoy for years to come. For those reasons, or perhaps just because I love a pretty table, even after many weaving projects, they remain my favorite item to make and one of my favorite gifts to give.

I've made many different place mats over the years. I made one set from fine linen thread, resulting in a finely woven cloth, appropriate for a more formal table setting. Others I made of thick acrylic yarn, perfect for informal meals. But my all-time favorite is a set I made from some discarded blue-and-white toile curtains. If this is your first weaving project, this trick might be perfect for you.

When working with fabric, printed cotton curtains are prettiest. Here are the steps to preparing your cotton fabric.

1. Press your fabric panels so they are perfectly smooth and lay them flat.

2. Following the length of the fabric, cut strips one and a half inches wide.

3. Once you've cut up all the fabric, sew the strips together end to end, until you have one very long strip.

4. Fold the edges in on both sides of the strip so that the edges meet at the center of the strip. Carefully iron the folded result so that you have a strip of fabric showing the right side of the printed fabric on both sides.

5. Fold again, this time along the center of the strip, so that the pressed edges join each other in the center. You should now have no unfinished edges showing. Iron again. By now your strip should be about three-eighths of an inch wide, which will be perfect for a weft yarn.

6. You will need a normal cotton yarn for your warp. (The warp is the taut yarn through which another yarn travels under and over to form the weave. In this case, your cotton strips will be your weft.)

7. Next, decide on how many place mats you want to make, and also their width and length. Then weave a small sample to determine the number of threads you will need to use for your warp in order to achieve the width you desire.

8. Once you've dressed your loom with the number of warp threads you need, you are ready to start.

Tip: When you make place mats out of different yarns, keep the following in mind: Place mats will likely get dirty with food stains. You can use bleach on white cotton and linen, but not on colors, and not on acrylics. Those spaghetti-sauce stains might be difficult to remove from light colors. On the other hand, bright, bold colors can camouflage many a nasty stain.

If you follow these simple steps, whatever project you weave will give you years of joy.

Happy weaving!

Carol Ann Martin

About the Author

Carol Ann Martin is a pen name used by author Monique Domovitch for Obsidian. Monique is a former television personality who divides her time between San Diego and the Canadian coast. She lives with her husband and their ever-expanding collection of dogs. When she is not writing, Carol Ann enjoys baking and beekeeping.